Whisper
My
Name

Whisper
My
Name

by
Ernest Hebert

Viking

VIKING
Viking Penguin Inc., 40 West 23rd Street,
New York, New York 10010, U.S.A.
Penguin Books Ltd, Harmondsworth,
Middlesex, England
Penguin Books Australia Ltd, Ringwood,
Victoria, Australia
Penguin Books Canada Limited, 2801 John Street,
Markham, Ontario, Canada L3R 1B4
Penguin Books (N.Z.) Ltd, 182–190 Wairau Road,
Auckland 10, New Zealand

Grateful acknowledgment is made to John Perrault
for permission to reprint a selection from his song
"Some Things Refuse to Fall," copyright © 1981 by John Perrault.
Published by Rock Weed Music (ASCAP). All rights reserved.

LIBRARY OF CONGRESS CATALOGING IN PUBLICATION DATA
Hebert, Ernest.
  Whisper my name.
  I. Title.
PS3558.E277W48   1984   813'.52   83-40685
ISBN 0-670-76200-8

Printed in the United States of America
by The Book Press, Brattleboro, Vt.

*This book is dedicated to my teachers
and especially to the memory
of David H. Battenfeld.*

Acknowledgments

There are people to thank. First and foremost is actor Tony Randall. Something he said in a television interview on the subject of fathers inspired this book, and indeed I took the liberty of giving a few of his words, as I remembered them, to my protagonist. I'd also like to thank Theodore Parent for his advice in helping me keep the legal and police matters in this book more or less in line with New Hampshire law and tradition, and John Perrault for his permission to use lines from his song, "Some Things Refuse to Fall." Finally, thanks, Medora, for hanging in there with me once again.

Contents

Author's Note

Because I've spent nearly all my life in Cheshire County, New Hampshire, its flavor seasons my fiction. But neither this book, nor my previous two books, are meant as commentary—political, social, or otherwise—on this region. Nor are the characters or the situations in these books based on real people and real events; they are figments of my imagination. My concerns are not the real lives of real people in real places, but those prisms of the intellect—namely, myth and metaphor—that magnify and clarify, but also distort, the facts of life in service to the understanding of it.

Whisper
My
Name

The Mall

The sound of the shower water beating against his skin reminded Roland LaChance of himself as a small boy listening to Old Joe humming coarsely against the drone of the family Ford station wagon. Only in the car, his mind on cruise, would Old Joe sing. Chance turned off the water, and the roar of a crowd from his portable television in the next room broke over him, quickly ebbed, and, following a split second of oppressive silence (when Chance heard Old Joe's hum die to a moan, signaling the onset of dark mood), he was listening to the water again, swirling into the drain, pittering from the shower head, drip, drip, drip . . .

"LaChance, I don't really want to send you a hundred miles to walk around a shopping mall," said Clovis Shard, editor of *The Tuckerman Crier* newspaper in Tuckerman, New Hampshire. "This is Mrs. Chubb's idea. But she's the publisher, and I'm willing to humor her now and then, as long as she keeps the hell out of my newsroom ninety-nine percent of the time. So, go. Walk the showcase of Magnus malls, talk to the people, ask 'em how they like it. Don't forget to sniff out the downtown, too. That's the

issue in Tuckerman: Will a mall leave the downtown a waste-
land of plywooded storefronts?"

As he talked, Clovis Shard ran his fingers through his crew
cut. It didn't matter to him that there were only four or five
gray bristles and two red ones on top of his head. Shard was
hardly aware of himself as a physical being, hardly aware
how sharply he contrasted with his rookie reporter, who was
young with black, unruly hair, a wiry body, and dark skin,
where Shard was middle-aged, bald, chunky, and fair. What
Shard was aware of was that his reporter was difficult to
handle. He wasn't the type you could bully, flatter, tease, or
even reason with. To get work out of him, you had to leave
him alone and hope he did the job. Shard suffered him because
he had the raw stuff to make a good newspaperman. He could
think fairly well, and he had an eye for detail, the ability to
grasp ideas without being swept up by them, and no gift
whatsoever for creative expression. What he lacked was
doggedness, curiosity. He seemed preoccupied; he spent hours
in the *Crier* files room; Shard didn't know what to make of
him.

Roland LaChance did not leave immediately for the Magnus Mall of Grenoble, New York. First, he stopped at the
Tuckerman County Courthouse, a place he had become quite
familiar with after several months on the job as the *Crier*'s
county reporter. He had spent many hours here attending
meetings of the Tuckerman County Commissioners, the county's legislative delegation, and numerous county committees,
and he had also covered occasional court trials. This morning,
however, it was not the *Crier*'s business he was on, but his
own.

"Anything? Anything at all?" he asked. He knew the answer
to his question even before he asked it by the tiny, sympathetic
smile breaking across the buck-toothed mouth of Charlene
Harris, the clerk helping him with his case.

"I'm afraid not," she said. "No couple or individual named
LaChance adopted any children in New Hampshire in the year
you say you were born, or in the two years following or the
two years previous. I've checked all the files."

"So, that's it."

"Yes, that's it. You're sure you were born here?"

"That's what my adoptive father said—conceived in Tuckerman County—let it out when he was drinking. Of course, he was such a liar, maybe even his Freudian slips were lies."

"And you came to live in Tuckerman County to learn the truth one way or another?"

Chance nodded, thanked Charlene, and left.

Genevieve's silence over his origins, Old Joe's deception—these remaining mysteries. Chance's efforts to find his natural parents had failed. All he had learned was that Old Joe had lied in telling him his records had burned in a fire in a county building. There had been no such fire in forty years. However, Old Joe was right about one thing: his records were missing. Maybe they did not exist at all.

It would have been logical for Chance to continue his search by questioning his relatives in Manchester, fifty miles away. But this he would not do. Chance wouldn't admit it to himself, but while he had come to Tuckerman to search, he didn't really want to find. In fact, he was oddly relieved at having arrived back where he started from—nowhere. He was relieved because something told him that knowing his origins might be more difficult to bear up under than not knowing. He had searched just enough to fulfill the requisites of his sense of responsibility. He would do little more. He would stay in Tuckerman County and wait and see how fate dealt with him. This was natural to him because of his name. As a boy he had come by the nickname Chance, and as time passed he had grown into the name, so that now, if he had any faith at all, it was in his name, living by it.

The light was gray and the air felt moist. Chance thought it might rain. He was still new enough to the area not to be able to distinguish a weather front from the haze that in the summer sometimes hung over the Tuckerman valley until late in the morning. So it was a surprise when his Subaru Brat reached into the hills that surrounded the city and plunged into booming sunshine. Out there was what Clovis Shard would have called an f22 day. Chance glanced into the rearview mirror. From this perspective, the valley haze took on the appearance of a cloud, its edges gold with morning sun, the light flowing along the perimeter like a golden brook. When he returned his eyes to the front, the image of a boy and a girl rushed to meet him: the boy in blue, in blue jeans and an open blue denim jacket, a Red Sox baseball cap on his head, a boy wearing condensed sky; the girl in a cotton print dress snug around her hips, hips that said "come here," bosomy, long, bleached-blond hair, her arm extended, thumb out at a rakish angle. Chance saw himself assume the image of the boy, and he was courting the girl, hitchhiking with her into another dimension, toward home, himself the sky, the girl the sun. . . . He braked.

The Brat came to rest about one hundred feet ahead of the hitchhikers. His thoughts were lost in the new awareness of the moment. He wondered why in the world he had stopped.

In the rearview mirror he watched them half-walk, half-run toward the car, and he saw that he had been wrong. The boy was a girl. She was short, plump, with a dirty, pimply face unguarded by makeup, about sixteen years old. The outline of her breasts, like fruit in soft, tissue wrapping paper, gave a touch of distinction to a filthy white T-shirt under the open denim jacket. Her hair was hidden under the cap. She would have been funny-looking had it not been for her mouth and eyes. She had a full lower lip and a delicate upper lip that pronounced a small "r" at its summit. Her eyes were a common hazel color, but they were large and glowing, at once suspicious and full of wonder. A serious mouth, serious eyes.

"You can ride in the back, or squeeze in the front," Chance said.

"Front, front—I ain't no cow being taken to market," said the bleached blond. She got in, and the dirty girl sat on her lap. The dirty girl studied Chance for a moment, turning her eyes from him and watching the road. The sadness about her was like the sadness of polluted water.

"Where you headed?" Chance asked.

"For bed and rest—been up all night," said the bleached blond.

"Partying," said Chance.

"Don't I wish. We work. Hospital."

"Nurses?" Chance asked. He was laying a trap. If the blond said they were nurses, he would know she was a liar. His habit of searching for lies in people was so ingrained, he had ceased to be aware of it.

"Shit, sheets, and blood—hospital laundry," the blond said, laughing at her joke. She peeked around the head of the dirty girl into the mirror and, despite the close quarters, managed to freshen her makeup. The dirty girl kept her eyes outward from the vehicle.

"Drop us in Darby Depot," the blond said, her voice thick with the local accent—Daaby Deh-poh.

"No car?" said Chance.

"Critter had a car. Engine blew up," the blond said.

"Critter?" said Chance.

"My fiancé. My word, I thought everybody knew Critter," the blond said.

"I'm Roland LaChance—Chance. What are your names?" He tried to direct his question to the dirty girl, hoping she would say something. He wondered whether there would be sadness in her voice.

"Nice to meet you, Rollie," said the blond. "My name is Delphina Rayno, and this is my sister, Soapy."

The dirty girl spoke then. Her voice was low and rich, and might have been musical, had not the words escaped with such effort, such pain. "Not today—today, no—no Soapy today," she said.

"Whatever you want, sweetie," Delphina Rayno said kindly, and then she addressed Chance. "Soapy don't like to be called Soapy sometimes. Certain words upset her. Sometimes she can talk okay, and sometimes she can't. Ain't nobody, least of all Soapy, knows when her talker ain't going to talk."

"What's your real name?" Chance asked Soapy.

"He took it. Won't give it. Leave Soapy be," Soapy said, her words deteriorating in an animal-like growl.

"Rollie, you pushed the wrong button. She's real touchy," Delphina said.

Delphina gabbed on about how unpleasant the work was in the hospital laundry and how they were falling behind financially and how she wished she had a nice big kitchen like her cousin Melba and a new stereo system, and about how she liked cats and maple wood furniture and the fact that she was dreading the coming of winter because there was no car and no money to buy a car, and Critter couldn't work on his car because somebody named Ike had all the tools, and she wished to hell Critter got the crazy idea out of his head that he wanted to be a farmer and would go back to Ike and his succor. Like a child, she talked with a certain familiarity, assuming that Chance knew everything she knew about Darby and her family situation.

Chance hardly listened. He was thinking about Soapy, about that name. Someone had stuck her with it because she didn't bathe. Why didn't she bathe? The oddity of the girl made him wonder about her with something like the innocent awe he had had for girls when he was fifteen. He tried to think of something to say to get her attention, but his very awe imposed a wall between his will and his ability to find the words he needed.

After a few minutes his mind wandered ahead in time to Grenoble. How would he shape his story? Whom would he talk to? His thoughts drifted away from business to pleasure. Maybe he would meet a girl at the mall. He ran a blue movie in his mind, yet even as the lurid scenes unfolded he knew they could never occur. He was too removed, too cold. Old Joe had chilled his adopted son with the manner of his dying.

"Lemme out—grrrrr!"

The shout, the growl, were followed by lower rumblings from the throat of Soapy and by anxious thrashings of her hands, like a startled infant. Chance slowed the Brat. Soapy grabbed the door handle on her side of the truck just before it came to a halt. Soapy and Delphina spilled onto the shoulder of the highway. Soapy's hat fell off. Long, shiny, clean reddish-blond hair seemed to tumble out in slow motion in the morning sunlight. The contrast between the dirty face and the lovely hair touched Chance, warmed him. Their eyes met. He thought later that if he could have spoken at that moment, she might not have run away. As it was, she turned from him with a blush, quickly put her cap back on, and ran into the woods.

"Come back!" Chance heard himself shout.

"She ain't coming back, Rollie. She seen something out there," Delphina said, weary now, resigned. "I better try to find her. You get going with your trip. This might take an hour or all day."

So Chance drove on alone, feeling a sense of wonder, of loss.

Chance spotted the Magnus Mall of Grenoble from the exit ramp that arced from the Grenoble highway bypass into a vast parking lot. The highway ran along the side of a hill, and the mall sat below, in the valley. Surrounding the mall were motels, restaurants, gas stations, a car wash, a place advertised as a "tire warehouse," and a great, sprawling, one-story aluminum-sheathed hangar-type structure that must have been an industrial building. A few farms remained in the valley; indeed, from the ramp could be seen fields of corn that gave the impression of agriculture encroaching upon commercial interests, rather than the other way around.

Pale green, shaped like important objects in nature such as flowers or star nebulae, things with a hub and spokes, the mall seemed to have issued forth from the valley soil, then to have created a nest of yellow-striped asphalt. Here Chance parked the Brat. He almost expected the mall to move, to creep forward and feed on the cars in the parking lot, tasting the Brat—and *ptui!*

The beast imagery vanished the moment he stepped between the doors of the mall. The message of the mall was immediately clear. He was to think he had sauntered into a village, vaguely Bavarian. Under a roof there were streets paved with brick and a movie theater and stores, some of which had white, wood-frame fronts faced with fake stone, resembling country houses. Sifting through the thick, slightly moving air were the *tink, twip, fee-woop* sounds of a video arcade. All in a row were fast-food specialty restaurants selling ice cream, pizza, burgers, and submarine sandwiches.

At the center of this main section was an ice rink. Speakers, which off the ice could just barely be heard, directed scrubbed rock music onto the rink. Chance's eye was drawn to a figure-skating class. A half-dozen girls in short skirts and leotards and two boys wearing black slacks and black turtleneck shirts followed the direction of a woman instructor with dazzling white skates. She was about thirty, blond and lovely but a little overweight, and her costume was tight. Occasionally a look of pain came into her eyes—or perhaps Chance only imagined this, for he was a good sixty feet away from her— and he wondered whether she was sad about outgrowing the clothes of her youth. She was not a strong skater, not particularly graceful; her skills were studied, worried. There was no doubt in Chance's mind that as a child, probably bullied by parents ambitious for her, she must have practiced figure-skating for hours every day without ever getting particularly good at it. He tried to picture himself gliding along the ice with her, but something prevented him from conjuring the vision. He could think it but not visualize it. He wondered whether the mind's eye could go blind.

Footways led off from the hub of the mall. He walked along one. On each side were stores. He strolled, and couldn't get over the feeling he was outside and that the mall's peculiar air was following him. Did people in malls discuss the interior weather? "Nice today, except air's a little slow." "Kind of chilly by the rink." "Take it easy." "You too." He looked up, expecting somehow to feel the warm wash of the night-light aura of a city sky. Instead loomed steel trusses and the rough concrete ceiling. It was as if the mall were a town that had sunk into the ground, and he was looking up at the underbelly of the earth.

The street flowed into a department store. He walked through several aisles, opened a door and blundered into . . . space.

The warm outside air pushed, the cool mall air pulled. He stepped back inside and returned to the rink. The student skaters and their instructor were gone, their absence having the effect of making him acutely aware of his isolation. He had the strong urge to strike up a conversation with someone, anyone, but preferably a woman. He looked around, seeing teen-agers coming and going in docile suburban gangs; young couples, she pathfinding, he lugging; families of men-led children and women-led men, the tribal body warmed and protected and secured by the misery of its collective company; women in pairs, lots of them, carrying sacks of this and that, whispering to one another like conspirators. No one alone. No one standing still. Everyone moved along by the invisible cop of the air. Here was a place designed to enchant and unpurse.

Chance stopped in the middle of a mall street and reflected upon his discomfort. He had been in malls before, happy, a shopper, a browser, focusing on this point of light or that. Now, without the sheath of the shopper's mentality, he found himself observing the mall through the prism of his own isolation, And he thought, There are no shadows here. The touch of air was strong now, not cool, not warm, but merely insistent, whispering to him, "Move on, move on." He wondered if other people judged him as he stood unmoving on the street. Did they think him a pervert? How would a pervert go about purveying himself in a shopping mall? The preposterousness of the question made his mouth crack involuntarily into an embarrassed smile, as if he had stumbled on his shoelace. Alone, still, grinning—surely he was subject to arrest; surely he was asking to be detained.

The air of the mall started him going again. Soon he realized that he was hungry. He imagined a restaurant, German in theme, lights predominantly yellow, with strong-legged, smooth-skinned, pig-tailed waitresses; he found himself craving wiener schnitzel. He'd sip a mug of dark beer, read the local newspaper, and sneak glances at the waitresses. There must be such a restaurant in the mall. But where? He'd have to ask directions. But from whom? He felt shy.

Chance wandered until he found himself at the end of one of the mall streets, in a J. C. Penney store. He spotted a pretty young woman behind a glass case that housed watches and calculators. She reminded him of Nora, his former girlfriend. He browsed her counter. He asked to see some watches. The fact that she was only three feet away, breathing, still, brought him pleasure. He slowly became aware that he was making her uncomfortable. He bought a standard man's Timex watch. Leave now, leave pure, without showing you had an ulterior motive, he said to himself. Finally, however, with a forced element of flirtation in his voice, he said:

"Say, I'm looking for a place to eat. Like food. You know, a good meal, a drink. People around."

"There's a whole bunch of food by the rink," she said.

He thought he recognized her accent.

"You from Pee-Ay?" he asked.

"Delaware," she said.

"I, ah, I, ah, I've never met anyone from Delaware," he said. His voice drizzled with a nervousness that must have sounded like malevolence to the clerk.

She stood silently, declining to continue this meaningless conversation. Should he congratulate her on her good judgment?

She was wrapping the watch. He wanted desperately to continue talking with her, remain with her. "I don't want a pizza or a burger," he said.

He knew now how he would manage the story of the mall for the *Crier*. He would talk to the manager of the store. He would contact local officials, asking them how the mall had affected their town. He would describe the mall as best he could, but he would be very careful to keep his confused feelings out of the article.

"There is a good sit-down restaurant on Sesame Street," the clerk said.

"How do I get to Sesame Street?" he asked.

"The end of Sesame Street is a long way off, a long, long way. If you're parked near the rink, it might be better to drive." The clerk's voice had dropped to a reverent whisper, as if she'd never been to the end of Sesame Street, as if it was on the other side of the world.

Her uncertainty, her awe at the extent of the mall, reminded Chance of himself wondering about the dirty girl, and he was remembering her hair, tumbling from the cap. He walked toward Sesame Street, cheered somewhat.

The Moose

When Delphina Rayno found the tracks of a large, hoofed animal (she thought it was a deer), she realized it was useless to go after her sister. Soapy would stay on the trail for hours, perhaps for the entire day. To a point, Delphina understood the reason for this.

When Soapy was twelve, she had come down with spinal meningitis. The disease had left her without words. The doctors said the fever had damaged her brain, and they wanted to enroll her in a special school. Their mother said no. Antoinnette Rayno didn't trust schools, but that wasn't the only reason she kept Soapy at home. The main reason was *him*. In Delphina's opinion, *him* continued to influence Antoinnette, even though he sent her little money and rarely visited. *Him* also influenced Soapy. *Him* did not wash, so Soapy did not wash.

It wasn't until Antoinnette died that Soapy changed. Even if she still refused to bathe, she did come awake in her mind. Delphina had done the best she could to help her. They would take walks, and Delphina would name things. *This is a tree. That's just pucker brush there. What you kicked is a rock. You find rocks low. Gravity keeps 'em down. A great big rock you call a boulder.* And so forth. Once Soapy knew the name of something, it came round into her knowledge of the world, and she would smile. Sometimes there were things she wanted to know for which Delphina herself had no words, difficult things, like why they didn't have the same father and why fathers didn't stay around the house. Soapy would want to touch a tangible thing, or if it couldn't be touched, touch something associated with it, as if the feelies on the tips of her fingers could help her name it. Thus it was that Delphina was quite certain Soapy was not pursuing an animal; she was pursuing knowledge.

For a moment Delphina wondered whether she should pursue Soapy, but then quickly answered her own question aloud, speaking to the road: "No! I got my own life, my own problems. Take Critter—now there's a problem." She looked west on Route 21, she looked east. A car drove by, slowed, and went on. Delphina decided she wasn't going to hitchhike. It wasn't a safe thing to do alone, especially when you were beautiful. She headed for Ike Jordan's Auction Barn, only a mile away. As much as she disliked Ike, he had that van, and, according to the Jordans' code of providing succor for kin, he'd have to drive her home. As Critter's fiancée, did she count as kin to Ike? Oh, well, she thought, if he don't give me a ride I'll piss in his eye. My gosh, she was tired.

Reggie Salmon had seen the moose on his Trust lands last night and was waiting for a call on the present location of the beast from Mrs. McCurtin, Darby's efficient town gossip. Hands behind his back, he paced to and fro on the long back porch of the great, sprawling summer house his grandfather had built in the 1920s. Now and then he glanced at the fields (leased to farmer Crabb), at the Trust lands beyond, and at the magnificent view of the Connecticut Valley below and the Vermont hills in the distance. He looked right through his wife Persephone, who was working in the garden even as they chatted.

"Are you sure Dot McCurtin didn't call while I was on my hike?" Reggie asked.

"The only call was from Garvin. Something about a mall. Does Garvin want to build a shopping mall?"

"I doubt it. A mall—my word. What would our moose think of a mall?"

Reggie Salmon held more land in Darby than anyone else in the town. People in the villages of Center Darby and Darby Depot referred to Reggie, partly in contempt, partly in reverence, as "the Upper Darby Squire" or just "the Squire." He was so perfectly proportioned that he instantly impressed strangers by his bearing, rather than by his size, and it wasn't until they were close enough to measure him against themselves that they realized he was also a big man. Reggie was aware of the impact he had on people, and he was also aware that the recent purplish-red streaks on his face increased rather than reduced his ability to hold their attention. To Reggie, the physical pain that lay in the path of his illness was unthinkable, the thought of death fearful, but the contemplation of disfigurement was almost pleasurable because it further separated him from the common run of humanity.

Persephone Salmon worked steadily in the soil among her flowers; she was in her forties, looked it, and was still striking. Her friends and relatives in Upper Darby could see how lonely she had become, how Reggie in his illness had left her, given her up for the company of the ghosts of his father and grandfather, up there on the Trust lands he worked so hard to preserve in a wild state, as if preparing a residence for his own passing.

"It's been years since we've had a moose in Darby," Persephone said. "I wonder what it wants here."

"I think I know the answer; he's doomed as a trout in a shower of acid rain," Reggie said. His tone told Persephone he was going to preach, so she shut most of his words from her mind.

"This is moose country," Reggie went on. "There were few deer in this land when the white man first came here. Now we have plenty of deer, few moose. Think of the white man's diseases that ravaged the Indians—syphilis, tuberculosis, smallpox. The moose, too, succumbed to a disease from an invader. White-tail deer manage to survive rather well with worms in their brains. They pick them up from snails they ingest as they feed in swampy areas. They then pass on the infection through their feces. Moose cannot live with the same brain worm. Moose die. Where you find deer and snails, you won't find moose."

"So our moose is sick," Persephone said.

"That's my guess," Reggie said. "He is most certainly a North Country moose, where the deer population is small, and he wandered too far south and got infected. Now he has neurological problems, and he's wandering, wandering . . ."

"Perhaps he's just lovesick. Isn't there such a thing as a wandering, lovesick moose?" Persephone asked.

"It's a little early for the rutting season to have begun. I'm betting on the worm," Reggie said, an edge in his voice.

"Go ahead, then. I'd prefer to imagine he's lovesick," Persephone said.

"Brain-sick or lovesick, the Darby moose is doomed," Reggie said, as the telephone rang.

It was Mrs. McCurtin. The moose had been spotted crossing River Road onto the property of the Hillary Farm.

In a field that undulated gently and irregularly as a haphazardly thrown blanket stood three men, the most prominent of whom was Avalon Hillary, the owner of the Hillary Farm. He was about sixty, a sprawling, wide-in-the-hips man wearing overalls, who might have resembled one of his Holstein cows were it not for his face, a deeply lined, perpetually worried face, intelligent, given to brooding. At Hillary's shoulder, like a bodyguard, was a swarthy boy-man also wearing overalls, Carlton "Critter" Jordan. He was holding a .30-.30 Winchester rifle. The third man, about forty-five, was one of those slender people who carry an impressive pot belly but seem to have no other body fat. Slung beneath his belly was a gun belt, on his head a blue wide-brimmed hat. This was Godfrey Perkins, the Darby town constable.

The men were watching the moose amid the cows.

"What the hell is he doing?" Critter asked.

"Organizing a harem," Hillary said, without humor.

Critter took another look. Sure enough—the moose had rounded up a cow here, a cow there, getting them to stand in a rough semicircle with him in the center, now and then sniffing their behinds. But there was no time for amour. Some of the cows wanted nothing to do with this tall, antlered stranger. The moose would bring a cow into the group and two would leave. He'd chase the deserters and the recent recruit would wander off. And so on.

"Goddamn, I don't have enough problems but what an intruder from Coos County has to come down here and get my herd into a compromising situation." Hillary was looking at the sky, Job complaining to his Holstein god.

At that point, the moose's antlers caught a tender place on the flank of a cow, and she let out a fearful whine. Hillary couldn't take it any longer. He rumbled toward the bull, waving his hands, attempting to shoo the moose. The moose watched the man carefully. He took no action until the man reached an invisible boundary that the moose had set earlier. Then he flared his nostrils, pawed the earth, lowered his head, and prepared for battle.

"Get the hell off my cows, you goddamn son of a bitch," Hillary yelled, but he knew better than to get any closer than about forty feet. He then turned to the town constable and said, "Perkins, get over there and shoot that son of a bitch."

"Mr. Hillary, you really don't want a wounded subject of that magnificence stalking your fields, because if I shoot, wounded is what he'll be. This .38 can do wonderful damage to a man, but to that, to that, it's going to be no more than a black-fly bite." Something had told Perkins that an officer of the law shooting a moose would result in bad publicity.

"Oh, sure—you bet," Hillary said, his voice dripping with sarcasm.

"I'd be happy to dispatch that animal," Critter said, sounding off proudly, like a marine who has just finished boot camp.

"Go ahead, Critter. Do the constable's job for him," Hillary said.

Perkins holstered his gun and stepped back. He rotated his index finger against his head, as if to say, Dairy farmers—they're all nuts.

Critter brought the rifle to his shoulder and took aim. At that moment a speeding Ford Bronco skidded to a halt on the shoulder of River Road, and the driver jumped out, shouting, "Hold on, Jordan! Hold on! Don't pull that trigger."

Critter lowered the gun, and Hillary spoke. "Mr. Salmon, I don't believe this is any of your goddamn business. Shoot the moose, Critter."

Salmon ignored Hillary and faced Critter Jordan, saying, "If you injure that moose with a firearm, I'll have you prosecuted under New Hampshire RSA 114A."

"That's right," Perkins said, getting on the legal bandwagon.

The streaks on Squire Salmon's face reminded Critter Jordan of fall foliage. He didn't know what to do, his body oscillating visibly between the will of his employer and the threat of the local aristocrat.

Hillary saw the uncertainty in him and interceded. "Put the gun down, Critter," he said. "No reason you should have to go to jail for this poor farm."

Then Hillary turned his attention to Salmon. "If I could hit the broad side of a barn door, I'd shoot that moose myself, jail or no, and I'd shoot the goddamn tires out of your bonneted pickup truck just for the joy of it."

Salmon was stung by the slight to his Bronco, but he responded as graciously as he could. "Avalon, I know how you feel—"

"No you don't," Hillary cut in. "These are my cows, my girls in a manner of speaking, and there they are, all nervous and getting sick, and being accosted by some antlered sex maniac come down from the Connecticut Lakes." Hillary paused to take a breath and, having gotten new wind, tacked from indignation to sarcasm. "You're an ecologist, Mr. Salmon, a lover of the birds and the bees and the trees and the fishes, you tell me what to do to save my cows from further embarrassment."

Salmon missed the sarcasm and offered a serious proposal. "I believe I do have a solution," he said. "Godfrey, get on your radio and call the state police. Tell them to notify the Fish and Game Department."

"Wonderful, Mr. Salmon, wonderful," Hillary said. "They'll take anywhere from half a day to two weeks to get here, and by then the moose will have petitioned the zoning board for a variance to establish a whorehouse on River Road."

Salmon caught Hillary's ironic drift now, arched an eyebrow, and harrumphed audibly.

Constable Perkins ducked into his police cruiser, apparently satisfied that in the Fish and Game Department he had, as it were, a pigeon to pass the buck to.

Hillary and Jordan stormed off, heading for the twin-silo barn that was the main identifying feature of the Hillary Farm.

After Godfrey Perkins completed his call to the state police, he stood outside, leaning against the cruiser with his arms folded. Reggie Salmon joined him, saying, "Magnificent beast, eh?"

It took Perkins a moment to realize Salmon was not referring to Hillary but to the moose.

"Mr. Salmon, how was you able to cite the RSA number on the moose-croaking law?" Perkins asked.

"Made it up," Salmon said. He smiled while Perkins broke into a laugh.

"I kind of feel bad for poor old Avalon," Perkins said.

"The world is full of Avalon Hillarys, full of cows, too," Salmon said, the smile gone from his face. "It is not full of moose. The moose is a rare and wild creature in our New Hampshire. It needs every advantage it can get . . ."

Reggie had more to say, but he was interrupted by the sound of machinery. Rumbling out of the barn, there came a backhoe with a bad muffler, farting and belching like some bad-mannered dragon. Behind the controls was Avalon Hillary. He was making for the moose and the harem, which had stabilized at fourteen cows. The noise got louder and louder as the backhoe approached. Salmon and Perkins slipped between the barbed-wire fence and started back onto the field.

The moose perked his ears in the direction of the backhoe, flared his nostrils, and lowered his tremendous antlered head. The harem dispersed. The cows ambled upslope somewhat, paused, turned back toward the action, and, having formed a grandstand of sorts, settled in to watch the show.

"See here," shouted Salmon, but quickly quieted when he realized neither Hillary nor the moose could hear him above the din of the backhoe.

As Perkins moved closer, he got a better idea of the size of the beast. It was enormous, snorting through two-inch-wide nostrils. Even its drool was of magnitude, like the whites of five dozen eggs. The moose of his imagination had always been of the Bullwinkle variety. In the flesh a moose was not funny, not goofy, not on any humanlike scale. It was like a statue. It was humans that were funny and goofy and little.

The contestants squared off, the backhoe coming forward slowly but menacingly, growling terrible threats. The moose anchored in one place, defending his territory, now and then kicking up a divot, snorting and drooling, eyes maniacal with fury.

Coming or going, the backhoe was a fearsome adversary. At one end was a wide scoop, at the other an arm with a metal shovel where a hand should be. Hillary's plan was clear enough. He approached scoop first, apparently planning to push the moose off his land, nudge him and nudge him again until he was exhausted, then perhaps pick him up bodily in the scoop and haul him away. The latter part of this plan would be difficult to accomplish. The moose was just too big to fit in the scoop. Still, Perkins gave the advantage to the backhoe. Too much weight, too much power, too much gift for plan in the driver's seat. He gave the moose no credit for imagination. He figured the moose would stand his ground stubbornly, thus making himself prey to the scoop. He was wrong.

The first encounter revealed that the moose had an advantage: nimbleness—that is, nimbleness when compared to the backhoe. On the first pass the moose simply sidestepped the charging backhoe like a matador. The backhoe roared by, then halted, its arm shaking with anger like a closed fist. The backhoe backed, turned around, and came forward in its charging gear. Again the moose sidestepped, this time not jumping so far out of the way as the backhoe chugged by. On the third pass the moose sidestepped and then make a pass of his own, probing with his antlers at the cab. There was a clanging sound as antlers brushed metal. The sides of the backhoe partially protected Hillary, but there was no top, no actual housing around the driver. The moose had found a weakness. The thing inside had flesh and bone, and if he could pluck it out with his rack, he might quiet the entire apparatus.

After the fourth pass it became clear to Hillary that this tactic was not working; indeed, it was putting him in more danger than he was putting the moose. The animal was wasting little energy in getting out of the way, and with his own thrusts he was getting closer and closer with his antlers. It was time to try something different.

Hillary now approached arm first. This confused the moose. He knew the enemy was in the cab, he knew the scoop was a more formidable charger than himself: all this made sense. But this large, awkwardly pivoting arm had no parallel in his experience; it made no sense. He could only watch it as it swung through the air, unreal, unnatural, oddly hypnotic.

Above the machine sounds now came a louder, higher-pitched, more terrifying sound, a bellow of pain from the throat of the moose. The shovel had knocked against his shoulder. He bellowed a second time, an angrier bellow, as if in response to hearing the sound of his own pain. Some cows scattered, frightened by the noise. Hillary followed up his advantage. The swinging arm clanged the antlers, came around again, and just missed the moose's head.

During the clashes the action had moved to a wet spot where groundwater perked up through the pasture. The huge wheels of the backhoe and the great hoofs of the moose dug up grass, and soon there was mud everywhere.

The moose was not seriously injured, but he was weakened. Hillary grew more confident. He turned the backhoe around and prepared to bring the scoop into play, push that g.d.

moose right off his property and show those cows who was boss around here.

It was Reggie Salmon, frustrated as a coach whose team is getting shellacked, who first noticed the new player on the field—Soapy Rayno, that plump, aphasia-ridden, dirty little teen-ager. She had come out of the woods just as the moose had. Reggie moved closer. He knew Soapy rather better than she realized, and he was anxious for her.

"Get away from there, get away. They'll run you over," he yelled.

Soapy stepped between backhoe and moose, her arms raised toward the animal. Hillary halted the backhoe and stood up, uncertain what to do.

Soapy began walking toward the moose. She didn't speak; she held her arms out in invitation. Soon Soapy was standing not five feet away from the moose. She looked ridiculously small beside the beast, and yet those extended arms gave her power. The moose became uneasy. This new threat was more insidious than the old threat with the swinging arm. The moose started to move sideways, circling. As the moose circled Soapy, Soapy circled the moose, gradually narrowing the radius of the circle. Finally, they were so close, she reached to touch the shoulder of the animal.

It struck Reggie Salmon that this was the payoff for Soapy. What she'd wanted was physical contact with the beast. The moose began to make complicated, high-pitched noises—sounds of fear. Soapy's hands spoke: *Touch, touch—I touch, you touch, I touch you, you touch me.* Reggie was fascinated, oddly aroused.

To the observers—Hillary, Salmon, Jordan, Perkins, the cows—there seemed then a blank spot in time. Soapy was touching the moose, stroking his hide, when in the next moment she cried out sharply, her voice piercing right through the sound of the idling backhoe, and she was on the ground, rolling, then up on her knees, her face and hands covered with mud, her cap having blown off. The cascade of hair, gushing forth, startled the moose, and he stepped back. Soapy, still on her knees, raised her arms again in invitation. The moose pawed at the earth, kicking up divots the size of hubcaps. Soapy looked him in the eye, and then the moose lowered his great head and charged. Soapy never flinched. She remained on her knees, waiting.

Reggie Salmon wished he had a gun. Perkins and Jordan weren't marksmen, but Reggie was. He had been on the rifle team in college, and up until the last few years he shotgunned for birds. He could have picked off the moose, probably not killed it with a single shot, but diverted it. As it was, Critter fired the .30–.30 in the air. And perhaps it was he who saved Soapy's life, or perhaps the moose never intended to gore Soapy, for at the crack of the rifle shot, the moose leaped right over Soapy and fled into the woods.

Soapy picked up her cap, tucked her hair into it, and left without a word, without a nod. It was as if only she and the moose had existed. Reggie felt a surge of admiration. He watched her hook her thumbs in the front pockets of her blue jeans and walk into the woods. She didn't even bother to wipe the mud from her face.

News

On the drive to the Salmon house, Chance thought about Soapy. He'd asked her her real name, and she had said, "He took it. Won't give it." This made him think of Old Joe and Genevieve. They had taken his name away and wouldn't give it back. Someone had taken Soapy's name and wouldn't give it back. He tried to imagine her cleaned up, wearing a dress, but the pictures in his mind were as fogged as a Tuckerman morning. Hoping for a glimpse of her, he watched the roadside until he turned off Route 21.

His thoughts turned to the travel directions he'd received over the telephone: "When you get to the village green in Center Darby, take Upper Darby Road and go three miles. You'll come out of the deep forest gloom onto a ridge with fields here, forest there. You won't see the house. It hides behind the trees. But I'll leave the Bronco as a marker at the head of the driveway."

Chance was met at the door of the Salmon residence by a woman about forty-five. She had full lips and hair like honey streaked with gray; she was less than average height, but she stood like a tall woman. Chance introduced himself.

Before she spoke the woman appraised him with her eyes, as if the effort of speech might cloud the judgment of sight. "Reggie is expecting you. I'm Persephone Salmon," she said.

Persephone brought Chance through a hall into a main room dominated by a rubble-stone fireplace. There was no wall-board, no wallpaper, no paint; the walls were paneled with pine boards, darkened over the century to a rich brownish-gold. The rustic appearance was turned inside out by the many paintings and drawings hanging on the walls, by the Oriental rugs, the oak rolltop desk, the elegant French Provincial furniture.

Persephone could see that Chance was curious about her house. "It's a hybrid place," she said. "Reggie's grandfather put it up, his mother collected the artworks, the furniture is mine."

Chance's eye found an 8-by-10-inch photograph of a handsome, well-built young man and a stocky youth sitting on a tennis-court-sized slab of granite. The young man was bare-chested; the boy wore a T-shirt bearing the outline of an atomic bomb explosion.

"Reggie and his younger brother Monet," Persephone said.

"They don't look anything alike," Chance said.

"Reggie's mother was a Prell," Persephone said. "The Prells are short and heavyset, the Salmons more elongated."

"Prells?"

Persephone laughed ironically. "We're inbred in Upper Darby. We have Salmons, Prells, Butterworths, and everybody else."

"What would you be?"

"A Butterworth." Persephone excused herself and left the room. She walked without making a sound.

Moments later he was shaking hands with Reggie Salmon. The grip was firm but damp, and Chance could smell nervous perspiration from the man. He was still handsome, but his face was marred, as if raked by the paw of a big cat with red and purple Magic Markers for claws.

They went outside. Persephone was working in the garden.

"I thought your article on the Grenoble Mall right on,"

Reggie said, steering Chance along a path that led into the field behind the Salmon house.

"So you said when you telephoned."

"Yes. I'm sorry to have sounded so mysterious," Reggie said, "but I wanted to talk to you about two separate items, one of which, as I promised, will be a major news story for you, and the other for background."

The path bent toward a stone wall between the field and the forest. Glare coming off the field was so strong that the grasses and flowers seemed to take on a metallic quality; Chance was relieved when they went into the shade of the woods. The path wound through a forest of birches, oaks, maples, and pines. Now and then Chance saw a maple tinged with color, summer bleeding into autumn.

The path wound up and up, until they reached a great expanse of granite. Chance recognized the area as the backdrop in the picture of the Salmon brothers. Reggie made for a certain spot. Here the rock was blackened from countless camp fires. The view opened up, and Chance could see the maternal farmlands of the Connecticut River valley and the Vermont hills beyond, indistinct as the abstract paintings in the Salmon house.

"We're still on Salmon lands, along the spine of the ridge," Reggie said, his voice full of reverence, the believer in the holy land. "I come here often, as you can tell by the scars my fires have made. I won't say I meditate; I just sit, look at the fire, look at the lands, feel the weather.

"When I was your age, perhaps a bit younger, I had a crisis—a breakdown. I couldn't make myself right again; in the end it was the land that made me right. I went on to get a degree in forestry, and I've spent my whole life managing the family lands. I've gotten a living out of the forest. I know how to make a forest pay."

He kept his voice low and measured out each word for its effect. The spell that the forest had cast upon Reggie Salmon, he cast reflected upon Roland LaChance.

"This is what we humans do: we make the land pay. As I

say, I'm as good at it as anyone. But I've always believed there was something more. Something more, even, than stewardship, which is necessarily limited by the mortality of the steward. For years I asked myself, What can I do to keep these lands whole, integral? The answer I came up with is the Jepson Salmon Memorial Trust Lands. There have been three Jepson Salmons—my grandfather, my father, and my son, who died as an infant. I want to perpetuate their names, as the land perpetuates itself.

"The Trust will consist of some two thousand acres: the Salmon lands, which I control, and other lands donated by other persons in Upper Darby. For example, my wife's mother, Trellis Butterworth, died early this summer; she left half her lands to her children, half to the Trust. The details haven't been completely worked out yet. But when the paperwork is finished, under the terms of the Trust, the lands will be managed for profit for the first fifty years, with the money going into a stewardship fund. After that the forest will be left alone. No logging, no development, no management, no hand of man. People will be allowed to trespass, but not to tamper. Nature will have her way. You can imagine the stumbling blocks involved—taxes, etcetera."

Reggie stopped to take a breath, gaze at the view. Chance knew he was leaving an opening for him to say something, ask a question. He felt dazzled, blinded, as one rescued from a well bursting into sunlight. "You want me to write a story?" he mumbled.

Reggie smiled. "Not on the Trust. Your story is down there." He pointed toward the valley.

"What?"

"The Trust is background for story number two, just so you know where I'll be coming from in the next weeks and months. I intend to be in the news as an adversary to what is *down there*. There, in the valley, notice the farm with the twin silos and the hip-roofed barn." Reggie pointed. "That's the Avalon Hillary Farm. I have information that the Magnus people want to build their mall not in Tuckerman, as we've been reading in your newspaper, but on that property. You can see how a mall would endanger something so rare and delicate as the Trust. Accordingly, I am declaring war."

Reggie went on to say that his cousin Garvin Prell, a Tuckerman attorney, had learned that another local lawyer, Charles Barnum, had been hired to represent Avalon Hillary in unspecified pending negotiations with the town of Darby, but that Magnus was paying the bills. That was enough to convince Prell and Salmon that Magnus wanted the Hillary farm as the site of the mall.

When Chance returned to the *Crier* office, he went to work. He telephoned Hillary, who referred him to Barnum, who referred him to a man named William Case, who said, "Well, well, well. I suppose now is as good a time as any to inform Mr. and Mrs. John Q. Public."

And with that Roland LaChance had his first big news story for *The Tuckerman Crier*.

By ROLAND LaCHANCE
Crier Staff Writer

DARBY, Aug. 18—The quiet town of Darby may soon become the shopping hub for several hundred thousand people.

Magnus Mall Group Inc., the company that has been eyeing Tuckerman as a site for a mall, has shifted its energies to Darby, a small, picturesque town twelve miles from Tuckerman along the Connecticut River. The company has an option to buy the 700-acre Hillary Farm on River Road in Center Darby.

If Magnus can get town approval for a zoning change, it will purchase the farm from Avalon W. and Melba C. Hillary, according to William W. Case, vice-president in charge of new construction for Magnus.

Case declined to release the purchase price, and Hillary refused to talk to a reporter from the *Crier*.

The mall will serve southwestern New Hampshire, southeastern Vermont, and north central Massachusetts, Case said. In addition, the mall is expected to draw from metropolitan areas in Massachusetts and Connecticut.

The mall will include two anchor stores (as yet to be named), some one hundred smaller stores, restaurants, a movie theater and a video games center. "The architecture will be strictly Colonial," Case said. "It will look like a New England village, complete with town green. The only difference between this and an actual New England village is that ours will be fully enclosed. It never rains in a Magnus Mall."

A special feature of the proposal will be a model farm, made from some of the existing Hillary buildings.

"People will be able to see cows being milked, chickens hatched, even pigs at the trough," Case said. "It will be very educational for children and vacationers."

If the mall is a success, the company may launch a second project in Darby that will include a convention center, a motel, condominiums, a park along the river, and an industrial building, which would be leased to a nonpolluting industry, Case said.

"This is an experimental concept in commerce," Case said. "Instead of building in an already crowded environment, we've picked an area where the population is minimal, but which is within a scenic half-hour drive of some two hundred thousand people."

Construction will begin next spring and will be completed in six to eight months, Case said.

The Hillary farm is zoned for agricultural uses, but Darby zoning laws do not prohibit commercial uses in the agricultural zone, Case said. Therefore, the company could go ahead with construction after meeting requirements for a simple zoning variance. However, Case added, the company doesn't want to locate where it's not welcome, and will formally seek a zoning change from agricultural to commercial at the town meeting next March.

Case sees little trouble with getting approval at the town meeting, even though a two-thirds vote of residents present is required for a zoning change. He said the mall will provide such tremendous tax breaks for property owners that he's convinced voters will favor the proposal.

"The mall will so broaden the tax base of Darby that if a homeowner pays $2,000 in property taxes this year, he'll only pay $1,000 once the mall is built," Case said.

Case declined to say whether the company would seek a variance to build the mall if the zoning change is turned down at the town meeting, but he did say the company probably would lean toward pulling out if the proposal is defeated by a substantial margin.

The move by Magnus puts the Tuckerman city government in a serious bind. Most city officials had opposed a mall in Tuckerman because of fears that it would draw business away from the downtown sector. If the mall is built in Darby, the city not only could suffer the deterioration officials are afraid of but also wouldn't profit from the tax revenues the mall would generate if it were built in Tuckerman.

The Thought of the Money

All during the drive to Tuckerman from the latest Darby Planning Board meeting Melba Hillary said nothing while Barnum and Mr. Case blabbed in the backseat of the Buick. Avalon Hillary was glad he had insisted on driving the two men to the Planning Board meeting from Tuckerman. He had told them he needed to return to the city anyway because Melba had some shopping to do. "Why take two cars? Save on gas. You fellas just hop in this boat. Plenty of room," he had said, and practically shoved them in. Had they suspected his insincerity? It probably didn't matter. They were used to insincerity on a scale that made him a piker. To them, insincerity was as common and natural and necessary as rain.

Avalon was afraid that if they had taken their own cars to the meeting, they might have ended up at the farm for a conference afterward, and he didn't want them there until absolutely necessary. He had met with Barnum a half-dozen times and told him everything he could about the people on the Planning Board and the town and all that, any damn thing he wanted to know, and Avalon trusted him, more or less, respected him, even liked him, more or less, but for some reason he didn't want him in his house—not Barnum or the engineer or even this Mr. Case, the big shot from New York. He couldn't say why, except that it had something to do with himself and his father and the land and the goddamn cows. These men might have an option to buy his property, but until the papers were signed the place was still a farm, his farm.

The drive from Darby to Tuckerman would give him a chance to think, and on the way back home to talk with Melba, alone, in peace, without the phone ringing, without Rexalle playing loud music, without his married daughters showing up at all hours to tell him that he was running his life wrong, without the voice of the farm itself whispering in his ear, "Fix that gate, doctor that heifer, cut that hay." At the moment Melba was silent. Not that she was shy. Not Melba. Usually, you couldn't shut her up. But here, away from the farm and the habit of the farm, the habit that busied the mind with ten million loose ends, here in the free zone of the Buick, she could think about the money—$2.3 million. Avalon didn't blame her. He, too, was thinking about the money.

He had tried to brood his way toward meaning, toward correct actions, the way he did when he weighed the pros and cons of whether to go to the bank for another loan. What was it going to do to him to leave the farm? What was it going to do to Melba? Melba who had never lived in another house in the thirty-nine years of their marriage. Or was it thirty-eight years? He had tried to conjure up the sense of loss that by and by surely must settle over him. After all, he had spent his whole life on the farm, after his father and grandfather before him, three generations with cow shit under their shoes; no more to come—no sons, no daughters with interest. But there was no sense of loss. There was only exultation, anger, and the money. The money didn't whisper. It shouted: "Listen, up! Until now, your life, Avalon, has been no more than an incident in the greater, longer-lived being of the farm itself. Everything you ever thought or did before this moment is out of time, not yours, belonging to them, your father and his father before him, and to it, the farm. I the money: this is the only thing of value to consider; I the money: this is truly your own thing to consider."

His chores were more wearying these days, as if his age suddenly had caught up to him. He could see more clearly his father's legacy: the two W's of farm life, work and worry; having to milk the cows every day no matter how he felt; having to herd the help as well as the herd; having to make bank payments on equipment that already was needing repairs. "On the farm, something's always broke," he heard himself say.

"What's that, Avalon?" said Barnum, from the backseat of the Buick.

"Nothing. Just talking to myself," he said, but the sound of his own voice and Barnum's reply brought the urge to talk, to mingle with his fellow man. He was about to take off on something, but he halted himself when he noticed in the rearview mirror that Barnum was impatient to continue blabbing with Mr. Case.

He'd wanted to tell them that it wasn't just the money; it wasn't just the fact that none of his children were interested in the work and worry of the dairy business. Heck, he understood that nobody in his right mind would want to farm in New England. It was that the business itself was discouraging these days, both for the spirit and the pocketbook. He'd always had the kooky idea that milk was good for you, that it nourished the children, that in a pinch—if the Russians dropped their bombs or something—why, you could eat the cow. But apparently he had lived his life wrong. The doctors, bless 'em, had decided that milk wasn't good for you, and the American people had said "Uh-huh." There was a glut of dairy products on the market. The goddamn government was sick to death of buying surplus cheese, and they were running out of places to store it. So what that at the far reaches of the earth babies were starving, crying for milk? You couldn't stop that. Logistics, politics, general evil plugged the teats—tut-tut. But never mind. The milk wasn't good for them anyway. Ask the doctors. Dump the goddamn milk in the goddamn gutter. The country would be better off with one less dairy farm. By shutting down he'd be doing a favor for all those other poor-devil dairy farmers, misguided fools; he'd be helping them make a living and hold on to that kooky idea that their work and worry was benefiting the world, the babies.

He wasn't afraid of leaving the farm, and he didn't feel like a traitor, though he was. There was no guilt, no hurt, no sadness, at least not yet. He supposed that one day the abandonment of a lifetime of work and worry and, yes, belief would ring down on him. But for now he didn't have a feeling about it, not even regret. Not counting the anger, which would probably go away once the money came, the only feeling was in the thought of the money, the exultation. There was just the thought of the money. It was difficult even to think about what he would do with the money. The money itself was not yet real. All that was real was the thought of it—$2.3 million. He wanted to shout the figure; as it was, he allowed himself the pleasure of whispering it. He glanced at Melba to see whether she had heard him. She had not. She herself was deep in thought, the thought of the money.

They would be millionaires twice over and then some. It would be difficult even to get rid of the money. At, say, ten percent per year interest, they'd have an annual income of $230,000, much more than he could possibly make keeping cows on his land. And that wasn't even draining the principal. There was no work in interest money, no worry. It just kept dripping into the bottomless pail of personal desire. Sinful, downright sinful. Somewhere along the line you were cheating somebody and didn't know it. He felt as though he were picking God's pocket—and that felt good. It was strange: When you depended on God, or nature, or whatever was out there, for rain or sunshine or protection from frost, why, you respected God and feared Him. But if you had the pot of gold at the end of the rainbow, you didn't care whether it rained. You neither feared Him nor respected Him. God was just another idea, like electric milking machines or current-use taxation.

All the while Avalon's mind churned, a part of him was listening to Barnum and Case in the backseat. They talked so much he wondered how they got anything done.

"The question is, Bill, are we going to come back at them asking for the zoning change, which I don't believe we need, or are we going the zoning variance route via the Board of Adjustment?" Barnum said.

Barnum was a jowly man with big, soft hands, hands that would be like shovels if he ever turned them to farming. Avalon envied the hands.

"Let's review this," Case said. "With rezoning, we face recommendations from the Board of Adjustment, the Planning Board, and the will of the voters. Correct?"

Case's voice sounded like somebody holding his nose, but there was no doubt he was in charge. Avalon resisted a vague urge to ask him how many suits he owned.

"Correct," Barnum said.

"The zoning variance is obviously the easier row to hoe, but the town laws being what they are—shaky—the variance decision could be challenged in Superior Court," Case said.

"That's what Harriman says, and he's got a point, at least in theory," Barnum said. "But as a practical matter, once you've got that variance and have established your use, that's it. From a legal standpoint, it would be difficult to prevent that use."

"Let's test the winds of that assumption," Case said. "If we take the variance route, we don't need the town vote to fly us, only the blessing of the Board of Adjustment."

"The Planning Board has to review the site plan, but they have to approve it if it meets their criteria. State law," Barnum said.

"Something tells me, and this is the drift I get from the rest of the officers of the company, that in the long run we'll get better sailing weather if we go for the full-course menu rather than the à la carte route," Case said.

"So you favor our present course—a request for a zoning change," Barnum said.

"I like the idea of a town vote," Case said.

"My own feeling is we're better off to try for the variance first," Barnum said. "If it fails, we can go to the people, via the zoning change. You've got two shots instead of one. Don't forget, we need a two-thirds majority. State law."

"A town vote is a good barometer of the body politic," Case said. "If it's overwhelmingly in the negative, the company might be advised to set up the kitchen in another part of the house."

"If I hear you correctly, Bill, Magnus might consider going someplace other than Darby," Barnum said.

"Well, yes," Case said. "Why try to beat a dead horse to death?"

"But Mr. Hillary's farm remains the favored location. Is that correct?"

"That is correct," Case said.

And on they blabbed. Hillary found their talk tiring and dreary, yet he was jealous too. A common quest made them such pals. He himself wasn't much for discussing a problem. His way was to think and brood and mull over alone, usually while doing chores. Thinks on his feet: that's a farmer. Eventually, he'd worry himself into a solution. Not always the right one, however. Then, too, there was the burden of knowing that having made his decision alone, he alone was responsible for it. So many times he would have been better off discussing a problem with someone. But he didn't have the knack for productive chit-chat. He became impatient; he had a difficult time respecting other people's opinions. These men, they just talked on and on and on without brooding, without mulling, without pain, without even thinking. Eventually, they'd stumble on a solution that probably would work out. They were like squirrels that hid their acorns, forgot where, then when the time came searched busily and found food hidden by other squirrels. Having reached a decision more or less together, they must feel all sweet and companionable at the moment of the find, Avalon thought. Later, if the solution worked out, each fellow would take credit for it. If it didn't, why it would be easy to blame the other guy.

Avalon didn't care that people knew he was selling his land. God knows, he wasn't ashamed of the fact; he hadn't committed a crime. What bothered him was that the word had gotten around town that something was up. Somebody had squealed. If there was going to be news concerning his farm, he wanted to spread it his way, on his terms. He didn't want to tell it to a bunch of gossips at a goddamn meeting run by some woman from out of town. He didn't like the looks of that reporter either. If he ever started talking to Rexalle, she'd tell him everything, including the price—$2.3 million. Holy cow! Every time that figure came to mind, it gave him a tickle. He'd done the right thing, hadn't he? Well, he didn't know, didn't care right now. So it went with age. When you were young, you had a nice definite set of rights and wrongs, like wrenches hanging over the workbench. You got older, you got worn, you saw "this" become "that" and "that" become "this"; you came to realize that a man always believes he's living his life right today, even if he was wrong ten years ago; you got forgetful about the joys of youth and fretful about the despairs; you came to be a good judge of men and weather, which made you see the futility of trusting either; you got atheistic, and that made you lonely; you got tired of doing the chores and cranky when there was nothing to do; you got sick with the ingratitude of grown-up children; you got no thrill from pretties, no disgust from uglies—a sunset and a flapdoodle, all the same. None of this seemed serious when he turned his mind to the thought of the money.

Avalon and Melba dropped Barnum and Case at the Ramada Inn in Tuckerman. Case said he wanted to talk to the other officers in his company before deciding what the next move would be. He then offered to buy him and Melba a drink in the lounge, but Avalon figured the two men really wanted to blab together unfettered at the bar, so he said no thanks, not bothering to check with Melba because he was afraid she'd be tempted to accept the offer. He didn't care much for drink, and he didn't like how Melba got after a highball—first gushy, then critical. Besides, he wanted to go to bed. These lawyers could sleep until seven or eight o'clock in the morning, but a farmer—never. He wondered whether after he had the $2.3 million he'd get the knack of sleeping into the dawn.

"How many mornings a year you suppose that we get up and it's still dark?" he said, when they were on the road again, heading for home.

Melba knew what he was getting at. "All of them, except for a week in June," she said. Which was not quite accurate but which got the point across.

"Just once, I'd like to miss the goddamn sunrise at Christmas," he said.

"Where you want to wake up on Christmas? Not this Christmas, but next Christmas, and the one after that, et cetera?"

Her question startled Avalon. After the sale they'd have to move out of the house. He'd thought about the money, but he hadn't thought about how the sale of the land and the receipt of the money was going to affect their lives—who their friends would be, the car they would drive, the food they would eat, the things they would do, where they would live. But Melba had.

"Don't know, don't know's I give a damn right now," he said, hoping to put her off.

"I have an idea," Melba said.

Her tone sent a chill along his spine. When she used that tone, it meant she had made up her mind about something. Melba was a strong-willed woman, who nonetheless let him have his way on most matters. But when she decided to go after something whole hog, why, that' was it. He too had a strong will, but he parceled it out daily to get the little things. She saved it up and unleashed it all at once to get the big things. He had never gotten used to that tone and those slowly spoken words, "I have an idea." They took the starch right out of him.

"Yah," he said.

"I want to spend Christmas where it's warm, where you can hear the ocean rock the Christ child."

"Yah." He was amazed at the religious reference; he thought she'd gotten that out of her system years ago.

"Avalon?"

"Yah."

"Let's take the money and buy a condominium in Florida."

Naming of Parts

She knelt, touched the paint line in the street, and whispered, "Yellow." With the speaking of the word, it was as if an understanding of the color had been transmitted from the road, through the tips of her fingers, to her mind. For a moment she basked in the glory of the knowledge of "yellow."

"Soapy? Soapy? You okay?"

It was Again Jordan, looking down at her, grinning, as Jordan fellows would when they were on the edge of uncertainty. Again had been her boyfriend briefly. She still liked him a fair sum, but he was too much a Jordan for her to want to get close to. Of course, if he had touched her heart, it wouldn't have mattered that he was a Jordan.

"I'm okay. Beat it," she said.

"Soapy—Soapy Rayno," Again said, smiled, whistled, and walked on.

She understood why he had emphasized the sounding of her name. He was telling her, in the Jordan fashion, that if he chose to he could wound her, using her name as a weapon. There was nothing malicious in this. He was merely informing her of his manly attributes; this was Jordan strutting. He would expect her to feel flattered by the attention, the effort made.

She didn't care what Again said or what anybody said. Let them call her Soapy. Let them believe she was a Rayno. She knew who she wasn't, which was more than they knew; when, finally, she knew who she was, they might never know her actual name, but they would sense the unsuitability of the other name—Soapy Rayno—and shrink from it.

Soapy was headed for the Tuckerman Transportation Center, gathering, as she went, courage by naming things. She extended her hand, and whispered, "This is a parking meter." She would rather have shouted, but there were people around, and she didn't want to draw attention to herself. "This is brick," she said, touching the outside wall of Schoenberg's Pharmacy. "That there is a durenem," she said, now angry with herself because the name of the thing (which was "window") had not found its way out from her mind to her lips. The trouble was she hadn't touched the window. In order to name something, it was best to touch it. Too bad you couldn't touch people. If you touched them they would hurt you, and if they touched you it meant they wanted to hurt you. People were afraid to touch because they didn't want to know each other's hurt—hurt held so much of the knowledge of the world. She touched the window and spoke. "Window . . . window; window, window, window. Window." There now. That was a good word. And having grasped the word and spoken it, she now felt its essence— window: place where light passes through a wall. Beautiful. Beautiful word.

She spotted the American flag waving gently in the breeze from its great pole at the base of Central Square. She had an urge to say "flag," so that she could possess knowledge of the idea of flags. She realized the danger involved. The flag was far away, out of reach. Then again, the moose had been out of reach, and she had touched the moose and understood its loneliness, its confusion, and drawn strength from the knowledge, even as it made her sad.

She spoke: "Dwinggle." Must try again. "That up high is high, high up, high up, high." *Climb it. Climb that pole, touch it—fabric, colors; touch.* She had to fight the urge to climb the pole.

She walked on, the idea of a flag out of her grasp. Mustn't get upset, mustn't get angry. When she got angry, she found it impossible to speak and sometimes difficult to think. She must remain composed, because she had a duty to perform today: buy a bus ticket. *Sell me a ticket. I got money. I saved it. When does the bus come? Where do I sit?*

She continued to make her way down Main Street, touching this and that, naming things.

The Tuckerman Transportation Center was in the Boston and Maine railroad station, a run-down brick and wood building constructed soon after the Civil War. Trains still moved freight in the Tuckerman yards, but a passenger train hadn't stopped at the station in twenty years. Soapy had never been inside before. Thus she was unaware of the church-pew benches carved with hearts and dirty words: unaware of the immensity of the bathrooms and the hundred-year-old urine smell, unaware, also, of Ed Weejun. The station now served as headquarters for the Tuckerman Taxi Company and as a terminal for the Vermont Transit bus lines, and Ed did double duty as taxi dispatcher and agent for the bus company.

Ed hated questions. People asked him the strangest things: Will I get mugged in Kansas City? He'd want to say, How in the world should I know? Instead, he answered such inquiries with, Ask in New York. He doubted whether anybody in New York knew anything, but the answer seemed to satisfy, and he did want to satisfy these poor souls who found it necessary to travel by bus.

Even while dealing with them, he never looked at the bus customers, but watched his flash board to see if the taxi phones were ringing (he didn't like noise, so the bells were disconnected), and therefore he heard the girl growl before he actually laid eyes on her.

"Something I can do for you?" he asked.

"Grrrrrr!" the girl said.

"Somebody put you up to this? I ain't nobody for a joke,"

Ed said, seeing the culprit now, a plump teen-age girl with pimples.

"Grrrrrr!"

"Get out of here. Get the hell out of here before I call the cops." Ed was dialing police headquarters and one of his waiting taxi drivers was about to grab the girl, when she backed up and scrambled out the door. Ed didn't see her outside, jumping up and down, growling, weeping, gnashing her teeth. Nor did he see the young man who had spotted her distress come over to help.

For a few moments everything was white for Soapy Rayno. It was like being on the side of a hill in the middle of a blizzard. Too much feeling; too little sight; no flat ground. And then a boy was holding her arm, speaking to her gently.

"It's going to be all right. You just lost it for a minute or two. It's going to be all right."

His voice lifted the storm, and soon she could see, and her feelings calmed enough so she could command them. She recognized the boy now. He was the one who had given Delphina and her the ride the day she had seen the moose.

"You got a baby truck," she said.

He laughed, and his mirth was like a hand stroking her cheek.

They walked downtown.

"I was going to have dinner. Are you hungry? Want to eat?" he asked.

The Chrysalis was a restaurant with a dual personality. The street door opened into a common hallway. From there you could go right, into a diner with red stools and booths with heavily varnished tabletops. Or you could go left, into the dining room with rugs on the floor, tablecloths, chandeliers, and wallpaper of fluttering monarch butterflies. On weekdays for lunch, a workingman might sit in the diner and enjoy the Chrysalis's famous coffee, a Western sandwich, and apple pie for dessert. On weekends the same man might put on a tie and bring his family to the posh side of the Chrysalis.

Soapy had never been in the dining room, and when Chance

automatically turned left in the hall, she felt a sudden surge of pleasure mixed with shame—shame that she was so dirty and common in this magnificent place. Yet she kept her cap on, kept the little beauty she had to herself. Then the butter-flies on the walls and the candles flickering on the tables whisked away her unpleasant thoughts, and she surrendered herself to the moment.

"Want a drink?" Chance asked. She liked his voice. It was nervous and uncertain, but there was no weakness in it, or stupidity, or cruelty.

"I ain't of age," she said.

"Do you like to drink?" he asked, and she nodded in the affirmative. "If we're discreet, I think the waitress will let us get away with an end run around the law," he said.

He ordered a double something, and they took turns sipping from a glass shaped like a birdbath. By the time the second double arrived, she was on the verge of crying with happiness.

He had asked her a couple of questions about her life, and she had frowned.

"I know it pains you to talk, so if you don't want to say anything, that's all right with me," he said.

She put her finger on the wings of the butterfly on the wallpaper, and said, "Not a bird."

"Not a bird—that's correct," Chance said.

"Name it," she said.

"You want me to name things. You touch. I name. Is that it? That is it. Not a bird, but a monarch butterfly."

"Monarch butterfly," she said, and with his help she named everything on the table—knife, fork, spoon, napkin, table-cloth, menu, wine list, candle, begonia flower (she thrilled to that word, "begonia"). They went through the things in his pocket—keys, fingernail clipper, quarter, nickel, dime, Swiss army knife, comb, press card, wallet; on the inside of the wallet were twenty-dollar bills, ten-dollar bills, a VISA credit card, a MasterCard credit card, a driver's license, and a pic-ture of his parents, Old Joe and Genevieve. She could see that it made him sad to name them, even to look at their images. Soon he was talking about his mother.

"She's not my natural mother," he said. "I don't know who my natural parents are. I do know I was conceived in Tuckerman County, and that's why I came here. I'm not sure why I stay; I feel strange and alone here, haunted. But I can't leave. Why am I telling you this?"

"You like to talk—I don't like to talk—you like to talk," she said.

"That's it—you're a good listener, Soapy," he said.

He coached her through the menu. She had been able to read once, but the illness had taken away that ability. She was getting it back, little by little, but she still had trouble recognizing words and the meaning in their arrangements. He read the entire menu with the prices, and she repeated everything he said. This exercise made her feel warm, close. When she decided on the chicken with the broccoli sauce, he showed her where the words were written, and she read them to herself, and then touched them and spoke them aloud over and over. He corrected her. She was having trouble with "broccoli." She kept saying the words until the waitress arrived, and she was able to order for herself. A triumph.

The meal was delicious. Instead of swilling down her food, she took her time; she was reverent toward the food, toward the situation. They had wine, so the booze buzz lingered through the meal. She watched him carefully, and she did whatever he did. She discovered that it wasn't difficult to eat out at a fancy restaurant.

They had just ordered coffee when Chance left to go to the men's room. Soapy looked around the restaurant. Some people were eyeing her; a young man snickered. She touched the butterfly on the wall, and said, "Pizmop." She didn't deserve to be here. In order for her to deserve to be here, she had to come around inside herself, and to do that she had to get her bearings; she needed her name, like the sky needs the North Star.

When Chance came back from the men's room, he found that Soapy had gone.

Searching for Soapy

Chance was just finishing shaving, when he was suddenly aware of the sound of the water running, and he was looking at his face, studying it, noticing the straight nose, the dark eyes, the long neck. The LaChances said they had chosen him in the cradle because he resembled their kind, New England Franco-Americans. The subject of resemblance became a nervous family joke. Genevieve said he looked like Old Joe, Old Joe said he was the picture of Uncle Alfonse (Alfonse had gone West and Joe had never set eyes on him), and Chance saw in himself Genevieve, like a mirror that reversed gender and turned back time.

"No doubt I'm somebody's bastard—but whose?" he said to the mirror, and now he was seeing Genevieve in his features. He was lonely for her. He had lost his natural parents at birth, and he had lost Old Joe in the worst possible way, and he had lost Genevieve to . . . what? Circumstance? He didn't know. He remembered seeing her on the day Old Joe removed himself from life. She had picked him up at the airport in Albuquerque, looking exhausted and dry, dry as the New Mexico landscape. Now, in his own face, he could almost see the tiny moraines of red dust in the wrinkles that departed from Genevieve's brown eyes and faded into her smooth, sun-pinked cheeks.

He had wanted to hold her, weep upon her as if he were a just-found child. Instead, he had said, "Your skin is dry." "It's the sun here," she had said.

Chance looked into the mirror now, saying aloud but softly, "It's the son here."

That night he went to Murry's for drinks with Terry Dayton, the *Crier's* city hall reporter. Terry had a date and left early. Chance didn't want to drink alone, didn't want to go home yet. He drove the streets of Tuckerman. The LaChance family had pulled up stakes a number of times, as Old Joe took jobs across the nation's school districts, pursuing his dream of becoming a school superintendent. During the travel Old Joe would be in a good mood, and Chance, floating on the warmth of Old Joe's optimism, would watch the scenery pass by as a bather dreamily watching the world from an inflated inner tube on a lake.

He was thinking about Old Joe, on the road, happy, grinning, talking about what a great place they were going to, when he found himself driving past Tuckerman Hospital. And now he was thinking about Soapy, the dirty girl who buried her lovely hair in a baseball cap. He remembered that she and her sister worked in the hospital laundry on the night shift. Impulsively, he pulled the Brat into the main parking lot of the hospital. He didn't know what he'd say to Soapy, but he'd had three drinks and he didn't care. It was enough that the idea of seeing her cheered him.

Inside, he threw up his arm before the neon light pouring into his eyes, then walked on. Eventually, he wandered down the hall of the obstetrics ward. From a huge window he studied the newborns. Some dozed like tiny sleeping Orientals; some lay awake staring, wondering, it seemed, what the devil was out there; some screamed for mercy. Then he got a whiff of sweat and perfume. He turned, and he was looking at a young nurse, perhaps even younger than himself, with chopped brown hair and skin as white as her uniform. "Did you want me to bring out the baby?" she asked.

Being mistaken for a father prickled Chance with confusing

twinges of anger, panic, and pride. He asked for directions to the laundry. It was in the basement near the morgue, the nurse told him.

Below ground, the hall was dimly lit. A red ax and fire extinguisher attached to the brick foundation set him to wondering what you were supposed to do with the ax if fire broke out. He followed the groan sounds of machines to an open door and went in. A wave of heat rolled over him along with the smell of clothes dryers.

Two women pulled wet sheets from a washer. Chance was about to speak when he was startled by a roar. Out of the corner of his eye he saw bodies cascading into a cart. He caught a glimpse of bloodied linen. The image of a baby spitted on a sword flashed in his mind. Then he heard the women giggle. Apparently, he had jumped back as laundry tumbled down a chute. He blushed.

"Don't mind me and Kate," one of the women said. "When you're down here in hell, anything different is fun."

The woman named Kate cackled. She was about sixty, wizened, bent, yellow of tooth. When her face came into the light and Chance could see her eyes, he realized she was retarded. The speaker was about fifty, full-figured and dimpled. It was to her he introduced himself.

"Welcome to hell, Chance. This is Kate," the woman said, patting the wizened woman on the head. "Say hello, Kate. And you, young man, are feasting your eyes on Fralla Pratt. But I don't suppose you come to see me and Kate."

"I'm looking for Soapy Rayno," Chance said.

"Soapy ain't here. Soapy quit," Fralla said.

Fralla sent Kate off to do some work, and lit a cigarette. Fralla seemed so grateful for the company, for the chance to take a break from her labors, that she gushed with talk.

"Soapy quit because Delphina quit," Fralla said. "Soapy was good with her hands. Most women are better that way than men, you know. They're more dependable, too. They don't drink as much, and they don't drop dead on you the way men will. The trouble with women is they get pregnant all the time. Soapy was a good worker, steady as she goes.

'Course Soapy didn't say much, and when she did, half the time it didn't make sense, so you didn't get to know her unless you watched her hands."

Most of the women Chance knew of Fralla's age—secretaries, clerks, minor officials, teachers, friends of his mother—were well-spoken, well-groomed, friendly but reserved before a young man such as himself; there was always a feeling in him that he was not dealing with the real person. Even a woman's makeup seemed like a disguise to him. But Fralla obviously came from a different class. She was coarse and direct. He found himself comfortable with her, comfortable even with the "hell" she worked in. With pipes exposed, machinery uncabineted, brick and concrete walls painted a dingy green but not paneled over, the laundry room, like Fralla, was clearly what it was and nothing else. He wanted to shout, "There is no lie here!" Instead, he asked, "Did Soapy take her hat off at work?"

"You've seen her hair, else you wouldn't have said that," Fralla said.

Chance said nothing.

"I used to tease her about the hat, but she wouldn't take it off," Fralla said. "So I never seen her hair, but from a strand here, a strand there, and—by gosh—from a clean neck, I guessed she had good hair and took care of it."

"Strange girl—beautiful hair," Chance said.

"I can see you are of the finest cut," Fralla said. "I bet you've been to college and everything. I wish my son Porky had gone to college. Might not be all balled up with the law and his own heart-wrenchings today if he had some education and a strong father around. Not that I'm saying he's guilty. He ain't. He fell in with a bad crowd. He's the kind will do anything for anybody who's nice to him. Me not including, of course. They never do for the mother; no one does for the mother. The mother is somebody you blame. . . . The Rayno girls don't come from what you and I would call good stock. Their daddy was one of those wham-bam-thank-you-mam men, who was gonzo before the girls were big enough to know him. The mommy marched about from bed to bed, which of course led to hitting the bottle. She was bottle killed. This is no secret now—I ain't no gossip. And the plain fact is the blood lines of the Raynos is mixed netherwise with the Jordans. Not that I have anything against the Jordans. They're as good as the rest of us in their own way. To be honest, though, I don't knows I'd like any of my kind to marry a Jordan. I even get a little squeamish thinking about Delphina and Critter together."

Fralla talked on, about her son, about the old days when she worked in the textile mills, about her failed marriages, about talk itself, how we all have to talk but nobody listens. She told Chance that Soapy lived in a trailer with Delphina and Critter in the town of Darby. Fralla didn't know where the trailer was, but she knew that Delphina rented it from her cousin, Melba Hillary.

Chance watched Kate wheel a cart loaded with dirty laundry to a washer, while Fralla put an empty cart under the chute. He watched as the two women reached into the full cart and pulled the dirty linen out and stuffed it into the washer. He kept looking for blood.

"Some of that must be pretty messy," he said.

"You learn to look before you reach," Fralla said. "I don't mind what I see, and the smell don't bother me. What I don't like is touching the sticky stuff."

"Blood?" Chance asked.

"Shit," Fralla said. "Blood dries. Shit don't."

With that, Chance returned to his apartment. He watched the rerun of last Saturday night's boxing matches on the sports channel. When he finally felt tired enough to sleep, he shut the TV off and went to bed. He had already decided to search for Soapy. There was no good reason for this. He was like a man lost in the woods, heading for a mountain in the far distance to prevent him from walking in circles.

Melba Hillary met the Brat as Chance pulled into the yard, took one look at him, pointed a hefty finger at the barn, said, "He's in there," and went back into the house, shutting the door behind her. Chance entered the barn with some foreboding. Animal housing was strange to him. However, once inside he was relieved to feel emanations of safety. The smell of cows and manure perfumed the cool, moist air. He found Avalon Hillary putting a bale of hay in a wheelbarrow.

"Goddamn, but you're a pest," Hillary said, not entirely unfriendly. "You call me up on the telephone, and now you come to my farm. I can't tell you anything about this land sale. Mr. Case is the spokesman."

"I know," Chance said. "I actually came to see Mrs. Hillary about the trailer she rented to the Rayno girls, but she sent me here."

Hillary looked tired, soul-tired as well as body-tired. One of the handles of the wheelbarrow slipped from his hand, and the bale tumbled out. He stood for a moment, deciding, then sat down upon the bale.

Chance chose the moment to act. He wheeled the barrow to the open barn door to the stack of bales, loaded a couple in the barrow, wheeled it past Hillary, and deposited it in a corner where he saw other bales.

"I need the exercise. Do you mind?" Chance asked.

"Be my guest," Hillary said.

The work elated Chance. This small chore he had so spontaneously assumed turned him away from himself to the smells of the barn, the look of its heavy, dark beams, and the feel of the eyes of the older man on him. The next sound came from a cow, moaning.

"Sick—udder problem," Hillary said. "They get sick just like people, and they complain like people, and they die like people. But they don't have any interest in improving themselves beyond the station of a cow, and of course in that they are not at all like people."

It was now Chance's turn to offer something in the conversation, but he said nothing. He was content to work. Hillary continued to watch, mildly amused.

When Chance was almost finished, Hillary asked, "So what do you want? To rent the trailer? A job?"

Chance pushed the last bale beside Hillary, sat upon it, and spoke. He talked about his encounter with Soapy. He didn't say outright that he was looking for her, but Hillary seemed to sense that he was reaching for something that couldn't be explained. The two men slipped into a temporary intimacy, their conversation lubricated by the velvety barn air.

"The Rayno girls lived on this small piece of land we own that borders the Salmon Trust," Hillary said. "Ten or twelve years ago I made the mistake of leasing that parcel to some hippies that wanted to camp out and farm organically. They converted a school bus into a trailer home. Ugliest goddamn thing you ever saw. When the lease was up, I says, 'Get the hell off my property.' They moved, but left the bus behind. I worried what to do with it for years, when one day Melba says, 'I have an idea.' Next thing I know, the Rayno girls moved in. Pretty soon Critter was residing there too, and knocking on my door for work. Said he wanted to farm. Wanted to get away from his old man was more like it. See, Critter Jordan was Ike's go-fer. Critter tried to strike out on his own, as a young man will. But he came to the wrong place. Critter's not cut out for farming. He's not lazy exactly, just made wrong for this work. Wouldn't you know it but Delphina found herself in a family way, and she quit her job. So they left, all three of 'em, headed back to Ike. He's got 'em housed in his auction barn. As to Soapy, I don't know. Poor girl's afflicted. What are you going to do with her when you find her, give her a goddamn bath?"

When he was about to leave, Chance said, "I don't think I'd care to farm, either, but I like the barn."

"Uh-huh."

"If the sale goes through with the Magnus people, will you miss it? Buy another farm?"

"How the hell do I know?" Hillary said. "I've never been without the farm. Nor was my father. I'll tell you this: I like contemplating the lack of it. I haven't filled the lack with anything yet, but I've got a good mull going on it. Look at this farm, the machines, the buildings, the ground itself— look at the wear. Goddamn!"

Chance came away from the Hillary farm thinking about Critter Jordan, a young man who had tried and apparently failed to escape the tyranny of his father.

The Burglary

Critter Jordan waited nervously for his father to get out of a meeting. He paced along the granite-slab steps of the town hall; he sneaked about in the corridors of the building itself, listening, but unlike his father taking no pleasure in eavesdropping for its own sake, only wanting to be near human activity; he fidgeted in Ike's Dodge van, repeatedly checking the glove compartment for the Ruger .357 Magnum Security Six pistol that his father kept there but, as far as Critter knew, had never fired. Holding the gun brought him a small comfort. He hated being alone; he hated being on the outer limits of society. He had pleaded with Ike to let him attend the meeting with him, sit with him, son beside father. Ike said, "You wouldn't know whether to sit with your daddy or Mr. Hillary, now, would you? You wait here."

His father was still mad at him for working for Hillary. Critter had wanted to say, "Look, Pop, I didn't go to him for succor, but for work. I wanted to try something on my own. What's wrong with that?" But instead he had found himself saying, "Mr. Hillary is a good man, kind of cranky, but he always took the time to explain things and he never bragged," hoping somehow that Ike would change and be more like Mr. Hillary. Ike had cracked him across the mouth. So he didn't talk about Mr. Hillary anymore, didn't think about farming or any of that. He merely accepted Ike's succor, biding his time for the day that he, like his father, could offer succor instead of seeking it, and thus could realize his Jordan ascendancy.

Critter was taller, more muscled, more wavy-haired, more regular-featured than his father. He was aware that by the standards of the world at large he was almost handsome. Yet this meant little to him, for in the Jordan code ascendancy was everything for a man. He had tried getting away, but his experiment in working for Mr. Hillary had failed. He didn't like the hard work, the getting up early in the morning, the schedules, the clock watching, the attention to detail, the finickiness.

Critter was nervous, in part because his sense of isolation, painful enough under ordinary circumstances, was now exaggerated by the fact that other people were congregating nearby. As he was on the edge of the meeting, so the Jordan clan was on the edge of society: this idea settled into him, not as a thought but as a discomfort. He was also nervous because he hadn't had acigarette in more than an hour. A pack of Marlboros was in his pocket, but he didn't dare light one. Ike would smell the smoke on him the moment they got in the van. It wasn't so much Ike's wrath that he feared as the pure boredom of having to listen to one of his speeches, the same words, the same preachy tone, the same hammer of responsibility swung at him. "You listen up," Ike would say. "This is for you to learn, or go to jail and disgrace my name. You don't smoke on the night you break and enter, you don't eat garlic, and you take a bath; you wear clean clothes, dark clothes, and tennis shoes two sizes too big, and afterward you throw the shoes away. You understand the point now? If you leave a track, your foot won't be indicted by the grand jury." Here Ike would pause, expecting him to laugh at the joke about indicting a foot. "A man who stinks will alert a dog sixty feet away, if there is a dog, and it will alert the household once you're in the house." Never mind that the building they planned to enter tonight was uninhabited. If Critter raised that point, Ike would say, "You should assume that all premises are inhabited."

The impending burglary itself was the main reason Critter was nervous. He was always uptight before a break, and though he calmed somewhat during the actual operation, he plunged into anxiety and depression later. He didn't know why, and he didn't bother asking himself why. He didn't like messing with the whys of self. Whys led to . . . to disturbances. And so while his anxiety nagged him, its possible sources did not. It did trouble him that at times, most times, his father did not seem to notice the unhappiness of his son. That made Critter feel abandoned, brought back the pain of his mother's abandonment when he had been a small boy.

Ike was smart and he was stupid. He could see right through a falsehood, he could find the weakness in an idea, he could blow up the flaws in an argument, he was a big spender of big words. Yet now and then he could be tricked into believing that a tampon was a cigar, and he carted around a handful of strange ideas like good-luck pieces. Ike would say with great conviction that the Russians caused a blizzard or a cold spell. If you explained to him that New Hampshire had bad winters before there was a Russia, he'd smile and shake his head as though you were the fool. He had that ability to win out, even when he was wrong. Critter supposed that, like his father, most people had blind spots in their understanding of the world, but the darknesses in his own family seemed to run deeper, wider. He used to wonder what his own blind spot was, until he realized he would never be able to discover the answer, since if he could see that blind spot, it wouldn't be a blind spot. With that, he had ceased to search.

When Ike came out of the meeting, he was smiling. Critter inspected the smile to determine whether this was one of Ike's mirthful smiles or one of his toolful smiles. His appraisal of the smile was inconclusive, so he risked a question.

"How'd it go?" he asked.

"Oh, the Planning Board wanted to know various things, and all your concerned citizens expressed their concerns, and old man Hillary rubbed his knees just like a farmer," Ike said. "Don't mean nothing, it's all rigged. 'Course they've got to pretend, I suppose."

"Sure, Pop," Critter said.

And, concerning the meeting, that was that. Critter didn't expect his father to say more, indeed was happy that Ike had so limited his remarks. Even if Ike had told him his own views or had talked about what actually had gone on at the meeting, Critter would have paid no attention. Ike lied all the time about everything, lied out of habit and humor. You had to learn to read Ike by the lines around the corners of his mouth, by how many false teeth he chose to show you (not by his eyes—Ike could lie with his eyes), by certain cracks in his voice. The words themselves were as worthless as virgins.

Critter wasn't sure why Ike was getting himself involved in the mall issue. As Critter saw the situation, either they would get a mall or they wouldn't, and there was nothing any Jordan was going to do about it. Therefore, it made no sense for a Jordan to waste energy on things like going to meetings. But Ike . . . well, Ike was Ike. He had his ideas and his reasons, and there was no accounting for them. Critter was guessing that Ike had no real interest in the mall, but had attended the meeting tonight to give himself an alibi for this night's work.

Once under way, Ike driving, Critter in the passenger seat, Crowbar—Ike's dog—snoozing fretfully in the rear, Critter sensed Ike sliding into his burglar being: quieting, growing sensitive as a guitar string, fire crackling in his eyes. From here on in, Critter determined that he would have to impose a calm upon himself, do what he was told and try not to make any mistakes.

He wasn't sure exactly what kind of operation Ike had in mind, but something told him it wasn't going to be too risky. The recent burglaries hardly seemed profitable, especially in light of Ike's other enterprises. It was as if Ike kept up his profession to stay in shape and to give him, Critter, the practice. Not that Critter wanted the practice. He had no urge to carry on in his father's footsteps. The life of a burglar didn't suit him. He didn't like sneaking around. And although he found it hard to admit, dishonesty itself didn't suit him.

In the old days, when Critter was just a boy, Ike would rent a truck and they would back up to a place and load it with everything they could get in, and then head for Connecticut, where a Mr. Geyser would give them money or exchange their spoils for spoils from other parts of the country, for Ike's auction business. But these days Ike didn't sell stolen goods to the public—too risky—and he drove to Connecticut only now and then. Furthermore, he limited his recent burglaries to specialty items—paintings, antique clocks, or jewelry. Sometimes Ike would take something just because he liked its looks. "Isn't this beautiful, isn't it juuust divine," he would say, in a voice that seemed to come from a tape recorder in his throat, for it wasn't his own. God knows what he did with those things. Occasionally he took nothing at all. Those were the creepiest times. He would look around, his eyes wild, his chest heaving like a kid's at his first hoochy-coochy show, and they would leave the house undisturbed, and Ike would be satisfied in a place inside himself that Critter did not want to know.

Ike turned off Center Darby Road and headed into the hills of Upper Darby. By now he was completely out of his meeting self and fully into his burglar self. The smile was gone, and the eyes moved restlessly, like a predator at dusk. During the transition Ike had been quiet, but now he would want to talk, and it would be all right to talk to him.

"Where we going, Pop?" Critter asked.

"I thought we'd look into Mrs. Trellis Butterworth's house," Ike said. "They cleaned it out pretty good when the old lady died, but I'm guessing they overlooked a few items of interest. Let me tell you a few things . . ."

Uh-oh, here comes a speech, thought Critter.

". . . these ritzy people need as big a septic tank as you and me. Right?" Ike was demanding confirmation.

"Right, Pop," Critter said.

"If there's one thing I've learned about this business," Ike said, "it's that greedy people don't see the gold nuggets at their feet when they're frisking the dead. Somebody dies and the kin divvy up the estate—if they don't sell it at auction— but they always leave behind the loose ends. Uncle Harry wants the Parker shotgun and the briar pipes, and cousin Mary Lou has had her eye on the Newport hutch for years. A death brings out the gimme in people. The whole family is all secretly thrilled at the demise of the deceased, happier than a state trooper with a billy club at a hippie picnic. After the fight to see who gets the silverware and the teddy bears, they take their winnings and go on home, more or less egotistical that they'd screwed some kin out of his egotism. Ain't nobody sure exactly what's left over—an old clock now worth twenty-five thousand or a primitive painting that I can sell in New York for fifty thousand." (Critter winced at Ike's gross exaggerations. Why did he have to lie at every turn?) "See, the beauty of this is that if we find something of value and we steal it, it won't mean nothing to the kin. They already got what they want. They won't even notice what's gone from what's been left behind. Or if they do notice, they'll think Aunt Suzie come and took it. What we get is a free steal. Now if there ain't nothing of value, why we just hook a knickknack for a souvenir or don't steal a thing, walk away grateful for the experience. This is can't-lose burglary."

"No risks, eh, Pop?" Critter knew the moment he had spoken that he had made a mistake.

"There's always risk. Risk is half the fun of burglary. The other half is the profit," Ike said.

Critter knew he was expected to acknowledge this wisdom, especially in light of his mistake, but he tried to refrain from speaking. A faint murmur of rebellion was sounding inside him. However, Ike's silence was thick and dark, and Critter heard himself seeking relief by regurgitating words Ike had fed him. "Why sure, Pop. There's risk in any business worth the effort."

"You take the banking business," Ike said.

"Even there, eh, Pop?" Critter resigned himself to listening to Ike brag about his dealings with banks.

"Who'd believe that a Jordan was worth a million dollars?" Ike said. "I'll tell the difference between this Jordan and all them others behind us, this Jordan is smart and he ain't afraid of work. The real estate business ain't an easy row to hoe. Mr. Banker is always on your back for a payment, and you're gosh-darned lucky to get Mr. Tenant to come up with the rent every month."

It was true, in a manner of speaking, that his father was worth a million dollars and that, in a manner of speaking, he'd worked hard for what he had. Ike had been buying run-down houses and fixing them, more or less, for the last fifteen years. In addition to his auction duties and his burglary profession, Ike gaffed a house-repair crew, made up mostly of Jordan kin, and he collected rent money, much of it also from his kin, and he wheeled and dealt with the banks, and he did his own accounting on his Radio Shack computer; for leisure, he read law books and art and antiques periodicals. Whatever his father was, he wasn't lazy. Critter himself was a pretty fair rough carpenter with the work crew, and his father depended on him to haul auction lots to the barn in Darby (Critter would say with pride that he could move a piano through a bathroom window), but he hadn't worked out as an auctioneer, the role his father had in mind for him, and he had also failed at collections. "You have to know who to threaten and who to beg," Ike would say, and Critter would get depressed.

What bothered Critter about his father's empire was that if Ike was a millionaire, as he was fond of reminding people, why was it that the immediate family still lived like poor Jordan folk? His stepmother, Priscilla, in addition to raising three kids in grade school, labored in Ike's auction business, operating the canteen at the barn on Saturday nights and making arrangements for pricing and transporting lots. (People preferred dealing with her to dealing with Ike.) Most galling to Critter was that Ike insisted she continue working part-time at the IGA market in Tuckerman. It wasn't just that Ike was cheap—although he was. There was something about his business methods that prevented him from profiting from his investments. It was only after some painful thinking that Critter had figured out why the millionaire had no money.

Ike had gone through an orgy of slum-house buying in Darby Depot, all with bank money. Having borrowed money, he had credit; having property, he had collateral for more credit; having depressed housing, he could get government-sponsored fix-up loans. But Ike never quite put into the houses what he'd intended. The houses remained slums, and therefore receipts from the rent he could charge were below the loan payments. To make up the difference between his income and his payments, Ike borrowed more money. A bank foreclosed on one property, and found that it had declined so much in value from Ike's management that they couldn't recoup their loses by selling it. The banks discovered they had no choice but to hang in there with Ike, hoping that somehow he would get his act together. Ike kept borrowing money; he was having a hell of a good time. But one of these days the banks were going to shut him off and take everything he owned. The trouble for Critter was that his ability to articulate the problem was just shy of his understanding of it. He wanted to say, "Pop, you're buying properties like a man sending himself chain letters," but of course he could not, didn't have the knack or the guts. The knowledge was just another burden to carry, and he had no means to shuck it off.

They parked at a sandbank about a half a mile from the Trellis Butterworth house. Ike raised the hood of the van. If, in the extremely unlikely event Constable Godfrey Perkins should happen by, Ike would tell him they had engine trouble.

They walked along the side of the road, the stars just visible between the trees that leaned over them like huge, menacing prison guards. If they saw headlights in the distance, they would duck into the woods and lie in the leaves until the car passed. The *tow-hee* birds were alert, watching them, criticizing them; peepers chirped on, oblivious to everything but their own weird music; a breeze frisked Critter like some perv copping a cheap feel; the burglar-being of his father stepped out lightly, silently, ghostlike. Critter hated all of this. Lurking out there were poison ivy and snakes and great yawning presences waiting to swallow him up, plunging him into a permanently dark, spike-strewn, slime-lined world. He wished he were home in the auction barn, watching television with Delphina, eating State Line potato chips, drinking beer, burping.

The Butterworth house was a great big place, Victorian-fancy and surrounded by screened-in porches, built in the 1920s as a summer home. The Butterworth family had occupied the spacious rooms of the first two stories; the maid, the nurse, the cook, the butler and gardener had lived in cramped quarters on the third floor. Ike claimed the Butterworths were still loaded with money, but you'd never know it from the way they lived—like hippies some of them, hidden away in Upper Darby in handmade houses with rough pine boards for siding. Only old Mrs. Butterworth had remained in the family house, the servants long since departed. "The cottage," as she liked to refer to her house, was falling apart. The sills were rotted; there was no insulation, the oil burner was a monster, and the house must cost a fortune to heat; the wiring and plumbing needed to be pulled out and replaced. Now that Mrs. Butterworth had passed away, the house had been put up for sale, but not the land. No takers so far.

It was obvious the house was unoccupied, but even so, Ike insisted they wait outside, listening, watching for signs of human life. Ike was a cautious burglar, had never gotten caught. But there was more to this waiting than caution. Ike liked it, Critter knew. The wariness jogged his brain. But for Critter, it was a time of agony. He began to imagine that a mysterious Jell-O-like creature of the deep woods had oozed into his shoe and was entering his system through the soles of his feet.

"Foot itches," he whispered to Ike.

"Shh," Ike said.

"Itches."

Ike clasped his hand over Critter's mouth. The hand was wet with tension and it quivered with Ike's suppressed anger. Critter could feel the Jell-O creature string out into his veins.

He wanted to scream, but he kept silent. Why? Why didn't he holler and walk away? He didn't like this question popping out of nowhere, and he shook it off. He was grateful when a mosquito landed on his cheek, because it gave him something to concentrate on. He could feel it circling on his skin, like a tiny cat preparing to sleep; could feel it insert its sharp tube and suck a drop of blood from him. He was calmer now. The real itch had ridden over the imaginary itch.

Finally, Ike motioned that it was time to advance. They walked around to the rear, partly because Ike usually found easier entry near kitchens and sheds and partly out of breeding, the Jordans by nature uncomfortable at front doors. Ike didn't like to break the hardware when he entered a building, because he might not take anything that evening, and if he didn't raise suspicions he could come back later. He got a kick out of knowing he had been in other people's houses, had deciphered some of their most intimate secrets without their ever having been the wiser. It gave him a feeling of power. Also, he didn't believe in doing damage to someone else's property unless there was a mature purpose—profit or revenge. Occasionally, if he had some equipment with him, he might snap a common padlock with bolt cutters and then replace the padlock with one of his own. He'd confessed that his only regret was that he couldn't see the look on the guy's face when he tried vainly to open the padlock with the wrong key. This was an example of Ike's sense of humor.

It was going to be easy to enter this house. There was broken glass everywhere. They crawled in through an open window. Ike clicked on his flashlight. The place had been vandalized, and beer bottles littered the floors. Apparently, local kids were using the house for parties and general congregation. Critter envied the kids. They were coming here to have a good time. Ike was outraged.

"I tell you, Critter, burglary isn't what it used to be," he said. "There's too many kids getting into it. In the old days, a burglar had as much respect as an armed robber or even a murderer. People knew you had your specialty tools and that you could tell art from hoke. A burglar in the old days would never leave a mess like this. You tell 'em, Critter. After I'm gone, you tell 'em that your pop was a clean burglar. If you don't tell 'em, I'll kick your ass all up and down the pearly gates. And don't you think I'll be downstairs from the pearly gates. I can sneak my way into anyplace, heaven included. Look at this: somebody took a shit in the corner. These kids today not only got no skill, they got no pride. They just break windows and drink the booze. They always get caught, too, because they're stupid. And then the judges let 'em go. What a disgrace. No wonder this country's hurting. If I ever find out you've been behaving like this on a burglary, I'll disown you . . ."

"Pop, I don't go on burglaries alone. You know that. I don't even like burglaries."

Ike seemed not to hear his son. "Let's pick up a little here. Poor Mrs. Butterworth. She must be turning over in her grave."

They spent about fifteen minutes piling up the beer bottles in a corner of the room, straightening up. Ike swept the poop onto a newspaper and threw it outside. Then they went to work, searching for valuables with their flashlights, Ike upstairs, Critter downstairs.

As Ike had taught him, Critter paused every once in a while, shut off the light, listened, and scanned the surroundings until his eyes were used to the darkness. What gave him the creeps about this exercise was that no matter how hard he concentrated, he never saw or heard his father. Ike could be where he had said he would be—upstairs—or he could be down in the cellar, or outside, or right in the same room, spying on him. Critter went through the motions of searching.

There wasn't much around, and he was glad. The idea that they might have to come back with the van and load it up gave him the heebie-jeebies. He didn't want to go to jail. No girls there. The little furniture that remained was 1940s stock, bursting with stuffing in places, probably full of mice. The antiques and appliances were gone. There were some plates and silverware in the kitchen, a couple of good pieces included, but no sets. They must have been cleaned out by the relatives. He imagined that Ike was upstairs in the bedrooms, looking here and there for that odd piece of jewelry, that overlooked painting or Oriental rug. He resented Ike for reserving the bedroom searches for himself, but Critter always found a reason to check them out anyway, and Ike didn't seem to mind that he followed in on his heels. Some bedrooms could get you stoned on woman smells, and some were stocked with terrific lingerie. It would be nice to bring back Delphina a nightie. It was a long shot. He couldn't imagine old lady Butterworth in sexy under things. Still you never knew. He was thinking that maybe Mrs. Butterworth had been a lezzie when the beam of Ike's flashlight cut across his eyes.

"Follow me, I want to show you something," Ike said, excitement in his voice.

Ike led him to the staircase and ordered him to climb. Critter had a good idea what was going to happen next—they'd been through this before. When he reached the third step from the top, he heard a creak with a slightly different pitch from the creaks in the other steps.

"Secret compartment. Right?" he said.

"He's a good learner—'course he had a good teacher," Ike said, his voice bubbling with pride. When Ike wanted to say something kindly or very mean, he always addressed Critter as "he" instead of "you". Critter knew Ike's compliment was due more to whatever he had found in the compartment than to the progress of his son as a burglar. Nonetheless, it thrilled Critter to hear his father friendly toward him.

Critter was curious now, and he watched carefully as Ike slid the stair tread aside, revealing a small compartment.

"Usually, what you run across in these holes is a bottle of booze that the old man hid from his old woman, but sometimes there'll be some valuables," Ike said. This was about as intimate as Ike could be. It was almost as if the two of them were close, Critter thought.

"What we got here, Critter, is papers," Ike said. "The beauty of this is the only other person who knew they were here is the one who put 'em here, and she's deader than a doornail.

Something to say hooray about, Critter. I ain't had a chance to go through all the papers yet, but I imagine some interesting literature will turn up."

"Maybe some money, too, eh, Pop?"

"Money. Money! How can you bring up money at a time like this?" Ike said, and his voice was cold again.

Crowbar

By ROLAND LaCHANCE
Crier Staff Writer

DARBY, Oct. 14—Opposition to construction of a regional shopping mall has formed along two fronts in the small town of Darby.

In the exclusive section of Upper Darby, a citizens committee—named SOD (Save Our Darby)—has been formed to fight the mall through legal means.

In the depressed Darby Depot area, auctioneer Isaac O. Jordan is circulating a petition opposing the mall.

"A mall is wrong for Darby on every ground, and we in Darby intend to prevent it with every legal means at our disposal," said Raphael G. Salmon, spokesperson for SOD.

SOD presently consists of about two dozen charter members from Upper Darby, Salmon said, but is open to any resident of the town. Dues of $10 are requested from members. The group is raising money to battle the mall in a court suit, Salmon said.

Magnus Mall Group Inc., which has shopping centers all along the East Coast and in the Midwest, wants to construct a giant regional shopping mall in Darby. The company has an option to buy the Avalon Hillary Farm on River Road.

"There's no doubt a mall will destroy the rural character of Darby, but SOD's opposition goes beyond aesthetic concerns," Salmon said. "We question the social, economic, and moral impact of such a large commercial venture on the health of our town."

Salmon challenged the company's claim that increased tax revenues generated by the mall will ease property taxes for homeowners in Darby.

"The mall will mean more people, and that will mean increased traffic problems, a crowded Darby Elementary School, and urban crime," Salmon warned. He predicted that expenses to deal with the problems will be greater than taxes collected from the mall.

Furthermore, Salmon charged that the mall violates the town's long-range master plan for growth. If the mall is approved, SOD almost certainly will bring suit to block construction, he said.

In Darby Depot, Jordan said he was circulating the petition to bring pressure on town officials to oppose the mall.

Jordan said a mall would raise property values and prices in the town, driving out people with low and middle incomes.

"Mrs. Chubb is sniffing around for information. Apparently, your stories on the Darby mall fascinate her," Shard said to Chance. "Maybe somebody in city hall has put a bug up her ass now that Magnus has decided to forgo Tuckerman, or maybe she plays canasta with one of the Upper Darby grand dames. Did you know she used to be a friend of Trellis Butterworth?"

"No, but what difference does it make? Mrs. Butterworth is dead," Chance said.

"No difference. Absolutely none," Shard said. "Mrs. Chubb gives me the creeps. Publishers should talk with the editorial writer once a week, and make sure the ads are paying our salaries, and stay the hell out of the newsrocm. . . . So fill me in. We've got SOD and that nut Jordan against the mall. Who else?"

"The people who live on River Road, but they aren't particularly organized," Chance said. "After that, it's uncertain. Most people I've talked to and the ones who've been speaking out at the Planning Board meetings are suspicious of Magnus, but at the same time they like the idea of paying lower taxes."

"The selectmen, of course, are gung ho in favor of the mall," Shard said.

"They haven't taken an official position, but they aren't hiding their enthusiasm over the prospect that Magnus is going to bring in big tax bucks," Chance said. "Other than that, I haven't heard too much support for the mall. As a matter of fact, given the opposition, I don't know how the Magnus people expect to get the required two-thirds vote at the town meeting."

"Did you ask Case if Magnus is worried about the proposal going down the toilet?"

"I asked him whether the company will ignore the town vote and go for a variance, as they've indicated they could legally," Chance said. "He said he was thinking positive. Magnus feels they'll get the vote they'll need. At least that's what Case says."

"You wonder why the hell they opted for a town vote when they could have tried for a zoning variance first." Shard said this aloud to himself, then turned to Chance. "Maybe they're banking on an anti-snob vote."

"There's no doubt there's resentment against the Upper Darby folk because of their money, not to mention their accents and tweeds and all that," Chance said. "And the selectmen have expressed public dismay over the Salmon Trust because it's sheltered under tax laws. But because people think Reggie Salmon is a snob and an environmental kook doesn't mean they'll oppose him on something so important as the mall."

"What about Ike Jordan? Where is he coming from?"

"It's hard to tell," Chance said. "He's a slumlord in Darby Depot, so I imagine he'd stand to gain from a mall. Just the

pure growth of the town will kick up his property values. Yet
Ike has got this petition opposing the mall. By the way, I'm
driving to his auction barn to take his picture."

"What the hell for?" Shard asked. He didn't like his reporters making appointments without consulting him first.

"He called me up," Chance said. "He's got a cute picture
idea, his dog wearing a 'No Mall' T-shirt."

He had driven past Ike's Auction Barn a number of times,
wondering why the huge, hip-roofed barn stood alone, no house
near it. Now, as he pulled into the dusty, unpaved parking
lot, an explanation came to him. Across the road was a stone
wall, a cellar hole grown in with second growth forest and a
pile of stones that might have been a filled-in well. The state
had put Route 21 right through the gut of the farm, splitting
the barn from the homestead. The farmer might have taken
the money from the eminent domain proceedings and started
anew beside the barn, but for reasons of his own—perhaps
the sight and sound of the highway disturbed him—he sold
the land and moved his house elsewhere.

Out of the Brat, Chance was met by a man and dog. Without
a greeting, the man knelt before Chance and started to dress
the dog in a T-shirt. The man had dark eyes locked deeply
into their sockets and sallow skin, but what Chance noticed
in particular were the man's grayish, ill-fitting false teeth,
teeth that garnished a nasty, inscrutable smile, a smile that
sent a shiver of revulsion through Chance. He'd had the exact
same feeling only hours earlier while listening on the telephone to a voice that was slow, cocksure, and condescending.
No doubt about it, this was Ike Jordan.

Two other people had come out of the auction barn; a younger
man, whom Chance guessed was Critter Jordan, and Delphina
Rayno. The bulges of a few pimples showed through her
makeup, and her lurid, red lipstick wandered beyond the
boundaries of her lip line. Yet there was something about her
that Chance liked. Perhaps it was the fact that she was looking
at Ike Jordan without fear, even as if she hoped the dog would
bite him.

Ike was having trouble with his task. The dog wouldn't stay

still. He wriggled and whined in fright at the T-shirt, this alien thing; his tail wagged frantically, advertising his embarrassment at the helpless fear he felt. He was a large crossbred hound that might have looked ferocious were it not for the huge, floppy ears, the whiny voice, the wagging tail shouting, "I'm harmless, I'm pathetic, I'm just a hound. Leave me be and I'll leave thee be."

"Crowbar, don't you want to be famous?" said Ike Jordan. The words, measured for menace, came out one at a time through the smile of the false teeth. The dog understood the threat and responded to it by standing perfectly still, his nervousness evident only by his quivering flesh.

Ike hit the dog anyway, slapping him on the nose with an open hand. Then he put the dog's head through the neck of the T-shirt and front legs through the arm holes. Once dressed, as far as Crowbar was concerned the alien thing had gone away, and he relaxed. His great tongue fell out of his mouth, he panted like an engine, and clear saliva dripped from the corners of his mouth. He approached Chance and sniffed his genitals.

The dog was comical enough to get his picture in the *Crier*, but the trouble was the message on the T-shirt—"Save Our Darby; Kill the Mall"—faced the ground. Ike hadn't accounted for this in his plan. At the moment he solved the problem as he always did, as Jordans had since time immemorial, by jerry-rigging.

"Critter, you and Crowbar are going to get your picture in the paper," Ike said, delighted with himself.

Lines of pain arranged themselves in Critter Jordan's face.

Ike positioned Critter behind Crowbar, had Critter grasp the dog's front legs and stand him on his hind legs. The message on the T-shirt could now be read. Chance focused the lens of the camera.

"Smile like you mean it, damn you. Can't you smile?" Ike said to Critter. Critter forced a smile.

"I'd give up my front seat in hell to get a look at farmer Hillary's face when he sees this in the newspaper," Ike said, and snickered.

Delphina, arms folded, watched the scene with obvious ill humor. Chance sensed her presence was adding to Critter's shame.

After Chance had taken several pictures, Ike marched the entourage into the auction barn. The musty, dank smell of rotting wood hung in the air like a death sentence for the building; sun twinkles shining through the leaky roof resembled starlight. Inside, Ike set up another picture for Chance's camera. He donned some reading glasses (which he didn't need), sat at a desk (which was for sale), and stared deeply at a scroll (which was empty of writing). This was to symbolize Ike perusing the petition he'd established opposing the mall.

"Did you want to interview me now?" Ike asked.

"No," Chance said, and Critter and Delphina took heart from the impertinence in his tone. Ike did not notice. Ike was already thinking of the next item on his agenda, a meeting with a banker. He did notice, however, that Chance was hanging around past his business.

"I think the boy wants a cup of coffee. Pour him one," Ike said to Delphina, then grinned his enormous false-toothed smile and left with his dog.

The moment Ike was out of sight, Critter said, "You ain't going to run that picture of me with Crowbar, are you?"

"If you want, I'll destroy it," Chance said.

"You will?" Critter said, happily surprised.

"I will," Chance said, opening the back of the camera and stripping out the exposed film.

The three of them burst into spontaneous laughter, caught up in a sweep of freedom from elders. Critter and Delphina did a little dance; Chance draped the film across his shoulders.

"He don't want no coffee. He wants a beer—let's get to the beer," Critter said, as if it were the Fourth of July. He and Delphina led Chance through a canyonlike corridor to a wooden staircase so steep it was almost a ladder. This led to a balcony, part of what was once the barn's hayloft. Here a door opened into an apartment. The place managed to hold both the old barn smells of rotting hay and new smells of fried foods.

"This is the parlor," Delphina said, as they passed through a cramped, windowless room. Two walls were paneled with fake walnut wood; two walls were shiny with aluminum vapor barrier over insulation; the floors were plywood. The furnishings included a cheap Danish-style sofa, an overstuffed easy chair, an enormous television set in a Mediterranean-style console, a small bookshelf bulging with paperback romances, and a dignified grandfather's clock in an oak casing, its face to the wall.

They halted at the kitchen table. Delphina put three bottles of beer on the table. Critter twisted the cap off one of the beers and gave the bottle to Delphina.

In his father's presence, Critter had been quiet, even meek. Now that Ike was gone, he was good-natured and garrulous. He talked with the same slow drawl as his father, the New Hampshire accent in lower gear, but there was no menace in his tone.

"Crowbar? Maybe he belonged to my Uncle Ollie, and maybe not," Critter said. "Uncle Ollie was king of us Jordans for a long time. He and Ike didn't get along. Ollie had some trouble, and had to seek succor from Ike. Ike was pleased. He started thinking he was the new king. One day Uncle Ollie stole Ike's beer and took off for parts unknown. Pissed off the old man no end. Nobody's seen Uncle Ollie since. Pop found Crowbar in the woods, said he was Ollie's dog. But the truth is, just because Ike says Crowbar was Ollie's dog don't mean Crowbar was Ollie's dog. Then again he might be. Ike's a smart liar. He knows a liar to be good has got to lie to everybody about everything, and has got to tell the truth now and then."

"Fathers all lie," Chance said. "They lie out of fear and a crazy idea of love."

"Yah, well, my pop is better than average at it," Critter said.

The subject of fathers oppressed Chance, and he felt the need to separate himself from the conversation, to be alone if only for a minute or two. He headed for the bathroom, but stopped to look at the clock in the living room. It was a beautiful thing, an antique, the name Clapp written in chalk on the inside of the delicate wooden case. The beauty of the clock made him vaguely wistful, and the wistfulness fastened him to the sound of the ticking, like a rhythmic rain, until he was listening to his own breathing, the stutter in it telling him there was something inside himself fiercer than the constant dull anger of his ordinary waking life. As Soapy struggled to find words, so Chance struggled to find feelings.

When Chance returned, he asked, "Where's Soapy?"

"Gone—went to see *him*," Delphina answered.

That night, Chance lay in bed, part of him watching the figures on his television moving about (speeded up, it seemed, because the sound was turned down), part of him thinking.

He had learned from Delphina that she and Soapy had different fathers. Delphina's father was Tommy Rayno—"the kind you wanted to hug one minute and shoot in the eye the next." Currently, he lived in Lewiston, Maine, unemployed and alcoholic. Soapy's father was a man of a different cut, educated, but a hippie outlaw. Delphina was age one, Tommy Rayno on leave from his marriage, when this new fellow was around briefly and made Antoinnette pregnant. He was long gone by the time Soapy was born. Years later he resumed communications with Antoinnette. Some kind of deal was struck. Soapy's father sent small amounts of money; Antoinnette allowed him to write letters to Soapy, telephone her, and even visit now and then.

He went by different names—Isaac Newton, Ichabod Newcomb, Malcom Newman, and finally the name that stuck, Newhawk. Antoinnette Rayno wouldn't reveal Newhawk's given name. She and Soapy fought constantly over this subject. Delphina wasn't even sure that Antoinnette herself had ever known the name. Apparently, Newhawk was wanted by the law, so he had good reason to keep his identity a secret. Delphina gathered that he had blown something up in the course of revolutionary activities and that someone had gotten killed. Delphina had only seen Newhawk a couple times when she was a child, and her memory of him was indistinct. He was a stocky man with a full beard, brown, stringy hair, and wild bloodshot eyes, "like little pizza supremes." Another thing about Newhawk was that as part of his rebellion against society he didn't wash. Somehow he had passed down this idea to his daughter.

Newhawk's last batch of letters were postmarked Burlington, Vermont, and Delphina was fairly certain that that was where Soapy had gone, although she couldn't for the life of her understand why.

The Illness

Persephone Salmon was enjoying the cool, dry breeze of her solitude when she heard her husband's Bronco pull onto their road from the hardtop. A moment later it seemed to her she could feel the air in the house thicken, sweeten, an inhibiting air somehow. This she identified as the air of Reggie's illness.

"Welcome home," she said, in spite of herself sounding like a housewife demanding an explanation from her husband of why he was coming in late.

He seemed not to catch her tone. "Home—no place like it," he said. He came toward her, and for a moment she thought he might kiss her. But he stopped, all at once wary, sensing she sought distance between them. She wished he would want to punish her for not loving him enough.

"How was the meeting?" she asked.

"The Planning Board of Darby is hopelessly adrift in the hands of that Cutter woman," he said.

Zoe Cutter, one of the new people in Center Darby, had been elected chairman of the board after Trellis Butterworth—Persephone's mother—had died. On the point of new people, especially ones with money, Reggie and Persephone could agree. New people tended to be aggressive,

arrogant, and ignorant of all of Darby but the topography.
"Who was at the hearing?" she asked.
"And what were they wearing?" Before she could react, he
added, "I'm sorry. I don't know why I said that. Mrs. Cutter
informed us at length what we already know: that our ordinances are poorly written, and that regardless of the voters'
action at the town meeting in March, the mall issue probably
will be laid to rest in the courts. She understands that SOD
is fighting for show, and Magnus is fighting for show. What
she doesn't understand is that a town meeting vote will go a
long way toward defining the legal arguments before the courts.
The show is everything."
"Was that awful Jordan person there?" she asked.
"Unfortunately, yes," Reggie said. "It's the new people in
town, the commuters, who by sheer numbers are going to
decide this, and Jordan and his anti-mall petition will only
alienate them. I wish he was on the other side."
"The Hillarys?"
"Avalon and his lawyer and the man from Magnus—Case—
were all in a herd, like Avalon's cows," Reggie said. "To
give you an idea how gripping this mall thing is for some
people, Melba Hillary showed up and didn't even bring her
knitting."
Persephone spoke reflexively. "What is so unusual about a
woman going to a public meeting? We may not have gotten
ERA, but we still have the vote."
"I didn't say it was unjust, as you seem to imply," he said.
"I meant it was unusual—your word, by the way—for a farmer's wife to play politics."
"I'm sorry," she said, although she wasn't. " 'Unusual' was
a poor choice of words. It was the fact that you remarked on
it so . . . so . . . voluminously that got me going."
She wanted to take back that word, "voluminously."
"Smugly" was the right word. "Voluminously"was pompous.
Her imprecision was his fault. He had the husband's knack
of suppressing the little woman's IQ.
Now he strode over and kissed her, on the mouth but without touching her. He stepped back and smiled faintly, cutely,

as if he had bumped into a pretty stranger and out of coyness and politeness was excusing himself.

"I don't know if I'm going to miss that or not," he said, "—picking me up every time I demonstrate the dollop of chauvinism that I have remaining from my inheritance."

Going to miss that—it was a cruel thing to say, cruel to her, cruel to himself, and she didn't want to take it. But she did, hating the anger in herself, hating having to keep a lid on it. She wanted to kick him, spit on him, or at least rail against him. He saw her flinch, and she was oddly ashamed.

She wished she could be more understanding, more loving. But since the doctors had told him his illness was fatal and irreversible, Reggie had changed. He treated her with a kind of minimum emotional maintenance, just enough to keep her running so she could do her job in the household, like the lawnmower. Despite this, she might still have loved him all the more, subjugated herself to his demands, if only he had remained familiar to her. But he was different now, even smelled different. The fear of death in him had hardened into a personal logic, a world view outside anything she had known, anything they had known as a pair. This was not the Reggie she had married, the Reggie who had had the nervous breakdown when his own father died, the Reggie who had liked to play pranks on his wife and who liked to talk about trees as if they were his close friends. This Reggie did not seem real to her. It was as if his mind had already passed on, and a dark angel had taken over his body.

She tried to be cheerful. "Lilith called while you were gone."

"What does she want? Money?"

As a matter of fact, their only child had asked for money, but darned if Persephone was going to give Reggie the satisfaction of knowing he'd guessed right.

"She's studying Marx at the college," Persephone said.

"Groucho or Harpo?" he said.

"The economist—Karl."

"They're all the same thing, Jewish comedians," Reggie said, with a mean-spirited chuckle.

"Please don't make racist jokes in my presence."

"It's because I'm not a racist that I can make the jokes. Is she coming home?" Reggie said.

"Reggie, she only lives twelve miles away in Tuckerman. Why don't you go and visit her?"

"We'd quarrel," he said. "I'd say: 'Why can't you live at home?' And she'd say she has to be on her own, to become her own person. Blah, blah, blah."

"You should tell her how sick you are. Don't get mad. You know you should," Persephone said.

"No. No, no, no." He was furious. It was as if she'd told him he was going to die and had laughed in his face. She saw the real Reggie now, angry and unreasonable, and she was cheered up. The air was clearing. They were close for these few seconds, a couple squabbling. She wanted to slap his face and cry and embrace him.

"There's no reason for her to know—not now, not yet," he said. "Why should she have to carry that burden? Tell me. Why?"

He was angry because she had raised the subject of his illness. He was afraid to talk about it, even to mention it. It was as if he believed that every time the illness was discussed he was further weakened by it.

Persephone said nothing but watched him, watched his mind working, watched him struggle to change the subject.

"It's best I don't see her, for now, Persephone," he said. "You know she'll just ask for money, and we can't afford to give her any more at this time. It galls me, Persephone. Our income is too high to get aid and too low to send her to a ... a better college."

The phoniness, the absolute desperate phoniness in him. She could feel her own anger bubble up, almost like a joyous thing, could feel it take over and splash words at him like acid: "We have the money—in land escrow. It would be nothing to sell a couple of lots. Let go, Reggie, let go, for God's sake."

"Don't for-God's-sake me. There is no God. ..."

"Who cares? Lilith could have gone to Oberlin."

"I care. That's who cares. There is no God. No Supreme Being who oversees our individual actions. There is only Nature, which cares for us in the ah, ah . . ."

"She was accepted at Oberlin, Reggie. And she liked the campus. She was in love with poli-sci and they . . ."

". . . the ah, ah, universal sense, not the individual sense. I am nothing, you are nothing, that rotting stump is nothing. Together we make up the universe . . ."

". . . So now she's at Tuckerman State, stultifying perhaps, because you're too stubborn to part with some of the precious Salmon property. . . . What do you mean, I'm nothing? I am something, everybody is something."

"You know absolutely why we're not selling land."

"The Trust, the pissy Trust."

"It's not a pissy Trust, that's not a good word. It was a sacred promise I made to my father and grandfather: that I would keep that land in trust, *au naturel*, for the Sierra Club."

"The Sierra Club is not sure they want it, and when your father held that gun to your head, it didn't matter because there was still money, land or not. Now there is no money. Reggie, don't you understand? We, the Butterworths and the Salmons and the Prells, we have lived the American Dream in reverse. We can't keep behaving as if we're rich. We're not rich. We're almost poor—well, almost middle class. We have to get our children—"

"Our child."

"All right, our child. We have to get her educated, in the best place we can, for her benefit. For her profit, Reggie. Nobody is going to hand her a trust fund—well, not one she can live on. She is a person, Reggie, much more real and full of potential than Salmon land. She is not nothing."

"I resent that word 'pissy,' " he said.

"Oh, I always use the wrong word. What difference does it make? You know what I mean."

And on they went, to no purpose but to expel the anger. In the old days, in the days before the illness, they would argue like this, fight until as if by magic the anger would be gone and in its place would be desire. In the old days it was almost as if they would stage fights as foreplay. But now it was different. There was no reconciliation. When her anger left, it sucked out the air from the room. She gasped with need. In the old days he would have come to her, gently as the morning breeze arising in the fields behind their house. But now he said, "I'm sorry, I can't," and went out the door.

"It's not that you can't, it's that you don't want to," she said, but he was already gone.

There it was: the middle of night, and outside her husband was prowling around in the forest like a coyote. What did he do out there? How could he even see? Was he practicing existing in the land of the dead? She wondered whether he had provoked the argument as an excuse to wander. But, no. He needed no excuse. He came and went at will, without telling her. She would be in the greenhouse watering the plants, and when he opened the sliding glass doors into the house proper, there would be only the warm glow of the lights reflecting off the gold-brown, pine-board walls. And she would whisper, "Reggie," and then louder, "Reggie," and the only answer would be the one-pitch song of mosquitoes he'd let in when he left.

She tried to return to the book she was reading, but it had turned sour on her. *Devik's Nighttime* was about an out-of-work actor hired to impersonate a woman. Male author. What crap. It was bad enough that men, for reasons she had never quite understood, fought to keep women from realizing their potential. Now they were trying to invade the gender itself. She put the book on a shelf. She knew she would never finish it. It reminded her that both she and Reggie—not so much Lilith—had bad spending habits, left over from the days when there was more money. One of her own abuses was to buy hardback books on speculation. It was such a great feeling—sheer power—to walk out of a bookstore with an armload of hardbacks, enjoying their weight and heft; such a great feeling to recommend a good book before the reviewers got to it, or to be able to say to Leslie Overture, "Yes, darling, I know. I read it." So what that only a third of the books would pan out. The house was littered with hundreds of half-read or unread books, all of them hardbacks. They both had a bias against paperbacks, although Reggie didn't read much. He claimed the paper wouldn't last. He said the small print wasn't good for your eyes. She criticized his criticism, seeing it for what it was, remnant snobbery, and yet she shared in it, too. A paperback book felt so slight in the hands, it was hard to take the words seriously; furthermore, it seemed to her that the homes of people who kept paperback libraries suffered from the dank smell of cheap paper that had captured the moisture of the surrounding air, and that the homes themselves were cheapened by the books.

She was strong. She could bear up under a bad mood, yet now she wished she could take something to buoy her. She rummaged about in the bathroom and found Reggie's tranquilizers, but one look at the pills gave her the creeps. She walked over to the liquor cabinet. She liked the effects of alcohol, stimulating and calming at the same time, like the ocean, but there were things about drink that revolted her. Hard liquor stank so, and beer bloated you, and wine—well, wine went with meals. Too bad you couldn't get alcohol in bite-size, *Whitman*-like chocolate samplers.

Persephone considered smoking some of Lilith's marijuana. She knew Lilith stored some in 35mm canisters in her camera bag in her room. But Reggie was sure to smell it when he came in, and she didn't want another argument, at least not about that. She didn't even like marijuana. Every time she smoked, she became keenly aware of the passage of her own personal time, experiencing, it seemed, the beach-blond hair of her childhood first darkening, then lined with gray; the blue of her eyes (like the wings of a spring azure butterfly, Reggie used to say) becoming diluted and lost in twisted-twig wrinkles like tiny bird eggs in a nest; the translucent blue of her veins through her white legs suddenly bursting toward the surface and deepening in color until they were purple.

Persephone turned to the telephone and almost dialed her

sister's number, until she remembered that Florence had a job now and a new motto: early to rise, early to bed. Or was it the other way around? No matter, it was eleven o'clock, too late to call anyone, unless to deliver a message—*Yes, it's Persephone. Reggie died a few hours ago. Yes, yes. The end was peaceful; he was prepared.*

She opened the stereo cabinet and snapped on the television. They kept it hidden like a family secret, telling themselves the sight of it was aesthetically displeasing. The truth was they were ashamed to have TV in their house. The thing somehow was a betrayal of the earlier, more elegant age. It could not converse, it had no manners—therefore it was not one of them; it refused to be inconspicuous—therefore it was not a servant; it was no good as a seat or a container—therefore it was not furniture; it couldn't make toast or cool juice—therefore it was not an appliance; it lacked beauty—therefore it was not art; it could not be ignored or incorporated into other activities—therefore it failed as household entertainment, as radio and the gramophone succeeded. (Reggie's father had called the hi-fi a gramophone, and Reggie picked up this affectation when they invested in the stereo system, and for years now Persephone had been saying gramophone herself.) If she had been asked just why the television was kept hidden, she could not have said, "None of your business," or merely shrugged off the question as irrelevant or impertinent. She would have been compelled to invent an answer. She might have said that she had nothing personal against the TV, but that there were some things you put on top of the cabinet and some things you put inside.

The reception here on the hill was much better than in the village, but since Reggie refused to desecrate the top of his house with metal, the antenna was installed in the shed, where it was not fully effective. However, on this night reception was good. But there was nothing on. There was never anything on. Never mind. She forced herself to watch. Pretty people in rooms full of new things, ugly soulless things. A car chasing another car. An explosion. A woman crying, holding a pistol now. Whoops. She'd missed something. The woman had vanished, and was replaced by the ocean. A beach. Lovely. Persephone soon got the effect she was seeking. The images on the screen served as a mantra. *Let's see now, it was five years since she had stopped doing her yoga exercises. Why had she quit?* The reason was lost in a tangle of memories. The day's clutter spilled out, and the milky white air of sleepiness slipped in.

Persephone nodded off for a few minutes and came awake somewhat when the volume increased during a commercial message. She pulled herself up and walked slowly to the stairs. She wanted to preserve her drowsiness, knowing that if she came fully awake, it would be hours before she could call upon sleep again. It was warm upstairs, and she stripped to her underwear. She lay supine on the bed and with tremendous pleasure stretched out her arms. It was nice lying here alone, so much room. Reggie was a large man, smothering sometimes. Why hadn't they bought that queen-sized bed she wanted? Had Reggie balked? No, that wasn't it. She had balked. It cost too much. They'd have to wait until Lilith had her degree. Persephone herself had gone to Smith, and Reggie to Dartmouth. Lilith was enrolled in a state college. So sad. She imagined she could hear the crickets of summer, calling for lovers. So sweet.

When Persephone awakened the next morning, Reggie hadn't returned. Perhaps he had died, killed himself. There had been a time when she would not permit herself such thoughts. Now they brought comfort. She went downstairs and was startled to find the TV still on, Reggie in the easy chair where she had sat hours ago. The crazy idea popped into her head that they had exchanged souls.

"Reggie," she whispered.

He turned toward her. "Came back from my walk, and couldn't sleep," he said.

"Poor dear," she said.

"I've been thinking," Reggie said. "I'm afraid of dying, not personally, mind you, but cosmically. I mean I'm not afraid of the end of me. I'm afraid that when I die, the world, or the

world I know—the world I helped make—will die, too. That
makes me afraid. It makes me believe there's no meaning to
it—life, I mean. I know that doesn't make sense, but it's how
I feel."

"Oh, Reggie. Oh, Reggie," she said, feeling the cool air of
the morning washing over both of them.

Ike's Amazing Machine

Ike Jordan was sitting on the toilet seat, a cereal bowl on his lap, Crowbar lying on the floor between his heels. Ike's false teeth were in the bowl. He was cleaning them with a medium-bristle toothbrush and Crest toothpaste. He took his time. He enjoyed brushing his teeth. It was uplifting work. So many in his family, like his wife, had rotten teeth or, like his mother, no teeth and undistinguished replacements. But his own teeth were jewels. He believed in the inherent superiority of these teeth because he had taken them in a successful burglary of the Lodge residence in Tuckerman, the Lodges being the richest family in Tuckerman County. And they weren't just rich people. They were "old rich." Ike knew the difference. The teeth reminded him that he was a successful man. He liked to prepare for the important events, such as, say, going to the bank for a loan, by brushing his teeth. Handling them, looking at them, seeing them sparkle gave him confidence. At the moment he was cleaning them to prepare for today's performance at the Darby Energy Fair.

The fair had been launched in 1974 by some Upper Darby folk as a reaction against shortages in heating oil. The first few Darby Energy Fairs had been devoted to wood heat only, but lately the fair had branched out, attracting merchants who sold solar heating equipment, insulation, and coal stoves. The fair had become an officially sanctioned town event. Reggie Salmon and his Upper Darby kin had surrendered direct management of the fair to the town, which each year at town meeting appointed a Fair Steering Committee. Admission was one dollar. Exhibitors were charged a nominal fee. The town reaped a small profit. The fair was held on the town green; in case of rain, in the town hall.

Back in the spring Ike had paid his ten-dollar registration fee, listing his exhibit vaguely as "wood energy," although he hadn't actually known what he was going to do. He had figured that he could work in some free advertising for his auction barn, but the main reason he had signed up was that this was a good opportunity to have some fun. As the time for the fair came closer and closer Ike Jordan brooded and brooded about what his exhibit would be. The idea of energy conservation was in fact peculiar to him, something that he had heard a lot about but had never actually taken note of. It wasn't until he was at the Darby dump one day and happened to see an enormous, sprawling maple-tree stump lying askew on the ground like a great octopus, that he had gotten an idea. He had borrowed a hoist and flatbed truck from his brother, Donald, in Tuckerman, and he and Critter had taken the stump. Now it lay on the town green, a sign nailed to it saying, "See this stump made into firewood by the amazing Ike Jordan Wood Splitting Machine." The sign had generated some interest, and Ike had taken bets that he and Critter would split the stump in under half an hour with the machine.

After he had cleaned the teeth he popped them into his mouth. He smiled to himself as he thought about his own cleverness. "Come on Crowbar, let's haul ass," he said.

He had half an hour to kill before driving over to the auction barn to pick up Critter, and he decided to spend that time boning up on Darby ordinances. There might be something he'd overlooked that would help his campaign to oppose the Magnus mall. Ike never wasted time. He had learned young that the difference between himself and his Jordan kin was that he was willing to work, to study, to probe the outside world. He had been determined that he was not going to be limited by the Jordan kinship, even as he strived for ascendancy within it. "Ain't it so, Crowbar, ain't it so?" he said, and the dog wagged his tail in agreement. When Crowbar didn't agree, Crowbar got kicked and Crowbar knew it.

Ike liked studying laws. He liked the words, he liked the power of knowing things that most people didn't, he even liked the paper and format of law books. He'd read the Darby zoning and planning laws and concluded that they were defective, out of line with the state laws, which superseded them. Therefore, it didn't matter too much what the Planning Board did or even what the voters did at town meeting on the mall issue. What mattered was which side would have the best lawyers in the court battles that would follow. Money bought the lawyers—and the judges. Therefore, in Ike Jordan's view, Magnus would have their way in Darby because they had the most money. There would be a mall, taxes would be lowered; being a property owner of considerable holdings, he would reap the benefits. For this reason Ike secretly cheered the mall, believed in its inevitability.

Ike's purpose in publicly opposing the mall was to bring grief to Avalon Hillary. He'd always had a vague prejudice against farmers, but after Critter had left him to go to work for Hillary, a deep anger against the dairy farmer had bubbled inside him. Ike didn't actually recognize his anger as envy of Hillary. The fact that his son had, as it were, gone over to Hillary and the fact that he had this sudden hatred of the man were like two separate, unrelated incidents. He concentrated on the grudge itself, rather than its cause.

There was another, less important reason for Ike to oppose the mall. It inflated his sense of self-importance to know that by opposing the mall he would be allied, in the minds of his fellow townspeople, with the Upper Darby folk. He liked high-class people, felt a sideways kinship with them. He had broken into enough of their houses and fenced enough of their furniture and art objects to recognize that high-class people had high-class tastes. Ike believed (perhaps correctly) that he was the first Jordan to recognize that there was such a thing as "taste," and it sent him surging to think that he had incorporated this idea in the Jordan mentality. He had an appreciation of beauty and craft and order handed down from the ages, if seized from the homes of the high class. He was a big enough man to be grateful to the high class for refining him. He could hold this thought only because of its corollary, which was that his admiration for the high class was reciprocated. He believed they saw in him a resemblance to long-lost kin.

By and by, Ike Jordan was going to announce his candidacy for selectman, running against Arthur Crabb. By defeating Crabb he could wound old man Hillary, who was Crabb's brother-in-law, and he could politically unite Darby Depot and Upper Darby. He knew he could get elected if he could recruit the support of Reggie Salmon, the leader of the Upper Darby crowd. Therefore, the task at hand was to demonstrate to Reggie that it would be to his advantage to help him get elected. This could be done; Ike knew he had the means. These thoughts sent him surging.

When it was time to go, Ike snapped his fingers, Crowbar came to attention, man and dog marched to the van. "You're a good mutt, even if you was brought up wrong," Ike said, and Crowbar jumped into the van as Ike slid open the side doors.

The relationship between Ike and Crowbar was not as common and simple as it might seem; in fact, like everything else about Ike, it was uncommon and complex. Downright strange it was. Ike had campaigned feverishly to persuade his kin that Crowbar had been among the dogs kept by Ollie Jordan, Ike's half-brother, and that when Ollie had disappeared and his dogs were loosed, he—Ike—had found his—Ollie's—favorite, Crowbar, in the woods, paws bleeding, tongue dry, body emaciated, and that he—Ike—had brought him round to health and vigor. Indeed, Ike had found Crowbar in that condition, but that the dog had belonged to Ollie Jordan was mere speculation on Ike's part. When he found the dog, Ike said to himself, "What if this were Ollie's dog?" That evolved into, "This most likely was Ollie's dog," to, "This was Ollie's dog," and now to, "This was Ollie's favorite dog."

Having control of Ollie's dog was part of Ike's desire for ascendancy in the Jordan kinship. One achieved ascendancy through the force of one's personality and through succor, the ability to provide for kin in need. Under the unwritten rules of the kinship, a Jordan was required to provide succor to any other Jordan. The seeker got shelter, the provider ascendancy. The menfolk of the Jordan kinship jockeyed constantly for ascendancy. It was more valuable as currency for status in the kinship than money, women, or property.

When Ollie Jordan had fallen on bad days, having been evicted from his shack in Darby, Ike had been only too happy to take him in. But Ollie had left his succor before Ike could claim his rightful ascendancy over him; in fact had left with all Ike's beer. Ollie had vanished. It was said he had taken his idiot son, Willow, and retreated into the woods. But as far as Ike was concerned no one knew whether Ollie was dead or alive, gone or hereabouts. As long as it couldn't be proven one way or the other, Ollie, in the eyes of the kinship, would continue his ascendancy over Ike. This was not something discussed or spoken of; it was merely known. There was nothing Ike could do about it except continue to exert the force of his personality, continue to provide succor. Ollie was a frustrating problem for Ike.

Complicating the situation was the fact that Ike had to vie with other Jordan men for ascendancy. It was challenging enough keeping Critter in his place as a son and not as a rival, and running neck-and-neck for the pinnacle of ascendancy in the kinship with his other half-brother, Donald Jordan, the county's premier junkyard proprietor, without having to battle with the ghost of Ollie Jordan. Therefore, when Crowbar came along Ike saw a cunning way of dealing with the Ollie problem.

By spreading the word that Crowbar was Ollie's dog and by caring for the dog and making it his own, he was laying the groundwork for a memorial service for Ollie's ascendancy. Ike hadn't yet quite convinced the Jordan kinship that Crowbar had been Ollie's dog, but he could feel the group judgment wavering. Once the kinship was persuaded that Crowbar was Ollie's dog, the kinship would require Ollie to come and fetch his dog, to maintain his ascendancy. This, in Ike's view, was not about to happen. He knew Ollie. If Ollie were alive, he would make his presence known. Ollie was not the type to leave the county, not the type to allow a challenge to his ascendancy go unmet. Surely Ollie must be dead.

Ike packed several lamps and a small bookcase in the van for deposit at the auction barn. He never made a trip without combining purposes if he could. He never wasted time. He might not have Donald's flair for impressing people or Ollie's raw force of character, but he was a worker, a collector, a smart son of a bitch, and a man of means—a millionaire. He could provide succor. This might not be all a man needed for ascendancy, but it went a long way. Ike Jordan was a highly successful man in the Jordan kinship even if his happiness and sense of fulfillment were under the siege of his ambition.

When Ike pulled into the parking lot of the auction barn, he paused to look at his barn, his ark—his secret ark. Ike carried many secrets with him. He liked secrets. They were almost as good as knowledge for giving a man an edge. The secret of the auction barn, or so Ike liked to imagine, was that it was a kind of latter-day Noah's ark, a great big boat, hull to the sky, floating on the slick of heaven.

Sometimes he'd say to Critter, "You and me and Crowbar, we're all upside down, you know, and it's only this old barn that's right side up. Someday, when this evil world goes ker-flooey, we'll sail away into the stars, you and me and Crowbar and the whole Jordan bucket brigade." The boy would be full of fear then, thinking he was crazy. This was good. As long as you could provoke fear in kin, you were ascendant. It was not good to make strangers fear you, however. Strangers could get violent on you. With strangers it was better to smile, show them your teeth, let them wonder about you. As long as a man was wondering, his urge to harm was suspended.

Ike fetched Critter to unload the van. Ike didn't like to do manual labor unless he had to. It was demeaning. You didn't

see the Salmon men or the Butterworth men or the Prell men
doing manual labor, unless it was to cut a few sticks of firewood or rake the leaves—sporting labor.

He had Critter deposit the articles from the van in the auction barn according to another secret plan. Ike imagined he
was stocking the upside-down ark for some future catastro-
phe, although he really couldn't imagine what that could be.
It did occur to him that even if his auction barn really were
an ark capable of floating away on the sky, its stock of second-
hand furniture and white goods would hardly be of use in
repopulating a devastated earth. He solved this problem by
imagining that there would be other arks to hold other people
and creatures in other places and other times ("other times":
this idea sent a thrill through him because it was beyond the
notion of "secret"; that is, it was a secret which even if revealed remained mysterious) and that his own ark would carry
on the culture of the high class through the many beautiful
things now warehoused inside, while at the same time it trans-
ported to safe haven the members of the Jordan kinship. This
was fair, this was fair—this was interesting. He liked the
fantasy: Ike the savior of his own kind, Ike the savior of high-
class culture. Despite these ruminations, Ike was not victim-
ized by his imagination. He knew his mental stunts were for
amusement alone, and he did not allow them to dewile him
in the world of people and things.

Ike brought Delphina to the Energy Fair, as well as Critter
and Crowbar. He needed Critter to help him split the wood.
Well, he didn't really need him, but he felt better when Critter
was around. Critter was handy; Critter was somebody who
had to listen to him; Critter's presence felt good, as a sheep-
skin on the van seat felt good on your fanny on a cold morning.
Ike had insisted Delphina come along because he wanted her
to circulate his petition.

Petitions were wonderful. Petitions supplied great political
torque for little effort. You could get practically anybody to
sign practically any petition. People would sign to be polite,
because they didn't want to look foolish at not knowing the
seriousness of an issue, or they would sign just to get rid of

you. Newspapers, for some reason, took a petition for information worth telling the world as a fish takes a fat worm. Best of all, a petition could make a public official scratch his ass when he looked at all those names of voters.

It was a nice day. It had been a nice fall so far, warm with southerly breezes. Ike sensed an open winter in the offing. Good. The crowds were bigger at the auction barn when the weather was kindly. He didn't like these cold winters that so many people bragged about in New Hampshire, as if bringing attention to a glass eye. (Or dentures, but Ike didn't have the ability to apply most of his insights to himself.)

Ike looked over the exhibitors on the town green. Most consisted of merchants who sold wood-burning stoves. Ike hated this system of heating. He had grown up in shacks and trailers heated with wood, and he knew about the work involved in cutting, splitting, stacking, lugging all that frigging wood, not to mention the discomfort of rising on a freezing morning when the fire had gone out, and the smarting eyes from smokey dwellings, and the vision-warping terror of house fires. He'd been in two, lost kin in several others. Never mind what they said about "air-tight" stoves and stinkless rooms and safe chimneys, Ike knew, he knew—wood heat was dangerous, uncomfortable, unpleasant, and ugly. Give him oil heat, or gas heat, or electric heat—anything but the dry, hell-heat of wood.

As for solar heat, he couldn't hate it, didn't have the experience of it to hate. But he was suspicious of it. For one thing, the coldest part of a winter day was when the sun didn't shine, and there were many days when it didn't shine at all. But there were considerations other than practical. There was something high-handed about the pitches of sellers of solar. It was as if they were scolding the founding fathers for not saying that a man ought to have the opportunity for life, liberty, the pursuit of happiness, and his own south slope for passive solar. The very idea that solar heat was touted as free disturbed Ike. There was always a price to pay; a man once he matured learned that as his first rule of business. Maybe solar heat gave you cancer.

A minute hadn't gone by when Critter skipped off with Delphina to the snack tent. Ike liked the idea of Critter marrying one of the Rayno sisters—good stock, kin stock—but he wished Critter weren't quite so head over heels in love. It made him lazy and stupider than usual. Ike decided he'd better separate them now, or else no work would get done.

"Unfeast your eyes from me. This ain't the time or the place," he heard Delphina say, as Critter leered into her blouse. Ike had to admit she was worth a leer.

"Come along, Critter, and help your poor dad," Ike said. "Delphina, I want you to hand out some of them petitions. Tell 'em we're going to save this town from the company store."

At that point Crowbar yawned audibly, and Ike turned his attention to the dog. "Be polite, be polite. This ain't one of Ollie's shacks. There's nice people here," he said.

Ike crooked his finger at Critter to come along. Delphina went off to hand out petitions. She'd do a good job. Delphina was smart, reliable. But God, she could dish out the shit. Women—you couldn't even hit them anymore, but what they went running to their social worker. Pretty soon they'd be testing for ascendancy. That was a disturbing thought. It made him stern-up to the fact that he was going to have to find a way to humble Miss Delphina Rayno, before she got too big for her bloomers.

"These women today are making the world an anxious place, eh, Critter?" Ike said.

"I suppose, Pop," Critter said, and then feeling his response insufficient to please his father, he added, "You're right, Pop. These women make the world a mighty anxious place."

"Of course I'm right. I'm right ninety-five percent of the time," Ike said.

Ike Jordan spotted Reggie Salmon, tall and stately as a tree in a city park. Something stirred in Ike's heart, as something must have stirred in the heart of his ancestors as they genuflected before idols. He called Delphina over, instructing her to present his petition to Mr. Salmon for signing. Ike wallowed with incredible comfort in the feeling of his lowness. Rasslin' constantly for ascendancy left him wary and tense much of the time. With Salmon, to whom he willingly surrendered ascendancy (there was nothing to lose: no one else would know; Salmon was outside the kinship, above it), Ike was able to relax, imagining himself in the presence of an immortal, helpless and therefore free from the need of the exhausting exercise of cunning. He could afford the luxury of those thoughts, because, in fact, it was he, Ike, who held the gun to the head of Reggie Salmon, thanks to Mrs. Butterworth. He wished he could explain these tricky ideas to Critter, if only to show the boy the versatility of the burglar's trade. But of course Critter was too immature to deal with such complicated issues. Someday, someday.... The "someday" brought back Ike's tenseness. When Critter finally had the experience to appreciate his father's work, he'd be challenging for ascendancy. Life was difficult, life *was* difficult.

Ike waited for the crowd to build before announcing a demonstration of his wood splitter. He noticed that most of the people who came to the Energy Fair were the new people in town. It was the same way at the auction barn. The new people, being far away from kin, were lonely perhaps; and they were curious about life in Darby. They turned out for sugar-on-snow parties, for Old Home Days, for bingo if they were past age fifty. They were more neighborly than the natives. Ike felt rather affectionate toward them, although when he prowled their houses at night he was appalled by their lack of taste. Their idea of art was a microwave oven, a VCR, a picture of Mount Monadnock.

One of the new people—he could tell by her clothes, her makeup, her bearing—approached him, smiled, and walked on. So it was with the commuter class—smile. Ike understood.

Then he saw Bob Crawford. "Bob, you want to pay me now, or you want to wait until I split that stump?" Ike asked.

"It's you that will be paying, Ike," Bob said, breathing out ninety-octane air.

Most fellows had backed off on Ike's offer to take bets on the demonstration. They knew he had something up his sleeve. But not Bob. Bob was easy to turn your way.

When Ike judged that the crowd had about peaked, he went to his van and returned with a bullhorn. "Ladies and gentlemen of Darby," he said, in his auctioneer's voice, "it's time for the amazing, stupendous, wondrous Ike Jordan woodsplitting machine."

The crowd gathered, and when Ike set the charges it became clear what it was Ike had up his sleeve—dynamite. He was tickled to discover that he had alarmed the Energy Fair committee. The chairman, Mr. Charles Henderson, who had married one of the Butterworth girls, approached him.

"Ike, you should have cleared this with the committee," he said, his brow furrowed with worry.

"Next year I will," Ike said.

"Come on, Chad, it's just going to be little explosion," someone said from the crowd. That brought laughter. As Ike had calculated, the people were behind him. Henderson retreated.

Ike looked around. He had the crazy hope that Avalon Hillary would be there and would waddle over to him, and say, "You goddamn fool, here's a hundred dollars of my cow money says you can't split that stump." But Hillary was not there. Ike felt a mild wash of disappointment.

Constable Perkins stood off to the side. He liked a good time and would make no trouble unless somebody put pressure on him.

There was a minor hitch after that. The poles on the van battery, which Ike was using as a power source to detonate the explosives, were corroded, and when he pushed the plunger there was only the sound of the breathy anticipation of the crowd.

"Critter, you dummy! Hook those wires up right." Ike grinned, exposing the full glory of his plate.

Ike could see on Critter's face his humiliation, but it merely registered with him as mild unease; Delphina's anger seemed like the consternating admiration of a woman put into her place.

Critter cleaned the battery, and then everything went well. Perkins aided in moving the crowd back, Ike pushed the plunger, the dynamite went off, the stump parted, and Ike Jordan collected ten dollars from Bob Crawford.

McDonald's

Chance had just entered the Tuckerman McDonald's Restaurant when he saw Persephone Salmon in front of him, isolated between the waves of people coming in and the undertow of those sucking outward from the serving line. She turned, apparently about to leave, when she recognized him, halted, and blushed as if caught in the act of shoplifting.

"You look lost," Chance said.

"I ... I've never been in a McDonald's before. I came to see, to see the light. No, I didn't mean that. I'm always choosing the wrong word." Her blush deepened to scarlet, then faded to a complex pink, like something you'd find in a stone from the sea.

Spontaneously, he offered her his arm, and she took it. They stood in line, arm in arm, like a couple on a date. She studied the menu posted on the wall behind the counter, and when the young woman with the pale orange cap shouted into the din, "Can I help someone?" Persephone was ready. "A filet-o-fish and a glass of iced tea," she said, speaking all the words crisply, except for "glass," which her breeding retrofitted to "gloss." Chance ordered a quarterpounder with cheese, small fries, and coffee. Persephone was unprepared for the gentle demand to pay up immediately, and she fumbled in her handbag. Chance rescued her by coughing up a ten-dollar bill for both meals.

She thanked him in a whisper, took her tray, and followed him meekly, taking in everything with innocent awe, as if she were an immigrant just landing on the shores of America. She asserted herself only when Chance tried to steer her to a booth along a wall.

"No, no, not here," she said, offended. "Over there, by the window, with the plants."

He had never noticed before that the Tuckerman McDonald's was dense with lovely plants, the floors clean, and the light kindly by the window. From here he could watch the cars creep by on the service road and feel a sense of calm that he was not out there; from here he could see across the road a huge tree, one of the few living elms remaining in Tuckerman. Beyond was some brush, then a small stand of poplars. The trees were bare, the ground brighter by comparison with its litter of freshly fallen leaves. On the elm tree was a sign: FOR SALE, COMMERCIAL PROPERTY, D. N. BARNUM, REALTOR. The last lot on the service road unturned by the bulldozer, it had little frontage but reached in for almost half a mile to the Tuckerman River.

"If I was Magnus, I'd get a dredge-and-fill permit and put my mall right there," Chance said, pointing.

"It's a pretty spot, with the tree and the wild undergrowth," Persephone said.

He watched her eat; she seemed uncomfortable using her fingers. The food moistened her lips, as if she'd touched them up with lipstick, yet there was a calmness and sureness about her too, or perhaps it was dignity, that made her rise above the McDonald's mob. He felt sort of honored to be in her presence, as if she were a movie star.

"What do they do with all this paper?" she asked, delicately crumbling the covering of her fish sandwich, placing it beside the napkin and carefully scrutinizing it as if it were a test shape for a future sculpture in metal.

"You put it in the trash can," Chance said. "From there it goes to the land fill, thence to the ages."

"I like the fact that everyone has to stand in line, that everyone gets treated equally. It's so democratic," Persephone said.

"McDonald's is a giant corporation that has discovered that the key to making millions is to feed people along the order of socialist principles," Chance said.

Persephone showed she did not like this remark by turning her eyes from him, passing them over the plants of the restaurant and then through the windows and beyond.

"Oh, dear, I didn't pay you for the meal," she said. "What do you want?"

"It's a little sadistic on my part, but I'd feel happier if you owed me something," Chance said.

Persephone thought about that for a moment, then looked at him seriously, as if actually noticing him for the first time. She dabbed her lips with the paper napkin. "This paper is coarse," she said.

They lingered over the meal, as if they were in some elegant restaurant overlooking an ocean bay. The convention that one got into and out of a fast-food restaurant pronto hadn't sunk into Persephone. As for Chance, he wasn't happy exactly, but he did feel suspended from his sense of time, and he liked that feeling.

He drew Persephone into a discussion about the mall. It was bad for the environment, bad for the social fabric of the town, she said, but her voice lacked conviction. Yet it took him a while to realize that it wasn't so much that she had no zeal for the subject as that her own spirit was bleak, as bleak as his own.

Later, after she had left, Chance felt his loneliness more intensely than usual. But his thoughts did not turn for comfort to Persephone Salmon, but rather to Soapy Rayno.

Newhawk

"It's nice that you don't have any creativity, LaChance—
I hate a prima donna—but couldn't you come up with a
creative story to get some time off? You're sick or your
Aunt Bowlinda kicked the bucket—something I can pass
on to the business office other than LaChance wants to go
to Burlington for one, two, who knows how many days,
simply because he wants to go?"

When Chance frowned, Shard went on, "This is the way
things are done. You don't just take time off from work.
You give reasons, even if the reasons aren't true."

"I thought you were a truth man," Chance said.

"You don't know how the world works, boy. The business offices of the world want reasons to paper their asses.
The reasons are supposed to be convincing; truth is not
relevant to the situation."

"But what about you, Clovis? What about you? You've
harped on me from the start to get the story right, check
everything out."

"You're missing something, LaChance. I'm not a truth
man; I'm a facts man. Give me the facts, I'll give 'em to
the people, and let them find the truth. Now let's get down
to specifics. You've put me in a position where I have to
invent a lie on your behalf to paper both our asses before

the business office. Better it be your lie than mine. After all, you're the one taking the time off."

"All right," Chance said. "I'm asking for one or two days off to take care of some personal things."

"Personal reasons are not as good as the flu or Aunt Bowlinda's funeral, but I'll take what I can get. Have a pleasant stay in Burlington."

When the Brat headed North on I–91 in Vermont, Chance was still brooding about the argument with Shard. He wasn't angry with him, or even with the idea of the office lie. He was depressed by what he took to be the lesson of the encounter: that certain lies supplied necessary make-believe gyroscopic reckoning as mankind hurtled through time and space.

After he turned off onto I–89 and reached the mountains of northern Vermont, he saw that fall had arrived here. The leaves were touched with color; there was a chill in the air. A sense of the season passed wordlessly through his mind— fall: it was as if in the uniformity of summer green, trees had felt the warmth and simplicity of green, like a soft, caressing emotion akin, say, to the muted joy of listening to Christmas carolers. The emotion was sustained and left no room for any other emotions and it was reached by silent consensus among the trees. Now that fall had arrived, the green had given way to stronger, more violent colors, felt by each tree separately, distinctly, disturbingly, as if with each burst of color the deep emotions that had been suppressed were rising up all at once, the trees feeling everything inside themselves, until exhausted they would shed everything, begin again bare in the season of white forgetfulness.

In Burlington, on the other side of the mountains, the city leaning on a hill against the shore of Lake Champlain, it was summer again, warm, green. The city surprised him. He had expected a comfortable, slightly backward place, like Tuckerman; but Burlington was hip, more like Cambridge, Massachusetts, than what he had imagined a Vermont city should be like.

With the sudden silence as he shut off the engine of the Brat he realized he had no idea how to go about finding Soapy, or what he would do if he did find her. He had only the desire, or perhaps the need, to find her, as a young mallard duck hatched in Canada has the desire and need to find a certain marsh in Louisiana. It was this purity in his desire for Soapy that had sustained him, given him not so much confidence as reassurance that inside himself there was something that was not cold. And he had it in his mind that because his motives were pure he would find her, because despite all evidence to the contrary there was something "out there" that aided and abetted good causes. But he wasn't going to find her, not in one or two days anyway. Burlington was too big, too spread out. If he hadn't been so weary of driving he would have turned around and gone back.

But he stayed, and as Clovis Shard had taught him, he pestered people, asked questions, behaved forthrightly as a young Mormon missionary. Chance didn't find Soapy, but that night, in a bar called Sneakers in Winooski, the next town over from Burlington, he found Newhawk.

The Newhawk name was well known in the Burlington area, and from bartenders and waitresses and street people Chance was able to gather a profile of Soapy's father. Newhawk was active in the antinuclear movement, but some members considered his support counterproductive because of his lack of personal hygiene and an explosive temperament that frightened people because there was a sense of controlled madness about it. Newhawk was a legendary drug user who had tried everything and survived. Newhawk was a moocher of heroic proportions. Newhawk had a mysterious appeal for women. Newhawk had no other name but Newhawk.

"This is nice, like when you're bare-ass in the rain," Newhawk said, finishing the drink Chance had brought him, a double Jack Daniel's served neat with a beer chaser. He had a full beard and long dark-brown hair ordered against his temples by natural body oils. He wore the same style denim uniform as Soapy, along with a bandana around his throat and worn but expensive running shoes on his feet. His teeth were yellowed from smoking and lack of care.

"I had an ulterior motive," Chance said. "There's something I want from you."

"I know what they say about me, that I'm dealing," Newhawk said. "But it's not true. I'm strictly a consumer these days. I have a philosophical problem with New Wave drug pushers. It used to be a spiritual thing, man. You sold it because you believed you were changing the world. Today's dealers are business people. They do it for the money."

"I don't want to buy drugs. I'm looking for Soapy Rayno," Chance said.

Newhawk paused, wavering, it seemed, between his better judgment, which told him to depart, and his desire to hang around for free drinks. Newhawk handled this minor crisis as always. He ordered another drink.

"What do you want from Soapy?" Newhawk asked.

"I want to help her," Chance said.

"If you want to help her, get her stoned," Newhawk said. "She's got this block, all this societal crap constipating her mind. She needs to loosen up. If I could get her back, keep her stoned for a while, I think you'd see an improvement in the way she talks."

"She already dresses like you, wears you to cloak her spirit," Chance said. "Do something real for her."

"You make reality with this," Newhawk said, and tapped his head with his forefinger.

"Anyway, she was here and she left," Chance said. "Can you tell me where she went?" He was tired and sick to his stomach from the stink of Newhawk.

"She took off on me," Newhawk said. "She had this crazy idea she wanted to homestead. I guess I'd made her a half-assed promise a few years back that we'd work some land together. I can't remember half the shit I say—she should know that. I tried to explain to her where I'm at today. I'm into, like, body and soul. Body is soul, flesh—the me-ness of me—is soul. You know what I mean? Of course you don't. You kids today are as uptight as bankers. She needed to loosen up, so I got her stoned, and something happened and she took off."

"Something happened?"

"Something is always happening, man," Newhawk said, and turned inward for a moment.

It seemed to Chance that he wasn't dealing with a man, or even with a being of flesh, but with a stink, a shape, a few colors in the mind left over from an acid trip.

"Who—what are you?" Chance asked.

"Shrapnel from the sixties," Newhawk said, laughed maniacally, downed his drink, and walked out the door of Sneakers.

Mrs. McCurtin

Mrs. McCurtin reddened her full lips, rouged her cheeks and displayed her conspicuous buttocks in tight blue jeans. It was only the presence of Priscilla, age four, and Melissa, age three, that lent an air of propriety to a meeting between the bachelor reporter and the house-bound mother who had modernized the position of town gossip in Darby.

When Clovis Shard suggested that Chance talk to the *Crier*'s correspondent in Darby, to get background on the town for future mall stories, Chance had realized that Mrs. McCurtin might also be able to supply information that could lead to Soapy. Shard had said, "Dot McCurtin can't write—in fact, won't write; phones everything in—but she's got a great news sense. She's the best town correspondent we have."

The McCurtins lived in a 1950's ranch house on the country road between Center Darby and Upper Darby. The backhoe-arranged granite boulders that lined the driveway still retained their spiritless pale beige color. Another hundred years or so and they would look like they belonged there.

Inside, the television played in the living room, the radio in the kitchen, and the emergency bands scanner and the children everywhere. Through these sounds conversed Chance and Mrs. McCurtin.

"Do Darby households do everything in the kitchen?" Chance asked. The coffee was instant; the chairs maple, cushioned by pads crocheted with flowers.

"Always have, don't know why," Mrs. McCurtin said. "The kitchen table's the social center during the cold seasons, the back porch during the summer. Used to be the front porch was where you sat to chew the fat on a summer night, but not anymore. Nobody walks anymore, so there's nobody to look at, nobody to talk about. Cars go too fast to mull over. So they window-in the front porches and use them as guest rooms, and socialize in the back. They don't even build front porches on the new houses."

"You sound like you've been here since the turn of the century," Chance said.

"I have, in a manner of speaking," Mrs. McCurtin said. "My family and Billy's family go back fifteen million years in this town. Sometimes when I talk, I can hear my mother's voice, and sometimes it's my grandmother. Sometimes only me. But this town has changed, even in my young life. Our local children move out, move on. Their parents die or get discouraged by the climate and move out, move on. Still, the town swells and swells from so many new people. Other people's dissatisfied children from other places come here. They're taking over the town from us poor natives. We're as pathetic to deal with the situation as the Indians of old."

The telephone rang. Mrs. McCurtin lifted the receiver, listened without saying a word for a full three minutes, then said, "I got somebody here, Frances, so I'll call you later," and hung up.

"I spend my days listening and talking into objects—the telephone, the CB," she said. "I don't complain, though. It's what I hear, what I say to who will care that keeps me from going crazy. . . . I almost did go crazy."

"The isolation out here?" Chance said.

"Correct. When I married Billy McCurtin, he fresh out of Burdett Business School and hired on in the insurance office in Tuckerman, and me in my high school graduation gown, we both agreed we wanted kids, bunch of 'em. I liked kids, still do, but I didn't realize their limitations, nor mine. I need people around, and kids are kids, not people. They take away eighty percent of your life and enrich what's left. I had two of 'em, bang, bang, eleven months apart. With Billy gone ten hours a day, I was going nuts here. I'm not one to park herself in front of the television, or read—God, I can't stand to read. And there's just so much housework you can do."

"So?"

"So a few years back Arlene Flagg, our town gossip, left Darby. The story is she ran off with a man, but nobody knows for sure. My goal in life is to find out. But anyway, when Miss Flagg absconded, I said to myself, 'Dot, look around, look around. What do you see?' The answer was: empty people. I said to myself, 'Dot, you can fill their lives by satisfying their curiosity about each other, just like Miss Flagg did.' I took the job. I'm still not fully accepted, but I'm getting there. I modernized the whole operation. CB, scanner, portable telephone so I can talk in the yard—I got all the equipment. This is why you came here—right? Because I know this town."

"Everybody knows that Dot McCurtin is the leading expert on Darby, New Hampshire," Chance said.

Having caught the compliment she was fishing for, Mrs. McCurtin blushed with pride. Chance knew it was time to start asking questions.

"Most of the voters live in Center Darby. Who are they?" he asked.

"New people, or local folks that have been away, to college and such, and so act like new people," Mrs. McCurtin said. "They're here because they enjoy country living. Most of them don't know too much that's true about Darby, and they don't care to find out. They see a rock wall or a gravestone, and they make up a likelihood about it which they repeat often enough that they believe it, or they buy somebody else's cock-and-bull story. They come to town meeting, but it's a game to them. Their main public interests are bare roads in the winter, good schools, and lower property taxes. Naturally they can't have all three, so they get frustrated. They like zoning laws—they're crazy about zoning out this or that. They feel zoning is insurance for the scenery. The newest people in town are the first ones to come up with ideas to keep the next batch out."

"What will they think about the mall? I mean, when it's on the line at town meeting," Chance said.

"Who knows?" Mrs. McCurtin said. "It was roads and cars—progress, as we say—that brought the new people here. Progress: they turn to it, they turn away from it, they turn back to it, and so forth. I've heard every opinion under the sun, but I don't know the answer and neither does anybody else, because the new people don't know. They don't know who they are. My guess is they won't find out until the town meeting. Whichever side is best at telling them who they are will win."

"What's your opinion on the mall?"

Mrs. McCurtin, who had just pulled her three-year-old from an electrical socket, stood erect, put her hands on her hips, and gave Chance a self-consciously flirtatious smile. "The impression I make depends on who I'm talking to," she said. "If I say what I truly feel about the mall, I'll lose the mouth and ear of half or so of the people of the town. This is not something your town gossip can afford."

"The mall issue has become that divisive, people not speaking to each other over their position?" Chance said.

"Oh, yes," Mrs. McCurtin said. "This town will never be the same, no matter how the mall is settled. It's already done its dirt to the Darby heart."

"You say most of the voters are new people, or local folks who have become suburbanized, but I thought Center Darby was a farming community," Chance said.

"Used to be, and looks like that, because so much of what you see is forest and farmland," Mrs. McCurtin said. "And farmers actually do own maybe two-thirds of Center Darby, but the fact is most of the smaller farms are run by part-timers whose main source of income is their jobs in Tuckerman. There's only—let's see—the Crabb place, the Boyle place, and Old Man Hillary's that pay for themselves as farms. And they're in trouble. The farmers still have some clout, though. Heck, Arthur Crabb is chairman of the board of selectmen. But the breed lacks in numbers. It's the new people, the commuters, that have the votes."

"What about Upper Darby?" Chance asked. He saw that she was flirting again with her eyes.

"There we have a different kettle of fish," Mrs. McCurtin said, breaking out into wonderment. "Years ago all that upland was spackled with sheep. The hills were not closed in by forest, as they are now. They were pastured. Just a minute..."

She broke off and left the room. It took a while for her to get back. She had to stop to change a diaper and answer the telephone twice. When she returned, she showed Chance a scrapbook.

"Look at this picture—1890 something," she said. The brown-tinged photograph showed a wood-frame house, bare of decorative plantings and even lawn grass. Foot-tall fields started at the front walk and rippled up into the hills, the pastures broken here and there by stone walls. A bearded man with muddied boots and a woman in a mountain of skirts stood on the steps, eyeing the camera severely. Beside them was a child, his face a blur because he had moved during the long exposure needed for the film of that day.

"My Grandfather Hiram," Mrs. McCurtin said, pointing to the child. "That's the Upper Darby of bygone days, sheep country. They might keep a few chickens, a pig, a milk cow, and grow vegetables. But it was the sheep that paid the bills. I come from Upper Darby stock. My father was a Marine from Maine, but my mother was a Flagg. So you see, I got some claim to Arlene Flagg's niche in this town, no matter what some of these people say."

"What happened to Upper Darby?" Chance asked.

"The sheep business went bust is what happened," Mrs. McCurtin said. "The soil up there is thin and stony. Not much good for anything else but pasture. No market for sheep, and the farmers got poor fast. A lot of them went west; others left for work in the textile mills in the cities. In those days you wouldn't commute from Darby to Tuckerman. Nobody had a car, and the roads were no good, especially in the winter. So they left Upper Darby, and the forest took over the fields. "We have now to look at Jepson Salmon. He came from New York, fat with stock-market money, and bought that hunk of rock known as Abare's Folly, over there in Darby Depot. Old Man Salmon knew something about geology. He mined that hill for mica and quarry stone."

"So the folly was that Abare sold cheap," Chance said.

"That's a ten-four," Mrs. McCurtin said.

Chance rose from the table, brushed past Mrs. McCurtin, who had just jerked her four-year-old from the refrigerator door, rinsed his coffee cup in the sink, put it away, brushed by her again, and returned to his chair at the kitchen table.

"Aren't you the homey one," she said, and went on with her Darby history lesson. "Mr. Salmon liked the view, liked the country life. He built a summer place, where his grandson Reggie lives today with his wife and cousin twice removed. The three families up there are all interrelated. Seems as if old Mr. Salmon's lady got lonely for her friends. So the Salmons sold land to the Prell family and the Butterworth family. That's how it all started, up there in the highlands."

"Why is SOD fighting so hard against the mall?" Chance asked. "It doesn't seem to pose any direct threat to Upper Darby."

"It's Reggie Salmon that's making that fight," Mrs. McCurtin said. "He's sick, dying, they say. The fight against the mall is his last stand."

Chance looked at the picture Mrs. McCurtin had given him. "What happened to the ancestral home?" he asked.

"The Butterworths tore it down and built anew," Mrs. McCurtin said. "It wasn't enough house for them. There's still a few Flaggs around town, but not a one of them lives in a generational house. Blame Providence, I guess." She grimaced. "Since Trellis died no one today is even living in the Butterworth house. Doesn't seem right, does it?"

"What about Darby Depot? Why is it every time I mention the name of that village people snicker?"

"That's our other side of the tracks," Mrs. McCurtin said. "Jepson Salmon built those houses on that narrow spit of land between the Folly and the Connecticut River as housing for his miners. Room only for a street, one row of buildings, and a rail spur that's grown in with puckerbrush today. His miners were immigrants, mainly, and the old-time Yankee folks were suspicious of them. The original stock is mainly moved out of Darby Depot, but because the houses are in such poor shape and because there's no acreage, why only the lowly still live there. Proof of that is in the fact that Jordans have taken it over."

There was a pause then. Finally, Mrs. McCurtin spoke. "Something else you want?"

Chance realized now that she had understood all along that he wanted more than background information about Darby.

"What do you think?" Chance asked.

"I have my sources. You're looking for Soapy Rayno," Mrs. McCurtin said, folding her arms like a gladiator over a fallen foe.

"Where is she?" Chance asked.

"I'd say you mean business, from the tone of that voice. Soapy's around. Joe Ancharsky, the storekeeper in the village, says she comes into the store now and then, walks in from the Hillary trailer, he claims."

"She's living there?"

"No, sir. Melba Hillary checked the place out, and she says nobody's living there. We don't know where Soapy is. I'm guessing she's staying in the woods."

The telephone rang again. While Mrs. McCurtin answered it, Chance put on his coat and prepared to leave. He was excited. He believed he would find Soapy that day. But Mrs. McCurtin wouldn't let him go. She waved him back to his chair. After she hung up the phone, she said, "I've answered your questions. Now, I have one for you. I've talked to Mr. Shard on the telephone a number of times. He sounds so masculine. I sort of have him pictured as tall, dark, handsome, about thirty-eight. Or maybe older, more distinguished looking. Now I know he probably doesn't look anything like what I think, and frankly I don't want to know; don't want to ruin it. Just answer me this one question: Would you say he's attractive?"

"Handsome as a movie star," Chance said.

Contact

Somebody's dream of goodness gone to sin, Chance thought, as he stood before the school bus trailer. The yellow roof and sides of the bus were blemished by fist-size rust holes, and the bus itself seemed about to slip off a wavy foundation of concrete blocks that had not been sunk below the frost line. A padlock barred entry to the front door. A couple of windows were broken, but some faded, tie-dyed curtains still remained, brittle as pastry. It was obvious no one had lived in the school bus since the Rayno girls had moved out.

He circled the bus like a suspicious animal trying to make sense of something it doesn't understand, something that actually is a trap. The sound of the tall, dry grass brushing against his trousers made him think he had been here before. . . . And he was a child now, walking with Old Joe, who was saying, "Look at the sky, see how blue it is," and then time had passed and he was watching a butterfly shaking its wings. Seconds later, or perhaps it was minutes or hours, he caught sight of Old Joe's face without its mask, seeing there the anger and the sadness, and he had said in alarm, "What is it, Daddy? Is it something from the sky?" Old Joe had wiped the anger from his face, like a drunk wiping drool, and slipped on his school administrator's mask and spoken through the false smile, "It's all right; nothing can hurt us here." And Chance had been afraid, a different fear than that evoked by the face behind the mask, a fear he could neither understand nor express, but merely felt as a downpour of light from the heavens. It was as if he were an uncomprehending child bathed in the light of a nuclear explosion.

Behind the school bus he reached a low rubble-stone wall thrown up by a farmer clearing fields perhaps two hundred years ago. Here began the forest and the Salmon Trust property. Chance looked up into the sky. Against the roughness of the land it looked ridiculously smooth, unreal. He wanted to get away from that feeling of sky, and he stepped over the wall and walked into the forest.

The land inclined upward, and he found a freshly trodden path winding through the woods. He had walked in only about a hundred yards, but he might as well have been a mile from civilization. Birds called, and the wind had a personal sound to it as it slipped its arms around the branches of trees, and he could smell the damp rot of leaves on the forest floor. He came to a small clearing. Hidden in the trees, about seven feet up, was a tiny house made of logs and salvaged lumber. It had a pine-board door decorated with evergreens, a couple of windows, and a sheet-metal pipe for a smokestack. A staircase of logs hewn flat on one side climbed in a spiral from the ground to a landing. The house itself, held up by five trees joined together by cross pieces, was perhaps ten feet long and eight feet wide, with a pitched roof of split-wood singles.

In the clearing was Soapy, beside a pile of dry, dead tree limbs that she had hauled to the site; she was bucking them up into stove lengths with a bow saw. She worked efficiently but without haste. She wore her usual denim uniform and her face was dirty, but the Red Sox cap was gone and her hair was arranged in a golden braid that fell to her waist. She had lost some weight. He had thought he would want to rush forward and announce himself. Instead he felt shy, unworthy, and he withdrew.

That night as he lay in bed, the TV on but with no sound,

he imagined himself forward and easy for pleasure. He watched Soapy through the leaves, and he was aroused by the dank perfume of the forest earth. He burrowed in this vision until the eleven o'clock news came on. But the next day it was the shy self that acted.

From a branch on the path to the tree house, he left his laundry sack full of groceries along with his picture. The next day the laundry sack was empty. He refilled it with groceries. On the fifth day he found in the sack a sprig of evergreens tied with a hair ribbon.

She was waiting for him in the clearing, sitting on a log beside the wood pile.

"You won't tell," she said, wetting the small "r" of her upper lip with her tongue; her eyes were worried.

"That you've built a cabin in the trees? No, I won't tell," he said.

"You still got the baby truck. I seen it," she said, with just the trace of a giggle. She didn't look at him, didn't need to, he realized. She'd been watching him these several days, had him pretty much figured out.

He noticed now that the Red Sox cap was back on, her hair hidden. He felt a jab of disappointment. It struck him then that the mild unpleasantness of this small emotion was the first time in months that he had felt anything directly. He had been feeling by radar, his everyday emotions obscured by the greater gloom hanging over him, their heat made tepid by the coldness of the gloom.

"You're talking, Soapy. You talk beautifully," he said.

"I practice. I touch things and I talk. I . . . I . . . Wait," she said.

He waited, watching Soapy struggle to find the words she wanted to say. "Easier for me here. Not so busy. Now you talk."

"I like to listen to you talk," Chance said.

"I have to think hard to talk. Hurts. You talk. Talk about things."

He soon discovered that she was hungry for news of the world. He told her what was in the paper that day. He recited the weather forecast. He fed her scraps of information about the town until at last, stiffly, as if discussing formal arrangements for strangers, he broached the subject that mattered to him.

"I haven't made many friends since moving here," he said. "I'm kind of, ah"—the word "wounded" wanted to spill from him, and it took an effort for him to dam it and find a replacement—"kind of *standoffish*. I don't mean to be. Maybe we could be friends. I'll bring you stuff out here. We'll talk. I won't bother you."

"Long as you don't tell," Soapy said.

Several days later Soapy asked that he inform her sister of her whereabouts. Chance drove to the auction barn. Delphina met him at the door. She saw that his eyes were on her stomach, and she said, "Go ahead, touch it."

Chance pushed gently with the tips of two fingers, afraid somehow that the full contact of his hand might establish a terrible intimacy between himself and the new life inches away.

"Big as a basketball," Critter spoke as he appeared at the door with his hello, a beer for that same hand on his lover's belly.

The firmness, the coldness of the glass on his hand in contrast to the warmth of Delphina's belly sent a shiver of appreciation through Chance, as if this, a realization of the complexity of life and mind, was a definition of beauty. He tried—and failed—to keep that thought at the front of his consciousness, as he was pulled by the tide of Delphina and Critter to the kitchen table.

"Little Jordan feller is working up his courage to come out into the cruel world," Critter said.

"It's a Rayno until the nuptials," Delphina said, a hard edge to her voice.

"When's the big day?" Chance asked.

"When the queen here makes up her mind to take the Jordan name," Critter said.

Delphina ignored Critter. She was searching Chance's eyes. When his discomfort was visible, she said, "You found Soapy, didn't you?"

On weekdays, after his copy deadline at eleven-thirty a.m., Chance would drive to Darby, tucking the Brat behind the school bus trailer so that it couldn't be seen from the road, and he'd hike in to the tree house. He'd stay an hour or two, sharing a lunch with Soapy before he returned to work. They would sit on logs around an open fire, while coffee water heated in a pot blackened by flames. On weekends he'd arrive in the morning and stay through the daylight hours. Sometimes he brought food, sometimes building materials ordered by Soapy. He also brought books and magazines. Speech was difficult for Soapy, but she could read some and she could hear and she could understand. Her most articulate means of expression were her hands. They were nimble and educated; they could bring round an idea by drawing a shape in the air. With Chance as her assistant, Soapy insulated the cabin, added a porch, built shelves inside, constructed an outhouse, and laid in firewood for the winter. Chance hauled wood, fetched water from the stream over the hill, and pounded nails now and then.

The woods and the work and the passing of time brought changes to Soapy. She was maturing, losing her baby fat; her skin cleared up; her face became more angular, her body more sculpted. No longer would one mistake her for a boy, even at a distance, even with the cap that was always on her head when Chance was about. Her most conspicuous feature remained her filthiness, but here too something was different. She wasn't dirty like a human being—greasy, machine-slathered, work-soiled. She was dirty like an animal—dusted, branch-brushed, weather-varnished. Nor did her body and clothes give off the sick, nervous, tired stink of the unwashed person of the town, but rather something of the essence of evergreens, earth, and air.

"You smell like trees," he blurted out to her as the fire

crackled between them. It was the first time he had said anything to her that could be construed as romantic. But she took
the comment as informational and responded in kind.
"You smell like the newspaper office," she said.

As the weeks passed, Clovis Shard noticed a change in his
rookie reporter—a certain tranquillity, a growing competence
in his work. Shard translated this as a reflection of job satisfaction, a satisfaction that Shard himself, as mentor, felt he
could take a measure of.
"I've been here and there in the newspaper business ever
since high school," Shard said to Chance one day. Chance felt
a pang of despair as he sensed a speech coming on. Minutes
that could be spent in the woods with Soapy would have to
be spent here, listening, falsely attentive.
"I've been a reporter or editor, sometimes both at once, in
Houston, Tampa, Baltimore, St. Louis, even Buffalo," Shard
said. "Never New York, I'll admit. But so what? You should
try a big-city daily after you've completed your apprentice-
ship here. We don't call it an apprentice program at the *Crier*,
but that's what it comes down to . . ."
"Which accounts for the low pay," Chance said.
Shard, soothed by his own voice, chuckled and continued
talking. "Big papers report big news. You feel part of the
bigness. Jeez, in East St. Louis a guy with a gun wanted to
shoot me. Really. He even got my home phone number. I had
to move—like all the way to Tampa. Where, wouldn't you
know it, one of the kids from my first marriage, although I
was married to my second wife at the time, got into a racial
incident, which I won't go into.
"Eventually, LaChance, it tired me out. I quit for a year.
Went to work scratching asses for the Fogarty PR people in
New York. See, I did get to the Big Apple, but I backed in.
That doesn't count. Good money, reasonable hours, the pleasant companionship of alcoholic, burned-out newspapermen—
I couldn't stand it, LaChance. So I went back into the pressure
cooker, for NewSSpot. It cost me a marriage.
"I said to Riley, the professional cigar chewer in Dallas, I

said, 'Riley, give me a paper, fifteen, sixteen thousand circulation, and I'll make it into the best small daily in America.' They sent me to the *Crier*. I thought I was going to be publisher, instead of the em-ee. I had my feelings hurt, but I thought about it, and I could see that the truth is I'm not the publisher type. I'm a nuts-and-bolts man who belongs in the newsrooms of the world . . ."

"A guy who owns only one tie," Chance said.

Shard seemed not to have heard, not to have noticed Chance edging toward the door. Shard talked on, wistful as an army veteran remembering Christmases far from home, "It's better this way. As em-ee, I'm involved. I edit copy, lay out pages, make policy, and kick ass. It's my paper, not Mrs. Chubb's. I know it, and she knows it. I'm happy with my station in life behind a VDT. I wake up in the morning and I say to myself, 'I like my job.' At night I sleep like a baby."

"Secure in the knowledge that you know the difference between 'infer' and 'imply,' " Chance said.

That snapped Shard back to the reality of the newsroom. "Yes, I've been meaning to talk to you about that," he said, the editor in him assuming command, the jack-in-the-box reminiscer stuffed out of sight.

Later, when Chance was alone thinking, he found himself touched by Shard's attempts to recruit him into the brotherhood of the journalist's trade. Shard had demonstrated that it was an honorable life, a productive life, bound not to place or person but to work and a modest code of ethics. He struggled to imagine himself twenty-five years hence, an editor of a small newspaper in, say, Red Bluff, California.

The leaves fell from the hardwoods. Sometimes they fell like a soft rain. Sometimes the rain itself fell, and the leaves fell like stones. Sometimes the wind blew them off the trees, swirling them into tiny cyclones.

"Oh, shit," Soapy said.

"What's the matter?" Chance knew what the trouble was— the sound of the clacking of leaves. It reminded Soapy that her cabin no longer was well-hidden. He had asked her what the matter was because he wanted her to express her fear. When she kept bad feelings inside, the feelings polluted her reservoir of language.

Soapy said nothing.

"Say it, explain it," he said. He took a handful of leaves and put them in her lap. Her fingers inspected them, turning them, crunching them, rolling the stems between thumb and forefinger. He had seen this disturbing studiousness before. It was as if in touching something important her concentration was so intense that it blinded her temporarily.

"They'll see me, my cabin—hunters," she said.

It was the eve of the two-week-long deer-hunting season in southwestern New Hampshire. Soapy feared exposure; she feared gossip, curiosity, leering eyes. She feared these things not so much for the obvious reasons—that she valued her privacy and didn't want to be put into a vulnerable position— but because she was afraid something would be taken from her, the solitude she credited as her healing medicine, to be taken daily as needed.

Most of the deer had moved up-slope to a broad shelf just below the ridge where young hardwoods provided browse for food and stands of hemlocks supplied bedding and wind-protected yards for surviving the winter. The wise hunters would hunt the ridges, but not all hunters were wise.

Chance and Soapy disguised the tree house as best they could, lining it with evergreen branches. Chance worried. This year's deer hunters might not find the tree house, but eventually a hiker, a snowshoer, someone would stumble upon it. The news would be all over town in twenty-four hours. But Chance said nothing of this. He said, "Two weeks and the hunters will be gone—hang in there."

Soapy waited. She stopped burning open fires and lit her cabin stove only at night. Without a fire the cabin was cheerless, raw. Cold November rains fell. Chance took Soapy for rides in the Brat, so she could warm herself by the heater. Sometimes they visited Delphina.

"Give it up out there, sweetie. Move in with me and Critter," Delphina preached.."You can stay on the balcony. We'll put a curtain up for you. It's almost like living outdoors, and you can work for Ike."

"Don't like Ike," Soapy pouted.

"Nobody likes Ike, Soapy. Nobody likes who they work for. Nobody likes anybody unless they got a leg up on them. You do what needs to be done because it need be. . . ."

The second Sunday of the deer season was a poor day for the hunters. There was no tracking snow, the skies had cleared, warm air had moved in, a mild breeze lounged in the trees. It was Indian summer.

"No ride today. Not cold. Up on the ledges. See west and west some more," Soapy said.

Chance translated. Soapy wanted to take a walk to the top of the ridge, to the ledges, where the view opened to the Vermont hills.

They bushwhacked up-slope until they came to the logging road that led almost to the ledges. They had walked another half mile when they heard the report of a rifle.

"Let's talk, let's make some people noises so we don't get shot," Chance said.

"I whistle, you talk," Soapy said.

So Soapy whistled and Chance talked. Soon he was caught up in his own words, as if (and this struck him in the telling) his goal was to tell everything about himself without thinking, that the spoken sum might quench his thirst for knowledge about himself. (He imagined himself pulling up a bucket of cold water from the dark of a well.)

"I had this crazy idea I could find my natural parents," Chance said. "I looked in the files of the *Crier* for clues; I hung around at the courthouse. None of it to any avail. The problem is: no name. I don't know the names of the people I'm looking for, and the name I've got, LaChance, doesn't seem to exist in state files on adoption. Sometimes I think Old Joe told me I was conceived here in Tuckerman County to throw me off his trail. I wouldn't put it past him. Actually, I don't care who my natural parents are. At least, I don't think I care. What I care about is the lie: a lie has been told me, and I don't know what it is, and it's like an invisible wall between my future and my past. I'm in a bubble spinning through space in the present; it's as if every day I wake up with amnesia. I grew up more or less normal. I would wonder: What is my name? Not that I suffered over the question. It was just one more vague concern. Then everything changed, and now I'm all emotion, or rather emotion wrung out, so there's nothing left but the rags of feeling. Something happened, Soapy. My father died—that is, Old Joe died. And he did an awful thing to me.

"I was in college at the time in North Carolina—Wilmington—and my mother called me and told me to come to New Mexico, that Old Joe was dying. Then he came to the phone. We talked. He'd been sick for a long time, and during his illness I had been thinking about a promise he'd made to me years before when he'd been drinking. He said that someday he would tell me the story regarding my birth. Later he tried to back out of it, said the booze had tricked his tongue, that he didn't know who my parents were or any of the details. I didn't believe him, but for years I never said anything. Then that day when I talked to him on the telephone I told him I was coming to collect on the promise he'd made me years before. Mind you, we'd never gotten along. I had the crazy idea this would bring us together before he died.

"I remember seeing my mother when I got off the plane, the red dust in the creases of her skin. I'd long ago given up trying to find out about my birth from her. I was convinced she didn't know, that Old Joe had stolen this baby somewhere, and said, 'Here, it's yours.' To me, though, she was my mother, and the red dust in her skin, the dryness in her skin, made me sad. I wanted to tell her I loved her, but for some reason I criticized her. We argued on the drive. I didn't care. I was beginning to sense a power. I sensed that Old Joe on his death bed couldn't lie. One look at my need and he would have to tell me the truth.

"We arrived at the house, and there was a big red boulder in the yard and cactus and red dirt. The place, the effect, it was like being in an old Clint Eastwood movie. I said, 'Nice rock,' but Genevieve was already in the house. I hustled to catch up.

" 'Joseph, Roland is home,' I heard her say, her voice full of false cheer. There was no answer. I was still seeing the boulder in my mind's eye when I read the panic on her face. I followed her into the bedroom. I heard her shout, 'Don't come in, Roland,' but I was already in.

"Old Joe was sitting up, his eyes open, his jaw slack. But it was his complexion that took hold of me. He was pale as milk. He hadn't even bothered to put the pill bottle away. It lay on its side, open, empty, on a stand beside the bed. I knew right then that he'd wanted me to walk in like that, see him like that. And I realized at that moment that I had been wrong about something. I had thought I hated Old Joe. But I understood then I loved him, had always loved him. I didn't hate him—he hated me. . . ."

At that moment Chance and Soapy were startled by a crashing noise. It froze Chance. And he watched, detached from time and event, without strong feeling but with interest, as if he were watching television. A deer had leaped in the road in front of them, paused, as if to pose for them, displaying her glazed eyes, her delicately muscled shoulder bright with arterial blood. The doe then bounded into the forest. At that point Chance's mind caught up with the passing of time. He turned toward Soapy. She was gone.

"Soapy!" he heard himself shout. There was no answer.

His mind flashed back to the first day he had met her, when suddenly she had run into the woods. Since then she had told him the story of the moose, so he knew now why she had taken off after the wounded deer—to touch it, to know it. He plunged into the brush after her.

He ran until he realized the uselessness of running. Neither Soapy nor the deer were in sight. He stopped, trying to listen for sounds from the brush, hearing instead his own heart pounding, and when that had subsided, hearing the gentle hush of wind in the trees, then silence, then the ghost-moans of the traffic on I–91 five miles to the west and below. He made himself calm down, to think. He couldn't just blunder about. He had to find a trail.

He returned to the spot where the deer had jumped into the road. Down-slope about twenty feet, he saw a brush stroke of blood on a branch. Touching, looking, even sniffing—although his nose was no good for tracking—Chance was able to read the signs of the frightened, panicky flight of the deer. Here would be a hoof slash in the leaves, there a dab of blood. It was intense work, at once nerve-wracking and extremely pleasurable. He put himself into it, and there was no room for fear or anger or even hope; there was only the trail. Following the animal he had become an animal.

He reached a dense stand of young hemlocks. One part of him had lost complete command of time, while another part of him reckoned with fair accuracy that about a half an hour had passed. The undergrowth was so thick that he was almost upon Soapy before he saw her. She was lying on the ground, looking up at him.

He was about to speak, but her finger came to her lips, signaling him to be silent. The finger was wet with blood. He lay down beside her, seeing now that her face and hands and blouse were red and sticky with blood.

She had found the deer, she had touched it, bathed herself in its blood.

Soapy pointed to an opening between the hemlock branches that reached to the earth. Chance could see the deer lying on the ground, two men beside it. Big men, father and son, the younger holding a rifle, the elder unarmed. And he could feel Soapy's presence, dark with blood and musky from the earth.

"Gonna cut it," Soapy whispered, as the older man unsheathed a knife. Her voice was low, her breathing rapid and warm. They drew closer together. Chance could feel the sticky blood against his skin. He swooned with desire and revulsion.

They could hear the men talking now, the voices distant yet clear, the father with the diction and accent of a rural New Hampshire native, the son's speech smoothed by years of higher education.

"Right below the heart," the father said. "A fine running shot, Freddy, I daresay."

"Lucky shot," the son said. He was standing a ways from the deer, his rifle in his hand, and Chance sensed in his voice a little of his own revulsion.

The father began to cut into the belly of the deer, the sight drawing Chance and Soapy into an embrace.

"I never liked the knife work," the son said.

"When it's alive it's a her or a him; when it's dead it's just meat," the father said.

There was an intimacy between the men that made Chance sorrowful, the sorrow increasing his desire, which was not strictly for Soapy but for something else, something intangible, beyond expression or even comprehension, something in his blood, or perhaps only in the idea of blood.

"Happy with yourself?" the father asked the son, his tone matter-of-fact, as he lifted a great glob of guts from the deer and laid it on the leaves.

The son laughed sardonically, and it seemed to Chance that there was something of his own sorrow in the laugh. "I never thought I would ever hunt again, and I never thought that you would quit," the son said.

"I quit hunting deer and bear and other common game," the father said. "But I'll still hunt a coyote or a traipsing dog."

Chance and Soapy were no longer listening. They were deep within themselves, brought together not by love or even by feeling, but by blood and leaves. It doesn't feel right, Chance thought. The pleasure is there but it doesn't feel right. *The stickiness . . . the stickiness . . . the stickiness.* And he was lost; it was as if he were inside the deer, bursting forth from her belly, killing her with his own life as it came into the world.

They returned to the cabin, ashamed. He did not want to look at her, nor she at him. What had passed between them was not lovemaking, but something else, a killing thing, and he could feel a deepening of the sorrow that he had heard in the hunter's voice, that was his own sorrow, that was the hunter's sorrow.

Silent Night

By ROLAND LaCHANCE
Crier Staff Writer

DARBY, Dec. 5—The Darby Planning Board voted 5–0 last night to approve the site plan for a regional shopping mall in the town.

However, in an unprecedented action that bears no legal weight, members voted 3–2 to recommend that voters at the town meeting next March reject the current proposal for a mall and establish a mall study commission.

The board has been holding hearings since Magnus Mall Group Inc. announced plans to build a giant regional shopping mall in this small town on the Connecticut River.

"The mall's site plan meets the Planning Board's requirements," said Zoe H. Cutter, Planning Board chairman. "We had no choice but to approve it. However, members felt the board should go on record regarding the mall."

Mrs. Cutter, Franklin A. Bridges, and Theodore S. Duhaime opposed the mall, saying the present plan is too big in scale for Darby and that the Hillary farm on River Road, the proposed location for the mall, should remain farmland. They'll ask voters at the town meeting next

124

March to reject a plan to rezone the farmland but to elect a panel to study the impact that a mall would have on Darby.

Arthur J. Crabb, the selectmen's representative on the board, and Marguerite Croteau favored the mall.

"Most of America already is malled to death," said Mrs. Cutter. "The people of Darby choose to live here because it is a quiet, pretty, countrified place that just happens to be close to urban amenities and culture. There is no reason to bring those amenities to Darby, since they already are available within easy driving distance. On the other hand, there is every reason to preserve the rural atmosphere, since when it is gone it will not be so available elsewhere."

Crabb, a farmer and chairman of the three-man board of selectmen, thinks the planning board erred by making a recommendation on the mall.

"The planning board is supposed to plan, not tell the townspeople how to vote," he said. "It's obvious to anyone who understands where the tax dollars come from that a mall is going to do wonders for Darby."

Crabb doesn't think the mall will disrupt the rural atmosphere for the town.

"It's going to move out one farm," he said. "It's not going to kick up the wildlands we have around here. They'll be here, mall or no. But the wildlands aren't going to pay to plow the roads in the winter or educate the children, not with the state's current-use law the way it is. It's going to take something like a mall to give us the tax base we need to keep the town afloat."

The planning board's proposal that townspeople appoint a study commission is pointless, according to Crabb.

"If they appoint a committee it won't amount to anything, because while the committee is studying the idea the mall people will have gone somewhere else," Crabb said. "The proposal should either pass at the town meeting or get beat, and die. That's how we do things in New Hampshire."

• • •

In the shower, the water beating on his back, Chance recreated his conversation with his mother last week, trying to figure out what had gone wrong. He had telephoned her to invite her to spend the Christmas holiday with him. From the start there had been a certain passionate unease between them. They were, he thought, like lovers holding back, each waiting in the hope that the other would make the first move toward spreading salve on some nearly unbearable common hurt.

"Is it snowing in New Hampshire? When you were a baby in Derry, Joe would pull you on a sled, and I used to like to listen to the snow fall in the trees."

"We had a whisper of snow last night, but the ground is mostly bare. It snowed hard a week ago, but it changed to rain and the snow went away. It's cold now, about ten degrees."

"It's dry here, cold at night, warm in the day. I love the sun, the dryness."

He had heard something in her voice that reeked of the Westerner's bias against anything east of the Mississippi, and it was this perception, he understood now, that had triggered his subsequent annoyance with her, his insensitivity to her, if that's what it was.

"It's supposed to be clear and cold for the holiday—no White Christmas in New Hampshire this year."

"How is your work going?" He realized now that she had meant his job. At the time, however, he had thought, for some fantastic reason, that she was asking about his effort to find his natural parents.

"It's not going at the moment. I've found that there was no fire that burned adoption records, and yet there are no adoption records on me. I don't understand this. Maybe you could shed some light on the subject."

"Oh, that. You've been looking up things on that."

"Yes, that. *That* is why I came here to Tuckerman."

"Okay."

"Can you help me?"

"I'm here, you're there. Ah . . . there *was* a fire, Roland. That's why you can't find the records. Of course there was a fire. They didn't have computers in those days, Roland. Everything was on paper. If there was a fire, there would be nothing left. Nothing."

"Of course."

"What are you doing for the paper?"

"The *Crier*."

"Yes, the paper there."

"I'm covering a big mall issue. A development corporation wants to put a mall in Darby."

"Darby?"

"It's a small town. Very beautiful. And they want to put a mall in it."

"Every place has a mall today," she had said, puzzled.

"You don't understand."

"I said the wrong thing. I'm sorry."

"Mom, fly here for the holiday. I'll pick you up at Bradley Field. You can stay in my bed, and I'll sleep on the couch. I'll show you the county and the newspaper office. Christmas Day we can drive to Manchester and visit Aunt Jeanne and those million other relatives."

There was a pause. He heard Genevieve clearing her throat, a sound like choking, and he recognized this as her preface to speaking an untruth.

"You know how I hate to fly."

"I don't know any such thing. You never, never before expressed a fear of flying," he said with sarcasm that screamed, *liar!*

"I'm terrified of airplanes."

"I don't believe you."

"I can't help it, Roland. You don't understand."

"Your fear is not flying. It's me, isn't it?"

"It's not that. It's . . . it's the heebie-jeebies. It's flying—I'm afraid to fly, honest. Flying gives me the heebie-jeebies."

"Mom. Oh, Mom."

"Roland, call me Christmas night. Call me collect. I have to go now. Someone's at the door."

"Okay."

"What will you do on Christmas?"

"I don't know. Visit friends."

"Roland? Roland?"

"Yes, Mom."

"I do love you. Please believe that. I love you, son."

He had believed her. She did love him. He had no doubts about that. Yet she wouldn't come to Tuckerman to see him. There was something here that troubled her, somebody here that knew her.

He shut the water off, and for a moment he forgot about his mother and thought about water itself—falling from the sky, seeping into the earth, freezing, melting, evaporating. Water was Mother, Father, and God carrying us away to an ocean sleep.

He dressed and set off for Darby. It was Christmas Eve.

He had promised Delphina he would deliver Soapy to Ike's annual Jordan Christmas party at the auction barn. It would be Soapy's first public appearance since her retreat to the tree house. He knew Delphina was right in trying to get Soapy to mix with people. Yet something in him wanted to keep Soapy isolated. He was afraid they, the *they* of the world "out there," would take her away from him, or perhaps that she would give him up in favor of them. And yet he was not sure whether he wanted her, whether he deserved her, not sure what remained of whatever it was they had. Since that moment in the leaves when they had surrendered to blood and earth, they had exchanged warmth for heat. He wished he could start over with her. As it was, he was not making her happy, nor she him. They carried on out of habit and heat. He wanted to tell her that he had sought something else from her, something pure and cleansing for both of them, and that he hadn't meant for them to end like this: sullen lovers. But it was as if a measure of her aphasia had afflicted him, and when he went to speak of these difficult things, there were no words to say what was on his mind. Soapy, too, had slipped. Her cabin, which had been neat and clean, was now as disheveled as her person; her ability with language had regressed to awkward outbursts. Lovemaking had not united them; it had tainted them.

Now, as they drove to the auction barn, Chance saw that Soapy had come alert, perked up. This disturbed him, threatened him.

A minute or two passed, and he glanced over at her and noticed her winter's hat, a wool toque.

"Why do you keep your hair covered when you're with me, even when we make love?" he asked.

Soapy said nothing.

"I deserve an answer," Chance said.

"Mine!" Soapy shouted, and shook herself, as if shaking something from her clothes.

Another minute passed.

"You're looking forward to this party," he said. He had not meant it to sound like an accusation, but it did.

"So what? Fun."

"Speak in complete sentences," Chance said. "Say, 'I'm looking forward to the party because I want to have fun.' "

"K-k-k-k you," Soapy said.

Chance knew what she meant, and he responded by turning on the radio. He drove on, trying to feel anger, loss—anything.

Later, Soapy spat out some indecipherable syllables.

"I'm sorry, I don't understand what you're saying," Chance said.

If Chance had taken his eyes from the road for a moment and turned them to Soapy's, he might have been able to determine that she was asking him to be nice to her, that she needed the calmness he once caressed her with and which now was a rough embrace. But Soapy had not the voice, nor Chance the ear to complete the circuit from her need to his understanding.

By the time they arrived at the auction barn, Chance had pushed Soapy out of his mind. He was thinking about socializing, losing himself in drink.

He had visited Critter and Delphina a number of times, taking the back stairs to the apartment, but he hadn't been in the main part of the auction barn since the episode with Crowbar, so its labyrinthian quality startled him anew, evoking in him an image: the auction barn as a computer-enhanced model of Ike's mind. Things of varying value and style and type and size were piled here and there, as if by plan, but to no apparent purpose but to confuse, to scorn the idea of meaning: ceramic kitchen pots with plastic patio furniture, fishing equipment with oil paintings, tires with Edgar Rice Burroughs volumes, aisles issuing forth, flowing into greater aisles, or lesser aisles, or dead-ending into metal beds stacked vertically, a traffic pattern resembling Boston streets.

Chance's thoughts drifted into the party. Two men with electric guitars were playing seventies disco music. Forty or fifty people mingled about, many of them already drunk, although it was before the dinner hour.

They found Delphina by the canteen. The sisters embraced. For a moment Chance felt a loss, an ache.

Ike Jordan wandered by, patted Delphina on the tummy, subjected her to his toothy, malicious smile, as if he himself had sired the child in her, looked Soapy up and down, chuckled, and went away without a word.

"If I had the courage I'd wipe that smile off his face with a shotgun," Delphina said.

"What did he do now?" Chance asked.

"He didn't do nothing new," Delphina said. "I just want to kill him on general principle."

Critter arrived then. "Howdy," he said, his breath smelling sweetly of alcohol.

Delphina tugged Soapy's arm, Soapy waved good-bye, and the sisters left. Delphina and Critter did not so much as exchange a glance.

"Chilly in here," Chance said.

"It was hotter than a fart last Tuesday," Critter said. "I don't know what to make of these Rayno girls. I says to Delphina after the engagement was announced in the newspaper, I says, Delphina, when do you want to get hitched? Know what she says? I don't want to get hitched; not presently. I says, Delphina, you're going to have a child. She says, I know it better than you. Then she says, like she was some Upper Darby bitch, I'll live with you as wife, but I won't marry you. I says, you won't live with me and have my child and not give

him my name. She says, I will. I says, one of us is bluffing.
She says, Raynos don't bluff; Jordans bluff. I says, I'm going
to kick your ass. She says, you kick me when I'm pregnant,
I'm going to tell a social worker, ha-ha-d'ha. I says, I'm offering you a gold band to signify our bond. She says, I'll take
it. I says, shit you will; no wedding bells, no wedding band.
She says, Critter, you're a daddy-whipped baby. I cracked her
one, then, right across the mouth. 'Course, I pulled up. Didn't
want to take her head off. She says to me real soft, if that's
the way you want it, okay, but keep your blows above my
belly. You don't want to hurt that baby. Naturally, I felt like
shit. I know they say it keeps 'em sound, but I don't like to
hit no woman. Hey, all I want from this miserable life is the
smell of pussy, the taste of beer, and a car. That ain't much
to ask, is it?"

Chance and Critter stood by the canteen drinking beer out
of bottles, watching the Jordans. Ike and a few other men
tended to the rotisserie of a pig over a portable gas barbeque;
some women worked a cafeteria line; several men stumbled
like Brouwer boors; there were kids everywhere.

"How about a little program on the players here?" Chance
asked.

"That over there that stuck the apple in the mouth of the
pig is my uncle Donald," Critter said, pointing to a slim, hard-
bellied man whose skin creases were given punctuation by
black automobile grease imbedded in them. "He runs that
junkyard over there in Tuckerman that the city is always
trying to close. I daresay nobody can swear with the iron that
my uncle Donald can. Young feller with him is my cousin
Again. See, Uncle Donald is a junior, and when he had a boy
he wanted to name him Donald. You wouldn't want to call a
man junior junior, so he says, this one is going to be named
Donald Again."

"I like the logic. Who's that?" Chance directed his eyes to
a woman in her fifties with long dark hair. She wore a colorful
ankle-length skirt. Perhaps a half dozen plastic-bead neck-
laces cascaded from her neck onto a white blouse. There was
a powerful sultriness about her.

"That's Estelle Jordan, the Witch, my grandmother, although nobody would think of saying, 'Hey, Granny,' " Critter said with a nervous laugh. "She's maybe the only human being still breathing that can face down Ike."

"Your grandfather here?"

"Could be anyone of several fellers here, or none of 'em." Critter laughed uncomfortably.

As Chance was leaving he got a glimpse of Soapy through a break in a side aisle. She had left the crowd and immersed herself in the merchandise. He saw her again and was taken by the look on her face: attentive rapture.

"Soapy," he called.

She slunk away from the sound of his voice. It was as if he were the house dick and she had just stolen something. She met Delphina at the canteen, gestured to her, and the two of them hustled up the stairs to the privacy of Delphina and Critter's apartment.

He wanted to see what had caught Soapy's attention, and he turned down the furniture-and-appliance-strewn aisle from where she'd come. Here, away from the din, the barn reimposed its sovereignty. Chance heard—or imagined he heard—the muted *wup-wup* of beating bat wings. He stopped when he arrived at the spot where he had seen Soapy. On the floor, squatting on four lion-pawed feet, was an ancient, oversized porcelain bathtub, its white maw marred by a green stain from the faucet cut-out to the drain hole.

He should leave. This party was for Jordans; Soapy was going to spend Christmas with Delphina and Critter; he didn't belong here. Yet, not knowing exactly why, he didn't want to leave. He strolled deeper into the barn, into the mustiness. Preoccupied, he took a wrong turn in Ike's labyrinth. For a moment he felt a twinge of panic, as one lost in the woods. That was followed by anger at himself for not paying attention, then a sort of cosmic anger—anger at God for his messy creation—then, abruptly, the pleasant sensation of suddenly getting one's bearings. He ducked between some boxes searching for a shortcut to the main aisle, and was surprised to find, sitting in a rocking chair, a woman about to light a corncob pipe.

"Park your ass and brood for a while," she said, as if she had been waiting for him.

"You're Estelle Jordan," Chance said, taken aback as if he were the one walked in upon.

"If they told you who I am, they told you what I'm called," she said.

"Witch," Chance said, to hear the word on his lips, and then introduced himself.

The Jordan Witch lit her pipe, and the sweet, acrid aroma surprised Chance. "Not pipe tobacco," he said.

"Wacky-tobaccy," the Witch said. "Ike don't like it. Scares him. Sometimes when I want to get his attention I blow the smoke in his face, but today I only mean to tease him. He'll smell it pretty soon, and he'll think 'Witch!' because I'm the only one with iron enough to smoke in his barn. This will remind him where we stand, him and me. Care for a pull?"

"I don't know."

"This toke is grown in my very yard. Organic. No chemicals," the Witch said. She held him with her eyes and passed him the pipe. Chance drew the smoke into his lungs.

The Witch took a drag, another, and she was stoned, in the manner of the habitual user—two hits and off.

"These Jordan men drink their pleasure," she said. "They say they want to get to feeling good, but the truth be they don't want to feel nothing. This here that we smoke widens the eyes for the rainbow and tunes the goose bumps so they sing like Fats Domino."

He and the Witch drew down two bowls. The sound of the auction barn bats, heightened to Draculan magnitude, signaled him he was stoned, but not before he jumped to his feet and threw his hand up before his face in defense. He lurched backward, banged into a crate, and thought he heard the Witch snicker. He turned to face her, to confront her for her impertinence, but she was gone. He wondered for a moment whether she had ever been there.

He canoed (or so it seemed) to the party, which was raging at this point. From nowhere had come a giant Christmas tree, perfectly proportioned, perfect in every way, glittering, exploding like fireworks. Christ and the Fourth of July. It was a full minute before it came to him that the Christmas tree was artificial. Under it slept children amid gifts. Or perhaps the children were the gifts. For whom? In the background, he heard some women singing "Silent Night." Where was Soapy? *Where are you? Why don't you take a bath? It's sheer vanity, vanity turned inside out. You understand? Of course you do. You understand everything. You can talk, too. You fake it, to . . . to . . . Why do you fake it? To set yourself off from the rest of humanity? You're stubborn, Soapy, ungrateful and unfeeling. . . .*

"Critter, this place looks like Mars—your father's a goddamn Martian," he heard himself shout.

"Have an ice-cold beer to celebrate—what the hell is it we're celebrating?" Critter said, and handed Chance a quart bottle of beer.

"The birth of the Christ child," Chance said.

"They say he was God, but I don't care," Critter said, his voice slushy. "What I wonder is: Was he worth a shit as a carpenter?"

Chance didn't answer. He'd thrown his head back, tipped the bottle, caressed the neck with his lips and tongue. When he finished drinking he told Critter about his encounter with the Witch, ending with the phrase "almost lost my cherry," and they both laughed uproariously. The alcohol glazed over the tension induced by the marijuana, and now he could enjoy somewhat the slight distortion of the high—the halo of yellow around the lights, the grotesque *choorah* sounds of men commiserating over drink, the fluctuations of his sense of time. The singing stopped, and he heard himelf pick up the hymn, half-humming, half-mouthing the words: "Sii-hi-lent night, hooh-ly night, all is calm, all is bright, 'round yon Virgin, mother and child." Or was it round yonder virgin mother? Or round yawn virgin? Makes no difference, he thought.

He lost track of Critter, found himself among a group of older men, where a bottle of whiskey was being passed from hand to hand in morbid silence. He stayed for two swallows. *Soapy? Soapy? Round yon Soapy, mother and child. Sii-hi-lent night, Hooh-ly night.*

Hello, Mom. Merry Christmas. Mary Christmas. Marry Christmas. Nary Christmas. Round yon sturgeon, mother and child. Hooh-ly infant so tender and mild. So tender and mile? How many tender miles, how many, Mom?

"Hey, feller, you know how to sing 'Silent Night,' " he said, poking a young hunchback.

"My . . . name . . . is . . . Turtle . . . Jordan. . . . I . . . am . . . deaf," said the man, in the robotoid voice of a video arcade machine.

"Who can sing 'Silent Night'?" Chance shouted.

"I . . . am . . . a . . . handicapped. . . . I . . . have . . . learned . . . to . . . speak . . . thanks . . . to . . . the . . . Tuckerman . . . County . . . School. . . ."

Soon a group formed, men and women, including the hunchback, and led by Chance, they sang, "Sii-hi-lent night, hooh-ly night, 'round yon Virgin . . ." *Virgin on the verge of gin: tender words, tender miles of words.*

I am tired of caroling now. Chance drifted away from the singers and found Critter. Or Critter found him. Difficult to tell in this great crowd.

"Lost and found," Chance said, and the words seemed richly laden with meaning.

"Ike's looking for me," Critter said, faking sobriety, the fun gone from his voice. "The son of a bitch wants to send me out for beer, I bet."

"Hey, Critter, what holiday is this: the Fourth of July or New Year's, or what?" Chance said, taken by the urge to dance. "Is this Times Square? Where's the big ball on the tower? Hey, Ike, your barn has no tower."

"He ain't going to find me. It's his party. Let him go buy his own beer. I ain't his go-fer."

• • •

In fact, Ike's thoughts were far from his son. He was in the van in the parking lot of the auction barn gloating, talking to his dog.

"Quite a day, Crowbar. Quite a lot of surprises. When Mr. Salmon arrives, everything will be perfect."

Reggie Salmon had agreed to support Ike's political ambitions. Ike planned to run for selectman against the incumbent, Arthur Crabb. Accordingly, Ike reckoned himself an ally, yea, a friend, of Mr. Salmon. Ike had used the paper from the Butterworth business to persuade Salmon into giving his support. Ike hadn't charged him anything, and therefore he figured Mr. Salmon would be grateful, and so he had invited him to his party to show there was no hard feelings. He could have compelled Mr. Salmon's presence, but that would have been coarse. When you had a gun to a man's head, you should either blow his brains out or show restraint. It was coarse to tease him, shoot his ear off. So he had left it at that, an invitation. Ike had convinced himself Mr. Salmon would come to his party, would be honored to do so.

Ike waited until he grew anxious for human company. "Mr. Salmon must have had car problems," he said. "Let's go back inside, Crowbar."

It dimly dawned on Chance that Critter was upset about something, his father probably.

"They all lie. You get used to it, Critter. They think it's love. Maybe it is. Maybe that's the answer. Lies are love. Lies are love. Liza Luv, may she love forever."

"The son of a bitch."

Chance saw Ike with his common-law wife. They were coming forward. Chance tried to look in Ike's eyes, to see if the auction barn was reflected in them, or vice versa—*vice versa? What did that mean?*—but he was distracted by the glitter of Ike's false teeth—*like something you'd find on the devil's Christmas tree. What a great thought—ummm! Liza Lies, 'round yon virgin mother and smiles.*

"The son of a bitch," Critter whispered, in his own mind

slowly freezing under the dry-ice grin of his father's false teeth.

"Have fun, boys, have fun," Ike said, and he put a quart of beer in each of their right hands, and then vanished in the crowd.

"Oh, Daddy." Critter leaned his head against the bottle and cried softly.

Sii-hi-lent night, hooh-ly night.

It was a great party. Best party Chance had been to since his undergraduate days—*undergraduate daze?* Where was Critter? Lost Critter. That boy couldn't stay found.

What a genius Ike was, consecrating Christmas in this giant manger. All these shepherds and kings bringing frankincense and—what was it?—myrr, or mirr, or mur? Must look it up. Must make a note to look it up. Must get pencil. He fumbled through his pockets, coming up with his car keys. They jangled musically before his eyes. Why was he holding his car keys? Was he going somewhere? No, they must be some kind of symbol. But of what? Something of great importance and power, something to do with the Christ child, born of Mary and adopted by the original Old Joe. Something like that. And then he glot a gimpse—got a glimpse—of Soapy. She looked shy, flirtatious; by gosh, she was flirting with someone.

Chance bulled his way through the crowd. Soapy was on the edge of the dance floor, looking up into the eyes of Again Jordan. In a swirl of light, Chance saw the young bearded face of Again transformed into Newhawk.

"Soapy!" shouted Chance. It occurred to him as he moved toward her that the air in the auction barn had jelled into a liquid, and that he was swimming. He and Again faced off. He reached through the murk and felt himself push flesh.

"Book out!" Again said, and returned the push. Chance could feel the man's breath, like metal. Or was this his own breath blown back at him?

Soapy stepped between them. Protecting whom? Chance lurched forward, half-diving, half-attacking, stumbling into an embrace with Soapy and Again, the three of them dancing

now in one of those magical changes in which enmity becomes
detente. Date-aunt? Wasn't this wonderful? Isn't this grand,
Soapy? Isn't this tactile? Tack-tile. A growl. Soapy was upset.
Everything is going to be all right. Let me touch you, heal
you. I heal you, you heal me.

Chance fell backward, cuffed on the ear by Again. Okay.
No big deal. He wasn't angry. He was not angry. Then why
was he doubling his fist, cocking it, throwing it, hell-bent for
the future? Amazing the thrill of the feeling of the doubled
fist exploding against the surprised face. Who was it that had
said, "only to connect"? What a great phrase. What a terrific
party. My word, it must be midnight. It must be Christmas.
The birth of the Christ child. Savior. Sii-hi-lent night,
hooh-ly night. Christmas. He must call his mother.

A moment later, when Critter grabbed him from behind
and pinned his arms, Chance came briefly to his senses. Again
Jordan was across from him, being restrained by Ike and
Donald Jordan. Between them, on the floor, was Soapy, blood
spurting from her mouth.

Persephone's Rebellion

Persephone Salmon wondered if other women did this: made themselves pretty before their mirrors in preparation for combat with their spouses.

She liked the sensuous feeling of the brush passing into and through her hair, slowly bringing out the shine. Once when she was a girl, her grandmother Prell had said, "Persephone has hair like honey," and grandfather had corrected her: "Not honey—money, the hard stuff you can't get anymore." The currency might be devaluing gradually from gold to silver, but it was still rich hair.

Combat aside, she was paying more attention to herself recently. Persephone didn't bother to brood about why. It was enough that after years of self-enforced plainness, she wanted to be pretty again. No, she thought, that's too much to ask. She wanted someone to smite into recognizing the ghost of her prettiness. She didn't care who the smitten was, or even to make contact with him. She wanted merely to see herself as a woman reflected back in a pair of eyes on the street. This would do in place of touch.

She had discovered that when she felt pretty she also felt strong, strong enough to face Reggie. Reggie, now in remission, obsessed by "the Trust," dripping with war lust in his squabble with the Magnus people, forging some kind of personal religion out there in the granite-strewn hills, had himself grown strong and must be met with strength.

When she finished brushing her hair, dressing, applying a dab of perfume between her breasts, she knocked on the door of his study, and said, "May I see you for a moment?"

"Hold on," he said. Rustling sounds. She imagined that he was shoving something in a drawer to hide it from her sight. As she heard him rise, then the sounds of his strides coming toward her, she stiffened involuntarily, as if she expected he might throw open the door and hit her.

Reggie gave a start when he saw his wife. "You're all dressed up," he said. It sounded like an accusation. She felt the sadness and anger in his voice like a haunting.

"I'm on my way to the college to talk to Lilith's adviser. I wanted to discuss it with you first," she said.

He knew something unpleasant was in the offing, and he pushed past her and shut the door so they wouldn't meet in his study, where her presence was an intrusion into his private world.

They went into the living room, and she took a seat at one end of the couch, tempting him to sit beside her even though she didn't want him close to her. She knew he wouldn't sit with her; she merely hoped that, by extending the invitation to join her, she'd poke the place deep inside where he had buried his feelings for her. He went right on past her into the kitchen. He was going to make her wait, punish her for dragging him away from his study, his thoughts.

She watched the fire writhing on the hearth. As much as Reggie preached conservation, solar this and solar that, he used up a tremendous number of their trees every year because he insisted on burning them in the fireplace instead of in a wood stove, which would be far more efficient. She didn't complain. She liked the fire.

The room was lovely, a comfort. Never mind the ugly incident surrounding the Christmas tree. Reggie had been sick, and then in Hanover for tests, and so she had bought a tree in Tuckerman, a pretty spruce from Canada. When Reggie was well again, he had removed the decorations, cut up the tree, and burned it in the fireplace, installing in the stand the usual balsam fir he cut in their own woods. She had watched her tree burn (as now she watched the logs burn), watched it twist and crackle with horrible intimacy. He had strained to be gentle. "Don't take it personally," he had said. "I don't have many Christmases left, and I want the ones I have my way, with trees from the Trust. It's a connection, understand, with . . . with things. Don't you see?" She didn't see. He had taken down her tree to punish her for the unpardonable sin of insensitivity to his own vanity. Where he had affected a breezy workman's air as he stripped the decorations and hacked at the branches with a hatchet, she had seen in him right-eousness, a quivering, evil sensuality and anger, like some parson of old burning a witch. And she, Persephone, the witch, had stood there, magical and strange, watching herself in the flames of the fireplace.

He returned from the kitchen with two cups of tea. She resented the fact that he had not bothered to ask her whether she wanted tea. But all at once, she did want it. Nothing would taste better than tea at this moment. It took all of her will-power to summon the strength to leave the cup where it lay on the end table.

Reggie had not been, technically, inconsiderate of her. He hadn't lost his consideration so much as altered it to fit dif-ferent criteria. It was as if he had put her in a category marked artifact or mummy or loved-one-gone-by instead of wife, and then treated her accordingly. If he brought her flowers—not that he would, but if he did—they would be presented, met-aphorically, not from his hand to hers but from his hand to a pot placed before her feet, as before a grave. Thus his every polite act made her feel ghostly, without flesh or feeling. How-ever he regarded her, it was beyond touch. He had arranged it so that she would lose her sense that she was flesh. Thank God for combs, lipstick, mirrors, underwear, things that de-pended upon the reality of you for their meaning.

"Well?" he said.

"Lilith has been accepted at Oberlin for the next school year," she said.

"I guess I knew that."

"I want her to go, she wants to go, I'm going to discuss transferring the credits and all with her adviser today," she said.

"Let me guess," he said. "You've been to the bank and borrowed money on our name for this venture."

"Not exactly, and I resent you calling it a venture. It's our daughter's education."

"I'm sorry for the offense, Persephone." He spoke in a sweet, low, soulless voice, buying time with apology, a time-honored tradition among the Salmons. He started to speak again, hesitated, and swayed from side to side—two Reggies warring whether to pry directly (the new Reggie) or indirectly (the old Reggie). Then, his mind made up, he launched his inquiry, but at the onset Persephone cut him off and spat her own words at him.

"Don't you love her, Reggie? Don't you want the best for your daughter? Don't you?"

He exploded, a controlled roar that rumbled out of his throat and that with all its fury and evenness seemed to silence for a moment her ability to think, to feel. There was only his voice and the blue winter light, like light from a supermarket, coming off the snow into the house through the windows. She almost wished he were out of control, slapping her face for her cruelty, but his voice remained even and hard. "Of course I love her. It's what you consider 'the best' that I think is wrong. All of us here on the hill have had the best, and what's our sum total as human beings? We have alcoholics that imbibe the best Scotch and addicts that inject the best drugs. We have women in therapy, men that can't hold jobs, and children crippled by misplaced idealism. All of us are afflicted with rampant snobbery, although none of us will admit to that disease. We can't seem to marry outside of ourselves, and when we do bring a new person into our orbit, we make him worse than ourselves. I'm thinking of Chad Henderson."

"I'm thinking of your brother, Monet," Persephone said

spitefully, and then was immediately ashamed. But Reggie seemed not to hear, or at least not to take offense. He struggled on to complete his mental run.

"As a class, we're like a decaying climax forest," he said, then paused to hook other metaphors onto his train of thought. "We're a class on the skids. Tracking Lilith in the same groove is not doing her a favor, it's paving her path to oblivion. The better course might be to nudge her into a different direction. Leave her be at Tuckerman State College, Persephone. Let her meet different kinds of people, do things we don't in Upper Darby, shake her up at an age when she can profit from exposure to the world."

So that was it. He wanted everything he owned going to the Trust, not so much—as he was fond of preaching—for the sake of preserving the land in its natural state, but because he wanted to limit the boundaries for the expansion of his own kind, hem them in, in the hopes they'd self-destruct as a breed. Sick, he had reckoned sickness in Upper Darby; dying, he had contemplated suicide for a class, all on behalf of some loony theory that the family bloodlines were hardening from cultural arteriosclerosis.

"Snob or no, I'll have my daughter out of that state school, into Oberlin," she said.

"How do you propose to finance this education?" The new Reggie had won the war.

And she had been right. He didn't care about Lilith. He only wanted to know where the money was coming from, in the fear that she had devised a way to nip at the flanks of his trust.

"I'm going to sell my inheritance," she said.

Reggie was shocked, speechless for a moment, and Persephone experienced a brief surge of ecstasy at seeing him stopped cold. Finally he spoke.

"That's a betrayal to the memory of your mother."

He looked at her then, his head cocked to the side, like one of those children at the workshop for the retarded in Tuckerman, categorizing her for his mental menagerie.

"I guess this Oberlin thing means a lot to you, Persephone," he said. The words were conciliatory, but the tone threatening.

"It does. I've been trying to tell you that for years, years and years, Reggie."

"I know I don't listen. I'm preoccupied, I guess." His voice had dropped to a whisper; my gosh, he sounds like Lamont Cranston, she thought.

"But I still have command of my reason. Persephone, why not hold onto the land and just wait for me to die. You can use the life insurance money to send Lilith to Oberlin."

"With all due respect to the efficacy of your disease, Reggie . . ." her voice, so loud compared to his, made her ashamed. ". . . you may just survive it. You may stay in remission for years. Only God knows."

She wondered whether he picked up on the fact that she had accidentally blurted out an old joke between them. They were both agnostics, and in their younger days, they would kid each other with that phrase, "Only God knows." She saw no recognition on his face, and she had to fight back the urge to burst into tears. She had to remind herself to keep her composure, so that she could continue to battle on behalf of Lilith.

She slid closer to him on the couch, attempting to force him to look at her face, to smell her essence, to deal with her as female flesh and blood. He did not look at her. He looked at the fire. After a moment of silence in which she could hear the fire sigh, Reggie said, "Okay, okay, if, ah, I find the money to pay for Lilith's education—your terms—will you keep the land? Please. I don't say you have to turn it over to the Trust, not right away. But hold the land; don't sell it. Think about the land, what it means; visit it, let it touch you, Persephone."

All that passion, she thought. How could he be so warm toward the bunny holes and the briars, so cold toward her? "Reggie?" She lowered her voice.

"Yes."

"Reggie, why don't you love me?"

"What?" He pretended not to hear.

"Nothing," she said. "Nothing at all."

In the end, Persephone agreed to put off sale of the land she inherited, provided that Reggie paid next year's expenses for Lilith at Oberlin. She had successfully blackmailed him. She should have felt triumphant. Instead, she felt guilty, sad, angry beyond her original anger, stricken inside by a new insight, as if self-knowledge itself were a debilitating disease. She realized that while her motives to educate Lilith were strong enough, sound enough, honest enough, they were overridden by her desire to command Reggie's attention, to trouble him.

Who is dying? she asked, as if there really were a God she could call upon. Is it I, is it he, both of us? She was visited by a vision from the television: insects that devoured each other as they mated. It seemed to her that after every encounter with him, she lost some precious life fluid. Now the vision was transformed into a creepy idea: Reggie's life force already had died. He lived off others, a vampire, roaming the Trust, roaming their bedroom. This strange notion seemed to have as much—and as little—validity as her rational explanation for her suffering, that it was merely stress from living with a terminally ill husband who no longer loved her. The only certainty she had in her feelings toward him was that she wanted to hurt him, to punish him for dying in slow motion in the middle of her life, and that at the same time she wished to make one last connection with him so that she might achieve some kind of salvation through mutual pain.

Persephone didn't like the feel of the state college. The attitude of the students seemed to her an unhealthy brew of conservatism and hedonism. The staff was full of those nouveau people, the upwardly mobile sons and daughters of working-class parents. She admired those go-getters for their intelligence, their unabashed ambition—was even a little jealous of them for the fact that having begun at the base of the hill, as it were, they could marvel at the views with each step upward, while she of course was cursed with comparing all sights with the panorama at the top; but she despised them

for their bad taste, their pretensions, their compartmentalized
wardrobes that included such things as specialty clothing for
golf. Thank God they hadn't caught on to Pendleton's yet. In
their own way they were more snobbish than her own class,
often measuring their personal progress by the things they
owned, by the proper performance of certain useless cere-
monial acts brand new to them but about which they behaved
as if they'd invented them (wearing whites during tennis, for
example), by the little ditties of knowledge they'd picked up
in graduate school, even by the sniffing vanity they took in
using the word "supportive" in place of "helpful."

Never mind that Lilith's adviser, Dr. Hadly Blue, only partly
fit this mold: it was, on the whole, accurate. Blue was a soldier
in that cadre of modern poets and novelists that taught English at every state college in America. He also was a recent
resident of Darby.

This was the first time they'd met on school business. She
was distracted by the mess on his desk, the slovenly way his
sports jacket hung on him, the ring around his collar. She
wanted to straighten up the place, grab his ear, and march
him to the barber's. Now she noticed his fingernails were
dirty. It was forgivable, even manly in some circles (she imagined), for a carpenter, a mason, or a ditch digger to have dirty
fingernails. But a college professor? Why was it that perfectly
acceptable-looking professional men moved to the country,
and the first thing to go in their cerebral chassis was their
pride in personal grooming? She wanted to shout, "What are
you trying to prove, buster?" Instead she said, "I take it from
Lilith's embarrassment, when I told her I was coming here,
that advisers don't talk to parents much these days."

"Eighteen-year-olds are supposed to be adults," he said.
"Some are and some aren't, but most parents, perhaps mistakenly, give them the benefit of the doubt, at least in regard
to campus matters."

She couldn't tell whether she had been rebuffed, and she
really didn't care, but it gave her pleasure to consider pushing
him to be specific just to see how he'd handle it, but of course
she didn't carry out this idea. She asked him for a report on

Lilith's progress. Blue was, at this turn, thorough and honest, and Persephone found herself grateful, even liking him a little bit. Lilith was not a brilliant student, nor would she ever be; but she was sincere and hard-working. She was quite talented in music but had trouble in the sciences. Recently she'd developed an interest in economics and political science.

"Am I being snobbish or impractical to ship Lilith to Ohio for her education, when we have the state college so close to home?" Persephone asked.

"You're right on," he said, and she stiffened at his familiar tone. "Lilith is not happy at Tuckerman. She'll do better at Oberlin, if for no better reason than that's where she wants to be. I hate to admit it, but I think it's best she leave the state college. You know about our troubles. The college is estranged from its money source, the New Hampshire Legislature; the administration is estranged from the faculty; the faculty is estranged from itself, divided between union and anti-union factions. The students? Many, like Lilith, transfer out. Not all of our students should be in college to begin with, but in these times, we'll take anyone. It's a Darwinian reflex for survival. The result is many of our courses revolve around—how should I put it?—remedial work. . . ."

She didn't want to hear the rest of it. He was suffocating her; it was as if Reggie had re-created himself in the image and likeness of Hadly Blue. Was this the way it was with all men: yakky, possessed by theories?

When finally she left, she felt an overwhelming desire for a cup of tea. Persephone had told Lilith that she was seeing Dr. Blue, but not which day. Nevertheless, she believed somehow that she would find Lilith in her room. She'd pick her up and take her to Perrin's, and they'd have an hour together. Lilith was not in her dormitory, and no one knew where she was. Persephone certainly couldn't go into Perrin's alone. Where to then?

With the TV On

"... amoeba-like," boomed the voice of Reggie Salmon, and with that Charles Barnum jumped to his feet.

The eyes of the meeting moved from the tall broad-shouldered man in the tweed jacket to the pudgy man in the tweed suit. Chance rolled the pencil between his fingers, and wrote on his notepad, "9:22 p.m. Maybe, finally, some action."

"Madam Chairperson, really, I must respond to Mr. Salmon's allegation," Barnum said.

"An amoeba is not an allegation," Salmon teased.

"Madam Chairperson!"

"Go ahead, speak, Mr. Barnum," Zoe Cutter said. The chairperson of the Darby Planning Board had an air of command about her. She was stylishly dressed, with fine features and smooth skin. (She'd had plastic surgery last spring, Mrs. McCurtin claimed.)

Barnum, in a practiced theatrical gesture, had slipped on his reading glasses as he rose to his feet, adjusting them so they rested more on the tip than the bridge of his nose. "I must take exception to the description of the proposed mall of Darby as 'amoeba-like,'" he said. "The statement is misleading. The shopping mall, with its main anchor stores and ancillary shops spiraling off, has been de-

scribed by Professor Granger Hoyle in the *Retailer News* as—
and now if I may quote from this scholarly article—'a self-
contained organism, the very shape of which is one of the
most naturally recurring in nature, as in, for example, star
nebulae and flowers."

"An amoeba is natural!—natural as rain," Salmon said,
coming to his feet.

"But an amoeba is neither sentient nor appealing, except
maybe to another amoeba," Barnum said, looking around to
see if his humor had been appreciated by the small crowd. It
hadn't.

"That's my point," Salmon boomed.

There was laughter in the Darby Town Hall. Once again
Reggie Salmon had made the Magnus people look stupid.

"Yes, but our point was . . ."

"Mrs. Cutter, I believe I have the floor," Salmon said, cutting Barnum off at the pass.

"Madam Chairman!" Barnum shouted, exasperated.

"I suppose I've let the running debate gallop off," Mrs.
Cutter said. "Mr. Salmon is correct, Mr. Barnum. He has the
floor. I allowed you to speak, Mr. Barnum, because you seemed
so anxious to get a few words in. Not that it matters much.
This is only an informal hearing. We're not going to vote on
anything. But to make the meeting flow with some decorum,
why don't you finish, Mr. Salmon, and then you rebut, Mr.
Barnum, and then perhaps we can hear from other concerned
citizens."

That drew a collective snicker from the crowd. Salmon and
Barnum had dominated the mall hearings. The earlier meetings had been packed with voters, but attendance had fallen
off as the issue became tiresome with familiarity, the battle
lines drawn, the arguments repetitive.

Chance stopped taking notes. There wasn't going to be anything new at this hearing. He had been on the telephone all
that afternoon trying to get a lead on what the next break in
the mall issue was going to be. Barnum, he knew, favored
asking the selectmen for a special town meeting on the Hillary
property rezoning issue. But Chance wasn't sure what Case

thought about this idea, and Case had the power, although Barnum, the local lawyer, did most of the talking at the public hearings. As far as Chance was concerned, Magnus itself didn't seem to be working terribly hard on what was a very expensive project. On the other side, SOD had been making noises about filing a court suit almost from the first, but so far had taken no such action. It was whispered around town that the Upper Darby folk behind SOD were just too cheap to put up the money for a court battle.

He watched Salmon and Prell gather their things. Separate they were dignified men. Together they resembled a comedy team, the tall handsome straight man with the marred face, his short, stocky sidekick cousin. Persephone Salmon had come to the earlier meetings, but no more. Too bad. She brightened up the gloomy town hall. He didn't exactly like Reggie Salmon, but he found himself rooting for him. Salmon was pompous and vain, and he talked too much, but his commitment to his family Trust lands was so powerful, so complete and consuming, so honest that Chance couldn't help being moved by it. Darby itself was moved. Even the Magnus people often found themselves treating him with deference or perhaps awe. Yet who knew what this would mean during a vote on the mall? It was going to be a secret ballot. Perhaps the townspeople would strike down the town father with the vote.

Chance gathered his things—pencil, pad, camera. Outdoors, the air was calm and very cold. A typical January night in Darby. He looked up at the bright stars. Shrapnel from the big bang, he thought, and headed for Tuckerman.

Since his breakup with Soapy, Chance found the hour after his newspaper deadline a difficult one. He felt at once pent-up and empty, like a balloon about to burst. He would drive around aimlessly in the Brat, eat, and return to work. Once in front of his VDT, he'd be all right again; which is to say, he would be detached from his own sadness. He didn't like dining alone at home, or in places such as the Chrysalis or Murry's where he would feel conspicuous in his isolation. Thus, he'd gotten in the habit of lunching at McDonald's, its impersonal hubbub masking his loneliness. It was there, at the door of McDonald's, that he saw a familiar face.

"I thought you didn't like it here—no wine," Chance said.

Persephone Salmon was startled. She turned and looked into Chance's dark eyes.

"I came in for tea," she said. "It's hard to explain. I went to the Chrysalis, and I had the feeling of a great elastic band squeezing me. I couldn't bear to go in. So I came here . . . for tea."

"Don't you want lunch?" Chance asked.

Persephone thought for a moment. "It's what, almost one o'clock? Yes, I suppose I must have lunch. I don't really want tea. I don't know what I want."

"Have lunch here with me."

"It's not tea that I want, it's wine—wine," Persephone said. With that, it was as if the two of them, having been put to sleep by a wizard with his own intentions, had been set free to awaken together in a garden, and it was June instead of January.

"I will have lunch with you, but not here—not here," she said.

Persephone ordered a filet-o-fish sandwich and Chance his usual quarterpounder with cheese. They took their lunches in paper bags to the Brat. Chance drove to a corner grocery and bought some champagne. They went to his apartment then, and there they dined.

"This is surprisingly neat for bachelor quarters," Persephone said, her skin glowing from the champagne.

"Do you want to smoke? Some people like to smoke when they drink or after meals," Chance said.

The absurdity of this remark reminded them of what was on both their minds, and they embraced.

Later, there was an awkward moment between them that was quickly resolved. They were lying in bed, and Chance's erection faltered.

"Do you mind if I put the television on? Lately, it's my mantra," Chance said. He didn't wait for an answer. He snapped on the small set on the table beside the bed.

"Is that boxing? I didn't know they had boxing on in the afternoon," Persephone said.

"It's a rerun, on the sports channel," Chance said, nicely firmed up now.

The sound was very low. Persephone could just hear the chatter of the announcers. Confident as ganders they were. She could see the screen quite clearly from her position on the bed. Reception was much better than in Upper Darby. Must be the cable, she thought. She wondered whether the shiny shorts of the boxers were made of genuine silk or one of those imitation fabrics, stitched in Taiwan.

Reggie's
Rebellion

Reggie Salmon was dreaming and he knew he was dreaming. He was in the Garden of Eden, and Eve was saying to him, "You see there is no God, per se. God is the garden, the garden is God." And he could see the eyes of the serpent were her eyes. No, not her eyes, his own eyes reflecting back from her eyes. *I am the serpent; the serpent is I, I in her.*

He was, he thought, awake now, and he could sense the presence of Persephone beside him, and he could see himself in his mind's eye touching her, breathing her in, embracing her. "Just a touch away," a voice said. "Yes, yes, I know," he replied, and reached for her.

And he really was awake now, and of course he was alone in the bed. It was morning, but still dark and he could see stars outside the window. *Winter dark, blue dark,* the words popped to mind, seeming wise and inscrutable, as the first remembered words of the day so often do.

He sat up, listening to himself. Before the pain, before the faint stirrings inside, there would be a sound, a sizzling, that would signal that his disease had returned. All quiet today. He was still in remission. This was a good moment. He was fully awake and he knew he was going to live another day, guaranteed of it. No sound, no pain to follow, no drugs to take, no death. A day, a gift. He wished he had a god to thank. No god, alone in his thankfulness. He imagined the light pouring into the trees of the Trust. *Thank you, thank you for one more day.*

When a man was sick and dying, loneliness became a fearful thing, the sound of scalding. Animals might go off to die alone, but not people. Yet, this is what Reggie planned. He had been slowly separating himself from his loved ones while he was still alive, instead of all at once at the moment of death. He steeped himself in the loneliness. The pain of it made him appreciate life.

It had been his idea that he and Persephone sleep apart. He had seen his infant son, his mother, his father, his grandfather die, the dying hanging onto loved ones, the loved ones hanging onto the dying. Hanging on was a mistake, he believed. For the dying, it heightened the fear of death even as it diminished the experience of death; for the living, it purpled the grief-scar with guilt. His way was better. As much as he loved Persephone and wanted to be with her, desired her comfort, he was determined to cut the ties of love and friendship that bound them. This was a cruel thing to do to her, he knew, but he believed it was best in the long run. She might be unhappy now, bitter when he finally passed on, but as the years went by, the last days would fade in her memory and she would remember what had been good about their marriage, their love. He fancied that he was readying her for independent living, thinking and doing for herself, searching about for an identity as a widow.

As for himself, he didn't want to hang on to life through others. He didn't want to go out scared of that final separation from loved ones. The connection between loved ones was life itself. Death severed the connection. He wanted to get used to the idea of being without love, to muffle the usual death clap that was the snapping of the love cord.

And, too, he was taken with the idea that there was another connection, more sacred than the one between persons, a cosmic connection. He doubted the existence of a god of the Christian stripe of his ancestors, but there was something out there, and he intended to make contact with it before he died. Perhaps afterwards, too. He was convinced that other people were like screens between himself and the something else. He wouldn't admit that it was God he was looking for, only that at certain moments he had an inkling, just an inkling, that he could hear . . . something. Cosmic music?

He threw back the covers, and stood barefoot on the bare pine boards. He could come darn close to telling the temperature outside from how the cold felt on the bottoms of his feet. He guessed it would be about five degrees below zero, a typical start to a January morning. Reggie put on his fleece-lined slippers and goosedown robe, and ventured into the hallway.

Usually, he padded off to the bathroom, and then downstairs to stoke up the fires. But today he paused at Persephone's room, their room once. Something was different. It took him a moment to determine what it was: the door was closed. Even though he knew Persephone was alone in the room, asleep or awake and drifting—at any rate waiting until the house was warm before rising—the fact that the door was closed suggested something out of the ordinary. He asked himself what that could be, and the answer came to him, like words in a legal document: mystery, intrigue of a libidinous nature. He wanted to peek through the keyhole.

Reggie Salmon had recently repressed his sexuality because it interfered with his larger purpose of preparing himself for the grave. He had been successful until now. Images of copulation gushed into his mind. He actually did peek, for just a moment. It was dark in Persephone's room, and he couldn't see anything. Of course. Still, desire filled him. Why not just burst in? After all they'd lived together as man and wife for twenty-two years. But he could not, would not. He had, as per plan, mentally divorced her. By the lights of his philosophy, it was not moral they should resume relations.

He turned away from the door. He forced himself to put his mind to his chores and headed downstairs to stoke the fires. Although there was an oil burner in the cellar, Reggie heated the house with a wood-burning kitchen range and fire-places. On a normal winter's day he would light the kitchen stove and the fireplace in the living room and library, which he had confiscated as his study. The rest of the downstairs was closed off during the cold months. The upstairs rooms were cold, and the Salmons slept under goosedown comforters. When company came, Reggie started additional fires in the fireplaces in the dining room and summer room. He ran the oil burner only when severe cold threatened to freeze the pipes. The Salmons had argued about fires for years. Reggie had made one concession. He allowed Persephone an electric heater in the bathroom.

There were hot coals in the kitchen range, so it was an easy matter to throw some sticks in and get the fire going. Soon the kitchen would be warm. As always in the morning, the fireplace fires were out, although the bricks in the hearths continued to throw off some heat. He stacked some dry pine wood on the coals, poured on a smidgin of kerosene and touched it off. Once the sticks were going well, he'd add some split hardwood and, finally, round logs up to ten inches in diameter.

The fireplaces soon burned brightly, orange and black drama, like a hundred monarch butterflies bursting out of their chrysalises. He wouldn't admit it, but he liked the rush to his nostrils of burning kerosene, sweet, corrupt, catching hold of the wood, engulfing it in flames. If there was anything he was going to miss, it was going to be this: fire.

He burned dry, white birch for quick, hot fires; oak and beech for slow, brooding fires; fruitwood for fires with color. When the coals were hot on the hearth and the draw strong in the chimney, he burned huge unseasoned logs, which lasted for hours and which, as the moisture in the cell walls of the wood boiled off, seemed to speak with hisses and crackles, like pompous legislators before the New Hampshire House. Amusing—a good fire was amusing. A good fire satisfied the eye's need for movement, color, surprise; it soothed the ear with harmless, meaningless chatter, like TV talk shows; it delighted the nostrils with exotic perfumes. An open fire did everything for you that a woman did, except that when you touched it, the pain from the burn came right away and not later, when you least expected it.

Never mind that the fireplaces used twenty cords of wood a year, and that you could heat the house better with wood stoves for six cords. He had plenty of trees on the Trust. So many trees that he allowed fellows to cut wood on the Trust in return for a percentage of their haul. He was burning the weed trees that shoplifted the light and nutrients from superior trees that would make good timber some day. Of course, once the Trust went into operation, no one would take trees from it. Nature, over a hundred or so years, would get rid of the first-growth trees, carry on his own work for a climax forest, if in slow motion. He planned to have himself buried on the Trust, so he would go on nurturing the forest. *Persephone, the trees of the Trust are like a garden. You pull the weeds, the grey birches and popple, and you favor the royalty, the white oak and yellow birch.* She couldn't—wouldn't—acknowledge that there were differences in the quality of trees. It wasn't that she was stupid. It was that she didn't care. This was one reason he resented her.

He heard her shushing down the stairs in her slippers. She could always sense when the kitchen was comfortable by the few zephyrs of warm air that worked their way up into the bedrooms, and she would rush down and back her bottom against the kitchen stove. Reggie headed for the library. He didn't want to visit with her. He wanted to visit with his fire. He started to shut the door behind him; then, surprising himself, he found that he had paused and was peeking through the slit in the door. He watched her hug herself as she descended, glide through the cool hallway and disappear into the warm kitchen. It seemed to him that she had exaggerated her discomfort in the cold to justify some old anger at him, and a charge of resentment stiffened his muscles. But at the same time he had caught a glimpse of the back of her calves beneath her robe—solid calves, tennis-player calves—and desire had blitzkrieged resentment, inviting tenderness to repopulate the territory. Reggie felt a need to apologize, although he wasn't sure why.

Resentment counterattacked. Desire fought hard. Tenderness looked on from a distance through binoculars. Fantasy attempted to negotiate a settlement: The woman he had resented all these months (years?) was not his wife but an impostor. Last night, the real Persephone had stolen into the room and reclaimed her body. Resentment retreated, and tenderness marched onto the battlefield. Tenderness courted desire. Desire got bored, and headed for the hills in search of action. Reggie was left empty, groping. What if Persephone were the one that had left in the night, and it was the impostor that had taken her place in the morn? What if the woman in the kitchen with the magnificent calves, warming her behind by the stove, were a stranger? Her behind! Desire returned. He could see himself reaching under the nightie and squeezing her buttocks.

Reggie frolicked in these thoughts for a few minutes, and then with an act of will shucked them from his mind. He had a routine to get into.

The fire was going well now. There was still some warmth in the bricks from last night's long burn, and no matter what Persephone might say it wasn't too cold in here, although it would be almost eleven before it was cozy. He sat in his easy chair with the Hudson Bay wool blanket on his lap, and he looked at the fire. After a few minutes, the fire seemed to grant him peace, and he immersed himself in the euphoria, until he could feel himself floating back up to the world of workaday perception. He did not beg the fire. He had enough experience with fire-gazing to know that if you looked too long, the euphoria would be, as the Catholics put it, transubstantiated into anxiety. He was chilly now, and he did his morning exercises for warmth—certainly not for health.

He glanced at his Orvis field watch. It was nine a.m. Persephone would be back upstairs now, washing, dressing, and he could have the kitchen to himself. He made some toast, which he doctored with butter and marmalade, poured some orange juice (he had it in the back of his mind that Vitamin C might save him yet). Last came the coffee from the pot that Persephone had perked. He'd miss that—the woman sure could make coffee. He gave a start. The thought regarding Persephone and the coffee had come to him roundabout and peculiar: it was as if she were the one who were leaving—dying—and not himself. He set the food on a tray along with a fresh napkin. Somehow a meal wasn't a meal unless you had real linen on your lap. He couldn't bear paper towels. They were ugly, impermanent; they were a terribly unnecessary thing to make from a tree.

He carried the tray into his study and shut the door. He preferred to eat at the kitchen table, because from the window the view of his field and Mount Ascutney beyond was superior to the view from his study of Persephone's dormant garden. However, if he ate in the kitchen, there was the possibility that Persephone might return before he had a chance to finish and he would be forced to commiserate with her. Well, perhaps he should. He wanted to: that was the problem. Before, he had been relieved in her absence, uncomfortable in her presence. Now he wanted to visit with her. God, he was restless. Like a teen-ager. He considered. Was the restlessness fear in disguise? No. He knew what fear was, and he knew what this was. This was . . . huh, he knew. "Persephone," her name came to his lips. No, he mustn't. Mustn't.

Reggie ate breakfast and went to work.

This morning he planned to go over his notes for the latest Planning Board hearing on the mall. He'd heard that the selectmen were going to come out publicly in favor of the mall. SOD planned to attempt to tarnish this act by advertising the fact that Arthur Crabb, the chairman of the three-person board of selectmen, was Avalon Hillary's first cousin.

Reggie shuffled through his notes, muttering the points to himself. He must remember to gesture, to vary his voice intonations, to speak with passion and, when necessary, with *com*passion; in short, he must remember to act. Some of his arguments might be flawed, but this didn't trouble him greatly. You didn't persuade people with arguments. You persuaded them with acting. His influence over the town was going to be based on how the people perceived his performance.

The telephone rang. It was Jane Stein from the radio station. Even though he knew she would put him on the spot, it was good to hear her voice—businesslike, yet feminine and youthful, rich with life as pond water with the spring sun striking it. She asked him what he thought of the new anchor store in the mall; she spoke as though the building were already erected, the store already holding a sale. Apparently Magnus's latest hot air about an anchor store was going to be today's news story on the mall. Every day the media found the need to hold up the mall issue before the public eye. He babbled his response, and Jane hung up, and he was alone again. For a moment, he was actually aware of the paper-wrinkling hiss of this morning's fire (no two fires sounded exactly alike) and then of the tiny dust particles basking in a bar of light coming through the window. He imagined bikini-clad bathers suspended in the sunlight, eyes shut, dozing, rotating their bodies to the tanning rays of the sun evenly as planets. Lovely—lovely. He reached into the bar of light. The dust skipped away as if afraid. You can't touch beauty, he thought, puzzling at the source of this insight, if that's what it was.

An echo of Jane Stein's voice stroked him deep inside, and he found his desire for a woman reactivated. He had an urge to get up and walk around, putter about the kitchen, or just stand before the living room with his hands behind his back. But he stayed in the study because, well, Persephone would be out there.

But his office today was no sanctuary. Persephone still weighed on his mind. He was angry with her, he desired her, he loathed her, he wanted to touch her; she was sexy to him as someone else's wife. He felt violently libidinal. What to do? What to say? What to feel? He analyzed the situation, concluding that what he craved was not Persephone per se, but a woman—any woman. That led to a mental picture of Billy Butterworth standing in front of him, drunk, telling a story Reggie had half-listened to. Billy, who was Persephone's brother, was one of Upper Darby's more wasted spirits—alcoholic, homosexual, in debt. All that Reggie could remember was Billy chuckling obscenely about an old whore that advertised in the yellow pages as a fortune-teller.

Reggie reached for his telephone book, thumbing the pages until he got to "f". Sure enough, under "fortune teller," there she was: "Witch Inc., Black Swamp Road." On the same page was a small ad: "The Witch for palms read, fortunes told; night readings extra."

That phrase "night readings" sent a charge through Reggie's loins, and he could feel his heart thumping in his chest. He was so excited it was as if he were a teenager again. He glanced at the phone: white-hot thing. This was crazy. So what? It was immoral. Immoral? He was a dying man. He deserved the last rites for his libido. He might get a social disease. Disease? He was already diseased. He had no intention of imposing himself upon a loved one, disease or no. In fact, a social disease would seal his resolve to keep to himself. He felt suddenly sad in his desire. Maybe he had made a mistake. Maybe he should break down and confess his love to Persephone. No, he mustn't. It would weaken him somehow, distract him from his work; it was bad luck. It seemed to him that a disclosure of love would catapult him out of remission back into the clutches of his illness. And of course his love would only lengthen and deepen the pain of Persephone's grief. You never had a whore, you deserve a whore, take a whore, a voice inside him said. It was all sooooo crazy. He felt giddy. Excited.

He dialed the number and almost hung up when he heard the two short rings on the other end, for he was realizing what a loony idea this was. What prevented him from hanging up was his good manners. It wasn't polite to dial someone's number, tease them into answering their telephone, and then hang up on them. The polite thing to do was to tell a harmless lie. When she answered, he'd excuse himself, say that he'd dialed the wrong number, and lay the receiver gently in its cradle.

It didn't work out that way. He heard someone lift the receiver at the other end, but there was no hello, no amenity. A great span of time seemed to elapse. (Later he figured out that his agitation had made two minutes out of two seconds. (Was this a hint on extending mortality?) In his mind he was shouting for an amenity. After all, he had done the right thing by following through with the call. Now whoever was out there should do the right thing by greeting him. However, in the end it was Reggie who spoke.

"Hello. Hello? Is anyone there?" he said in hushed, civilized tones.

"Howdy," said a woman in a perfectly calm voice with a strong, rural, New England accent, with absolutely no come-hither nuances. He had been wrong. This Witch person was strictly a fortune teller. Maybe a night out, in a strange place, getting his fortune told, maybe such fluff would cheer him up, calm him down. Maybe that's what he needed.

"Yes, I'm calling about a night reading?" he heard his voice hike up to a summit. "I was referred to you by another party," he went on, wondering whether she could hear the awkwardness in his tone.

"I ain't no spring chicken, you know that, I hope," said the Witch.

Dear God, she's an old lady, he thought, but pressed on. "Naturally I know that. But I desperately need a night reading. What are your terms?"

"It depends on the kind of reading you want; I go by time mostly," she said, and quoted him a price per hour. Then without a quiver in her voice she quoted him prices on "regular readings," "oral readings," and "rectal readings." "Specialty readings" would have to be negotiated, and he'd have to bring his own specialties.

"I used to carry specialties," she said, "but they just clutter up my mobile home and remind me of work. Bring your own, if you got 'em."

Specialties—what in the world was she talking about? The answer came quickly to mind: whips, handcuffs, ropes. He imagined Persephone now, trussed up. She was somebody else's wife and she had been unfaithful. The husband had hired him to punish her. Reggie was powerfully aroused by these thoughts and at the same time ashamed, the shame adding an ingredient more compatible with desire than anger had been.

"I don't have anything like that," he said, perhaps too stridently.

"It don't matter to me one way or the other. It's your reading," the Witch said.

"This afternoon at four o'clock?" he proposed.

"Nope. I've got to bring my grandson to a Cub Scout meeting at three-thirty, and I won't be back here until suppertime," the Witch said.

Cub Scouts? Good Lord. How dare she have a family life. It was unholy. But who was he to judge? He felt a need to say something wise here, something uplifting, something forgiving; but he couldn't think straight.

"This may be my last reading. I'm ill. Truth is, the doctors say I'm dying," Reggie blurted out.

"They're all dying," she said mysteriously, with the aplomb of an immortal.

"Uh-huh."

"You come on by," she said. "I'll give you a reading you can take to the Beyond."

Reggie and the Witch agreed to meet for their date at eight p.m. that night, and then she gave Reggie directions to her mobile home. It was, she said, the only building on the only road going off the blacktop toward the swamp itself.

Before hanging up, she asked him questions, "You like a clean reading, you like it gamey, you like strong scent, or what?"

Her matter-of-fact tone had relaxed him somewhat, but it took a moment before it dawned on him what she'd meant. "Bathed, definitely bathed, and lightly—that's lightly—perfumed," he said authoritatively, the professional john now, oddly proud of himself.

"I hear you, Mister," the Witch said. "You give me a name to remember you by, so's when you come to the door to call I'll know to open it."

Reggie wasn't ready for that one. "Ah, call me Ishmael," he said.

"Okey dokey, Ishmael. See you at eight o'clock tonight," the Witch said and hung up.

Reggie breathed deeply. For the first time in his life, he thought (actually it might have been the twelfth or thirteenth time), he felt completely free; he had done something totally on his own, for himself only, in which duty, honor, family, and land played no role.

"Whoop-de-do," he said quietly, almost reverently.

Persephone having left on some errands, Reggie made lunch for himself. He pasted some pâté on a slice of bread, slabbed mayonnaise on another slice of bread, joined the two in a sandwich, and ate it with dill pickles and Pinot Chardonnay. Persephone had long ago stopped harping at him for eating rich foods. These days she even brought home some of the delicacies he craved.

After lunch, he took a brief nap on the couch in the living room. It seemed to him that he could just detect Persephone's essence in the fabric. With that, he was falling gently as an astronaut into a deep chasm of dream-light. When he reached bottom he found a silent, rushing river of liquid granite, bright glitter in the gray stream, cold to the touch. And he was awake again, and he could feel a chill in the room. Half an hour had passed. He hadn't stoked the fires since rising, and clouds pouring in from the west had prevented the usual warm, solar benediction that came in the middle of winter days.

Reggie replenished the fireplaces. The work warmed him before the fires warmed the house. He poured a small glass of milk and raided Lilith's chocolate chip cookie jar. Persephone hadn't returned, so he sat by the fire in the living room, looking out the window, eating a cookie. A few snowflakes were tumbling down from the sky. Good. He liked watching snow fall. If there was no wind, it was gentle, soft, a caress; if the wind blew, it was rough, hard, a wrestling match with an old buddy. The weatherman was predicting three or four inches. No big deal. Not that even a blizzard would keep him from his date tonight. The threat of bad weather would give him an excuse to drive the Bronco. With its four-wheel drive, the Bronco could bull through anything the New Hampshire storm gods could conjure. Fighting the snows from the Bronco, keeping the wipers going, aiding the defroster with a gloved hand across the windshield would be stimulating foreplay.

He should do some more work on the Magnus business. He hauled out the papers, looked at them, and then said, "to heck with it." He was in a holiday mood. He didn't feel like doing any work. He wanted to play, to think, to commiserate with . . . with whom? With what? Nature. That was it. With nature. He decided to take a walk in the Trust, hike up to the ledges and make a cup of tea.

Reggie changed into Canada Gray Trousers, a turtleneck sweater, and L. L. Bean hunting boots with rubber bottoms and leather uppers. The small orange day-pack he always took to the Trust was already stuffed with the basics: a compass, medicine (just in case), pot and cup, nylon tarp, dry socks, matches, candle, tiny Hank Roberts cooking stove and mini-grill for cooking over an open fire.

He had bought the cooking stove when Acronum Bentley, the Sierra Club consultant to the Trust, had made it clear he thought it bad form when hikers wasted natural resources by building open fires. Reggie realized this was a fine argument when you were talking about troops of hikers coming and going. But the Trust was not a public hiking spot—at least not yet—and an open fire now and then, made with dead branches, wasn't going to upset the ecology. The blue, unexciting flame of the cook stove had showed Reggie that he was as addicted to open fires as other men were to alcohol or drugs or women. However, he continued to carry the Hank Roberts stove out of what he regarded as sort of etiquette insurance. If Acronum or others of his ilk (cousins both literally as well as figuratively) happened to show up, here at the house or, as was possible, in the wild lands themselves, he could heat them a cup of tea, heat it their way, and prevent the unpleasantness of a petty philosophical specter looming over friendly chit-chat.

Reggie set out, taking his time, walking slowly. He still had much of his natural strength; the sickness had worn him down in another way. His stamina had diminished. It used to take him half an hour to walk to the ledges, and that was without drawing a deep breath. Today, the walk took forty-five minutes, and he was darn near exhausted when he got to the top. But it was worth it. Here he could see, see as the gods saw, from a height.

He stood there huffing, looking off in the distance, stirred by the air and the view, yet not seeing it—because he had seen it so many times before—not seeing it, feeling it rather, in tremulous union with it, as an artist is with the scene that he wishes to transform as his own on the canvas, his view, stirred by the fact that nature itself (he refused to refer to nature as "she," as "mother") had created the view, his view, soul nurturing thing, from a wound.

The view was made possible by a long sloping shelf of granite where no trees could take hold. In the days before the white man came, there had been a thin covering of soil here, gripped tightly by the roots of trees. Farmers settled the area, raised sheep on the lower slopes. Wolves carried off the sheep to briars on the ledges. One day the farmers burned down the hill to drive out the wolves. The forest came back, but not to the ledges. The wind had whisked the soil off the granite. The loss: plant life, wolves; the gain: a view, his view.

The granite slope suddenly steepened, then pitched straight downward for about thirty feet. From his spot at the summit of the ledges, Reggie could just make out the tops of stunted hemlocks, their roots snaking across the granite in search of soil and water. Below, the land was more kindly, and birches, red maples, and oaks competed with the hemlocks for space. Lower still was a stand of tall, straight white pines. They would be ready to harvest in another ten years. It occurred to him that he could log them now and raise money for Lilith's college expenses, at least for a semester. *So, there was a scar in the view; the view was a scar.*

His view, almost exclusively. Never mind that he owned it. The point was that only he beheld it. That was what was important. There was a path leading up to the ledges, but it was too far to walk for the casual beer-drinking set, and, because it was just a cul-de-sac from the main hiking trails, the hikers paid it little attention. A view such as this, for its full impact, had to be experienced alone. If you were walking on Fifth Avenue in New York, looking in the shop windows, or if you were at a clambake in a field in Center Darby, other people quickened the experience. But the view from the heights was different. Whether you gazed out from the top of the Empire State Building or from the summit of Mount Monadnock, you wanted the view for yourself or, occasionally, to show off your view to someone special, which was the same thing as wanting it for yourself. Although in theory you might be all for public access to the heights, during the actual moment of gazing you resented the bunch of strangers beholding what you beheld. A rare view should be beheld rarely. A fantasy from early manhood, the year of his breakdown, came to Reggie's mind. He was making love to a mysterious woman on an unknown mountain peak and they were rolling off, falling into space, interwound.

He brushed the snow off a pine log that years ago he had dragged to the spot. He had peeled off the bark to slow down the rot, and the sun had weathered the log gray. He removed the tarp from his pack, folded it to make a seat, and placed it on the log. He started a small, hot fire of dried hemlock twigs, added some bigger sticks, and straddled the fire with the grill. He scooped some snow into the pot and watched it melt, first to slush, then to water. There were bits of the forest in the water. There was no such thing as pure snow, pure water. Water always contained something; water was the primal container. When the water was boiling he dropped in a teabag. He was proud that he used "plain old Orange Pekoe." After the water had darkened, he removed the teabag and threw it in the fire. He put the pot on the log and kicked the grill over, then watched the hot metal cut the snow. He picked up the grill, the heat gone from it, and returned it to the pack. He fed some more sticks to the fire to cheer himself, to have some near sound in counterpoint to the far whisper of the snow coming down from the sky. He performed these acts with exaggerated, self-conscious care, the better to savor them. When he knew the tea would be cooler, the aluminum of the pot bearable, he sipped the tea. It satisfied.

Only now did he lift his eyes to the view. Here in the woods he had mastered the ability to stay intent on one small event at a time, so that the clock slowed, so that he had no need for other people, no need even for his own company. Here there was only the third being that was created from the union of himself with whatever it was, nature, the outdoors, that courted him, that he courted, when he left the house and took the path to the ledges. He didn't know it, didn't care to know it, for it was different in union with himself than in its raw state, and he wasn't interested in that. He was interested in this: this being, he/it, themselves, a third gender; and in this: the view, the fire, the ritual of the tea, their mating ceremony.

The view: tiny snowflakes falling gently, winds calm—a piddling storm—in the distance at the end of the world, the dark shapes of the Vermont hills brooding in the snow like huddling hens, Mount Ascutney completely obscured and therefore nonexistent, the sky itself nonexistent, in the foreground the lands of the Trust, trees flecked with snow, fresh snow somehow bluer than older snow, fresh snow containing the ocean, between the wooded slopes of the Trust and the distant Vermont Hills, the Connecticut River valley, maternal in its aspect, directly below, the river itself, in a half-moon turn, bordered by hardwoods, then giving way to snow-covered fields—Avalon Hillary's fields. Hillary, darn Yankee farmer . . . Magnus. Oh, shit! They were going to build the shopping mall right smack dab in the middle of his view. Oh, shit! A philosophical question came to mind: If you die and they change the view, had there ever been a view, a you?

He was very tired when he came down from the ledges. Persephone had returned. She was puttering around the house, cleaning up, singing to herself. She seemed in a good mood. He built up the fires and lay down on the couch for a moment, and when with a start he awakened, it was dark. Had he missed his appointment with the Witch? He glanced at his watch. It was only five-thirty. His next thought was: What would he tell Persephone? What lie? He didn't want to lie to her. He had never told her a lie before, except kindly lies, like the ones you told to children about people going off to heaven when they died. Once he had praised her taste in picking stainless-steel silverware for a wedding gift, when in fact he had been revolted by it.

As it turned out, he didn't have to lie. They were eating dinner, as usual without conversation, without even eye contact, listening to "All Things Considered" on the radio, when Persephone announced that tonight she was going to Tuckerman to do some shopping.

"You'd better take the Bronco, it's snowing," he said.

"That's a good idea. Are you busy this evening?"

He was suddenly suspicious. It was as if she knew what he was up to and she was trying to get him, not to admit it, but to debase himself with a lie. He shrugged, gagging on his anger.

"Are you feeling well?" she said.

"I feel fine, just fine," he said, straining to keep his resentment from showing. "I may get restless here, all alone, and take a ride myself."

He hated himself for that phrase "all alone," playing for sympathy, so hypocritical.

"If you're going someplace, maybe you should take the Bronco," she said.

Now he resented her all the more. Either she had been insensitive to his "all alone" whine, or she had chosen to ignore it.

"You take the Bronco. I insist," he said.

The meal proceeded in silence, he nervous, upset, straining not to show it, she serene, calm. And beautiful, glowing. Why did she look so beautiful? Was it his imagination? Did he see beauty that had always been there? Was she more beautiful today for something that had happened to her? If so, what? And why so calm? The answers to these questions came upon Reggie Salmon as swift and hard as a slap in the face. She had accepted the fact that he was dying—she was going to be free from him, free. Sometime today she had buried him.

Sow a seed; it grows. A terrible loneliness descended upon him. He wanted to reach out to her, strike her, hurt her, anything to demonstrate that he was still alive. He tried to gather up the resources to express this feeling. He was still searching in himself when Persephone left, taking the Bronco.

Persephone wasn't gone long when Reggie's anger and confusion began to fade. He was so stupid, so mean. Why was he so mean to her? At heart he loved her. He wanted to tell her he loved her. He wanted to hold her, dance with her, as in the days when they were young. He'd formed this insane plan for dying, and it was so full of hurt and meanness to both of them.

Before Reggie could develop this line of thought, he was distracted by a mental image of the Witch. Not that he had ever seen her. He hadn't. My word, all he knew about her was that she was a grandmother. He hoped she wasn't too tough-looking or haggy; he hoped she didn't sound stupid when she spoke. The image that he conjured of the Witch was of his Aunt Sophie, as he had known her forty years ago. She had been a heavy woman, large-boned and generously filled out with flesh, but she'd had soft, smooth skin the color of ivory and she always smelled good, and she was exquisitely feminine, wearing jewelry that jangled and frilly things that looked pleasant to nuzzle.

When he was a boy of about thirteen he'd seen her nude. He was restless—even then, restless—and he'd taken a walk one evening to a far corner of Grace Pond (named after his own mother and one of two ponds in the Trust). There he had seen Sophie and Uncle Glenn skinny-dipping. They had come out of the water—Sophie giggling, Uncle Glenn hee-hawing like a mule—embraced for a moment on the narrow beach, put their clothes on, and left. And that was that, a fairly common summer occurrence in the boondocks of Upper Darby. But it had changed Reggie's life, edging him toward manhood. After that he nearly swooned with desire every time he saw her. Several years later, it was no accident that Persephone, when he first started to court her, had been on the heavy side and with fair, smooth skin, although by the time they married she had slimmed down.

Sophie Druid (her mother was a Butterworth) had married Glenn Kauffman in New York. They were professional intellectuals, left-wingers actually. Something disillusioned them—Reggie wasn't sure what—and they moved to the cottage near the pond, launching an early venture into self-sufficiency. They were aided by the fact that Sophie, even during her socialist days, had never divested herself of a small horde of stocks from her family. Glenn had an operation to make him sterile, the couple lived frugally, the dividends trickled in, and the two of them had got through life without ever holding jobs.

Theirs was a nice little acre of land. But it was also a problem. The place was deep in the Trust, and Reggie didn't like the idea of an island of private property in the wild lands. Reggie had worked out a plan to buy the cottage and convert it into a caretaker's station. They could borrow the money using the collateral of the Trust, and pay it back from revenues generated by the Trust. When Trellis died, Reggie decided now was the time to buy the Kauffmans' property and ease them into Trellis's house. This would make everybody happy. Uncle Glenn and Aunt Sophie would have a change of scenery in a bigger and more splendid circumstance, without the burdens of home ownership; the Butterworth children would have their mother's house in good hands; the Trust would have a welcome addition. But Uncle Glenn and Aunt Sophie proved surprisingly stubborn, even hostile. They granted that the Trust was a noble idea, and they agreed that his offer for the property was a fair one. But they refused to sell, simply on the basis that they liked it where they were. They didn't seem to understand that they would be happier in Trellis's house.

Aunt Sophie no longer stirred Reggie. It wasn't the fact that she'd aged that troubled him. Her hair was silvery and her hands a bit gnarled from arthritis, but she was still pleasingly plump, still round and firm at the bosom, skin still smooth. What bothered him was that she'd lost the leer to her eye;

she'd become jolly over the years. Jollity and sensuality did not partner well. It made him sad to sec her, sad for his own lost, darn-near-forgotten boyhood.

It had stopped snowing when he slid behind the wheel of the Volvo. The temperature had warmed to just above freezing. Not enough snow had fallen for the plows to come by, but the roads had been salted, and the asphalt was black and wet. There would be no driving problems. He wished there were a blizzard out there, and that he was behind the wheel of the Bronco.

He tried to think about sex, resurrect the desire that had surged through him this morning, but he felt curiously dead inside. He felt as though he were going to the wake of an old friend: full of feeling deep down but numb, dentist-office numb, on the surface. Furthermore, the ability to conjure, to see the dancing girls in his mind's eye, had left him. He was rooted to the moment, to the evidence seeping in from the outside world. All that registered were the dull, persistent reports of routine sense perceptions: each corner to be navigated, the sickly sweet new-car smell (which had lingered for years), the soft-hardness of the feel of his hands through the gloves on the steering wheel. This, he thought, is a preview of hell.

When the highway merged into the Tuckerman bypass, he looked at his watch. Fifteen minutes had passed. He stopped to gas up, anything to break the tedium. He continued east, his senses now anesthetized, and the next fifteen minutes flew by and he found himself at Black Swamp.

The moon was out now, and he could see the swamp clearly. Tree stumps stuck out of the snow. In the background, looming, was Mount Monadnock. Above that the moon, departing clouds, stars. "Blue light," he whispered.

He turned off the highway onto Black Swamp Road, and then the dirt road that led to the trailer. He parked in a short driveway behind a new, four-wheel-drive Subaru sedan. Apparently the Witch made a pretty good living giving readings. The trailer sat up on concrete blocks. It was not one of the newer models, and he was glad it was night and the faded

color of the old trailer could not accost his eye. Beside the
trailer was a shed, then the swamp and the sky.

Light inched through the curtained windows of the trailer.
He could feel the air changing, the winds turning around from
the north. It was going to get colder in the next few hours.
Good, he thought.

Before he reached the door, he heard a voice, calm, direct,
female. "Give us your name," said the Witch.

"Call me Ishmael," Reggie said.

The inside was messy, as women are messy, crammed with
knickknacks, weed pots; and the woman had a passion for
color and texture. On the walls hung beads, bunches of dried
grasses and flowers and herbs, baskets, macrame, and prints
of the more popular Impressionist painters—the usual Monet
lily pads (he thought about his brother) and Van Gogh skies.
On one wall was an oil painting in progress of Black Swamp.

"You paint?" he said.

"Customer done that," she said.

He looked at her, puzzled, curious.

"I like to barter," the Witch said.

"You mean you exchanged, -erup, it, for artwork."

"Sure, why not?" she said.

"It's not done," he said, referring to the civility of swapping
sex for art.

"He's taking his time—who can blame him?" she said, referring to the fact that the painter had not finished the work.

Reggie sat down in a comfortable but extremely ugly chair,
ersatz Colonial; across from it was a matching couch. Had
she bartered sex for cheap maple furniture?

The Witch was dressed like a hippie girl of the 1960s, with
a long, flowing skirt, a white blouse, and beads. Of course,
she was much older than the hippie girls had been, perhaps
as old as himself. Her hair was still black, though, with just
a few streaks of gray to prove she didn't dye it. She had star-
tling amber eyes, full of motion; intelligent eyes. The eyes
said, Be still, everything is going to be all right.

"Did you bring a bottle?" she said.

"Should I have?"

"Most of 'em do," she said, looking at him closely, sizing him up. Somehow he thought this was for the good. She was experienced. She would know what to do. It was incredible. He felt excited but not in the least bit aroused. Rather, he was curious, boyishly so.

"I'm going to guess and say you ain't been around this scene too much," she said.

"Never," he said.

"Let me spell it out then, so's you don't get this confused with your home life. I ain't your girlfriend, I ain't your wife. You don't owe me nothing but money. I don't want no satisfaction from you. Just the money. A lot of these new ones think they got to satisfy. They get these ideas from their wives and their girlfriends and the young whores these days that think the world owes them an orgasm. Unless you're the type that gets satisfied by satisfying the other one, let me tell you, it can be sad for you to try to satisfy a whore."

"What do you do when you have a customer who insists on satisfying you?" he asked.

"Why, I go along," the Witch said, with a little laugh.

There was a pause. She was looking at him. He imagined that she was trying to decide just what in the world he wanted from this encounter.

"I confess I am a little nervous," he said.

"Want liquor? There's some in the kitchen," the Witch said.

"If you have beer or a dry, white wine, that would be nice. I'm not much for hard liquor."

She went into the kitchen and returned with beer foaming from a long, slender, elegant glass. Delight registered on his face. She'd already figured him out, he thought. Somehow she knew he hated drinking beverages out of bottles and cans, and that he had an aversion to glasses with handles on them. He sipped, and sipped again. He was relieved that he didn't despise her, didn't despise himself. Still, he should be getting down to business, but he didn't know what to say, wasn't sure just what he wanted out of this . . . this whore. In fact, at the moment he couldn't think of her as a whore. She was a person he had met, who was considerate and who deserved consideration.

"You like music?" she asked, and when he nodded his head, she reached into a cabinet and gave him a carton of tapes. He was grateful. It gave him something to do. He rummaged through the awful rock 'n' roll, the sentimental country and western, the pretentious bluegrass, until he found some classical music. He picked Beethoven's Ninth Symphony, handing the tape to the Witch. Then, as if she'd cast a spell over him, the music was playing without him being aware that she'd put the tape in a machine. This seemed like magic to him, and he decided to preserve the illusion, the mystery, the tension, and not look for the speakers but accept the music as coming out of the ambience, as he would if he were at the ledges.

She was kneeling beside his chair. She seemed to sense that he'd overcome his beginner's nerves. She touched his arm. He liked the stroke of her fingers, the way she looked on her knees.

"How about some toke? I bet you like that?" she said, pinching his tricep.

He had used marijuana off and on for years. It had been introduced in Upper Darby by Corinth Prell, who had attended Goddard, and by his own brother, Monet. He smoked occasionally when he was taking medication, because it helped alleviate the nausea, but little for recreation in recent years. Marijuana was out of fashion up on the hill, replaced by that old standby, booze. At the moment, however, marijuana seemed like just the right garnish for this experience.

They smoked from a corncob pipe. She liked it. It was her vice, he could see.

"Home-grown?" he said.

"Home-grown. Brings you up the mountain kinda slower than you'd like, but lets you sled down by the seat of your pants at your own speed," she said.

Time passed. He didn't know how much, didn't care any more than he cared where the music came from. For all he knew, the weed was from the IGA, Beethoven had come back from the dead to conduct the Boston Symphony Orchestra in the next room, or the Devil himself was in there readying punishment for Reggie Salmon—he didn't care.

And she was close to him now, her hand on his chest, her breath in his ear. She smelled faintly of flowers. He could see those flowers, bursting open like fireworks in slow motion.

She was opening his shirt. Somehow she'd managed to douse the lamps, and the only illumination came from a tiny plastic Christmas tree. It had dancing colored lights, and a pulsating star on top. Hallelujah! He reached into her blouse. Her breasts were large and hung low, the nipples long and slender and firm.

She undid his belt—"Hoist them buns," she said—and he raised his bottom. She pulled down his trousers and underwear in one fluid jerk. She was all tongue and gums. No teeth; no busy hand; no head against the stomach.

She sensed a crucial juncture, and whispered to him, "Want to do it, or finish this way?"

"Do it. I want to do it," he said.

They went—that is, she led him—to the next room, a cramped bedroom, cramped because it was dominated by a huge water bed. She kept the lights off. He knew better than to ask for them on—the lady was not young.

Off they went, chasing nesting eagles. Wonderful. He remembered her words about not worrying about her satisfaction. He found the birds, high in a tree, mating.

Afterward, he thanked her. "You're welcome," she said, and asked for the money. He paid. He drank a beer, they talked— he couldn't remember about what—he made a date for the following week, she wished him well.

"This is about the third-best I've ever had," he said.

"I would have guessed the second," she said, and kissed him on the cheek.

It was true, and yet he couldn't get over the feeling that it could have been even better if his date had been with Persephone: wife, mystery woman, complete stranger.

Surprisingly, Persephone was not home when he arrived. He was going to wait up for her, but he was too tired. He stripped and went to bed. Just as he was dozing off he heard her come in. He met her on the stairs in his robe. "Did you have a good shopping night?" he asked.

"Better than you can imagine," she said. "Did you go for a ride?"

"I did and I listened to music," he whispered, to muffle the clang of the lie against his temples.

"That's nice. Verdi?"

"Beethoven. The Ninth."

"Exciting, but tiring: that's Beethoven," she said.

"Yes. Did you buy anything tonight?"

"No. We looked, we tried on dresses and such."

"That's nice," he said.

"Good night, Reggie," Persephone said, went to her bedroom and shut the door.

Her use of his name washed him with sadness.

Reggie Salmon awakened the next morning to the sizzling. It was more intense than in the past. He was surging out of remission; he was going to need a miracle to survive long enough to make the March town meeting.

Barnum's Proposal

As Charles Barnum was looking at the menu at the Chrysalis Restaurant he was remembering his doctor's furrowed brow, and his warning to eat less, drink less, and quit smoking.

"They have a great shrimp salad here," Barnum said.

"Uh-huh," William Case said. "It's intriguing, isn't it?"

"Actually, I've never tried it," Barnum said.

"No, I mean the intensity of the opposition on the mall," Case said.

"Squire Salmon," Barnum said. Case's voice was so sharp, Barnum feared they might be overheard and he kept his own voice low, in hopes Case would get the hint and pipe down.

"Could we offer him anything?" Case said, deliberately avoiding eye contact.

"Well, I don't know." He didn't like the direction Case was leading him.

"This is a land-poor fella, is it not?" Case said.

"He'd call the police," Barnum said.

"I'm not talking about a bribe, Barnum. I mean only to show him we're not ogres at Magnus. Is not the Squire warehousing nuts for a pet project? Would he not feel warm toward a business supporting that project?"

The word "bribe" reverberating through the restaurant had triggered Charles Barnum's nervous stomach. He could feel the acids in it threatening to devour the host unless some food was introduced.

"The forest Trust," Barnum said. "I have a colleague who is friendly on the squash court with Garvin Prell, my opposition brother, and I might persuade him to feel out the territory."

"Okay. What are your thoughts about our other Darby adversary?" Case said. He was smiling now.

"The local auctioneer, Mr. Ike Jordan," Barnum said.

"Who is this guy?"

Barnum felt on steadier ground, and his stomach relaxed a bit. "The Jordans are people out of step with society as a whole," Barnum said. "The relevant consideration is whether his opposition is meaningful."

"My instincts tell me to let the auctioneer ride his hobby horse," Case said.

Barnum nodded in agreement. The waitress was delivering food at the table next to them. He tried unsuccessfully to catch her eye. Selective sight was one of those annoying skills of those in the service industry.

"You said on the phone you had a proposal," Case said.

"I suggest we ask the selectmen to call a special town meeting in two weeks," Barnum said.

"Well, hello," Case said, and Barnum took heart from the surprise in Case's voice.

"The regular town meeting is fraught with pitfalls, Barnum said. "There are dozens of local issues. The mood of the meeting can go any which way. It's a crap shoot, Bill. A special town meeting will give us a clean agenda and a smaller, more attentive crowd."

The waitress arrived, greeted them, then looked to Case for the order.

"I'll have the open steak sandwich with a side of french fries. But before, bring us a round, please. I'll have a Dewar's with soda."

"The same," Barnum said.

Partings

Following their usual fare of McDonald's food, champagne, and sex, Chance and Persephone Salmon sat up in bed, watching the sports channel on television. Sunday night's basketball game between the Boston Celtics and the San Antonio Spurs was being replayed.

"So Larry Bird was a Hoosier before he was a Celtic," Persephone said, responding to a comment by one of the TV announcers. She had spoken only to hear her own voice say the word "Hoosier."

"Yes and no," Chance said, taking her seriously as usual. "Yes, he's a Hoosier because he was raised in French Lick, Indiana, but he played his college ball at Indiana State, which made him a Sycamore between being a Hoosier and a Celtic."

"My own people came from Scotland—Celtics all," Persephone said. "But as to the question of Hoosiers, what is a Hoosier? How was the English language so lucky as to come upon this word?"

"Who knows?" Chance said, seeing now that she was playing. "It's enough to be or not to be a Hoosier without the issue of origins to cloud it over. You like Larry Bird?"

"I've decided I don't care for basketball," she said. "It has too many ups to justify too few downs, and anyway it doesn't reach for the id the way a sport should. I like boxing. Boxing goes right to the quick."

"No boxing on the sports channel this afternoon," Chance said. "It doesn't matter to me what's on. I think of television as a container to empty the contents of my mind into."

Ten minutes later Larry Bird scored from a region referred to by the announcer as Three-Point Land. Chance wished Persephone had still been there to appreciate this exploit.

Persephone was gone for good. She had broken off their affair to devote herself full-time to Reggie during his last days.

"So here I am," Chance said to the television set. "No Persephone, no Soapy—just me."

He sipped the remainder of the champagne. The pleasant afterglow of the sex was still upon him, and he didn't feel that bad, he thought—not all that bad.

It seemed to Chance, thinking about Persephone, that they had never actually touched. It was as if they had discussed lovemaking instead of actually making love. They were dreamers who had stumbled upon one another on the common, but insubstantial, ground of their respective dreams, dreams whose ends were out of sight in opposite directions. He didn't regret that he had lost her; he regretted that he would remember her indistinctly. She had returned to Upper Darby to be with Reggie, to care for him, to help him die (he had insisted he wasn't going to spend his last days in a hospital bed), and finally to bury him. Chance envied her. He saw in Reggie's dying an opportunity for Persephone to incinerate a part of her past in the pure heat of servitude. He himself had no such opportunity. Old Joe had sneaked out of his life, Genevieve remained mysteriously estranged from him, Soapy had been a mistake, Persephone a dream.

And he was hearing an energetic voice from the television set: "The Iceman stops, spins, sets, shoots, tickles the twine."

Chance left his rooms for the closer confines of the Brat. He drove around Central Square, down Main Street, up Main Street, back around the square and down again, and so forth, like some teenager on the prowl for a pickup. Never mind that it was the wrong time of day, the wrong time of year. It was too cold for street people, and the park benches on the square were empty. It was too early to watch the shopgirls and secretaries leaving work in their high-heeled shoes. There were no touch-hungry twenty-year-olds drinking beer and smoking pot in TransAms, lounging on the parking-metered median strip of Main Street. Cars and trucks and vans and bicycles moved like blood cells through arteries, unimportant in their singularity, it seemed, but rather contributing in their flow to the life of a greater creature: the city. A few shoppers came and went from the five-and-ten-cent Jupiter Store, Bacon's Jewelers, Carla's Boutique, Schoenberg's Pharmacy, Blastos's Newsstand, Hinkle's Travel Agency, and Robichaud's Singer Sewing Machine outlet. He wondered which would be lonelier, aimless driving amid aimful shoppers here on Main Street, or aimless walking amid aimful shoppers in an enclosed mall? Maybe it didn't matter. Maybe human happiness and misery sought their own levels irrespective of changes in the environment and culture, short of war or other extreme circumstance. Maybe that didn't matter either. Maybe people tear down and build out of a command from that greater creature, whose libido is set in concrete, supported by steel, sided with aluminum, shingled in asphalt, accessed via glass.

He was driving around the square for the third time when the flow of traffic forced him toward West Street and Route 21. He took this as a sign. Without plan or preliminary thought, he was headed for Darby, for the auction barn and Soapy Rayno.

All at once his mood turned inside out; he was cheerful, optimistic. A picture came to mind of Soapy sitting on the porch railing of the tree house. (Actually, she had never gotten around to putting up the railing, but they had talked about the project.) He watched himself walk up the ax-hewn stairs and take her hand. The picture dissolved into recollection. They had cut firewood together and scooped snow into the coffee pot and tossed twigs into campfires; they had exchanged words as if nouns and verbs were things, valuables from the ancestors; they had come together without touching. (At the moment it was as if the weeks following those minutes in the blood-soaked leaves hadn't existed.) And there had been something else. He searched in memory for it, rummaging about in images of brooks, birches, and boulders until it came to him: union with the forest. Since the breakup with Soapy, he had lived in town, worked in meeting halls and offices, played at the YMCA, relaxed before the TV, conversed in bars and living rooms. His emptiness at parting was due as much to his separation from the forest as from Soapy. Or perhaps, in the way that was important to him, Soapy and the forest were manifestations of the same spirit, two separate breaths of one spirit. He needed *it*—her; he fancied that Soapy needed him.

Somewhere between Tuckerman and Darby he lost heart. His optimism became thin ice on a pond, he a child running across it, trying to reach the other side, the ice beginning to crack under his feet. But he rallied by thinking, scheming. He would patch things up with Soapy. After all, he hadn't meant to hit her, hadn't meant even to hit Again Jordan. He might apologize, not for himself but for his wandering fist. No, that wasn't enough. He had to do more, feel more. Otherwise Soapy would never take him back. He wasn't sure what he would say to her. He wished that Soapy would come to him.

Ike's van was parked at the main entrance of the auction barn. Critter and Crowbar stood, waiting, it seemed. Three giant posters had been slapped against the side of the barn that faced Route 21. They said, "No Mall 'T All," "Ike Jordan for Selectman," and "Vote Ike, Save Darby."

The Brat slipped in next to the van. Chance could tell by Critter's reserved greeting that his father was nearby.

"Ike politicking, or what?" Chance asked, to make small talk.

"Fiddle-farting around," Critter said, throwing a nod in the direction of the barn. "We just moved a Duncan organ inside—bohunky thing—and Ike's brooding about where to put it."

"Be seeing you at the special town meeting?"

"Not likely. Never registered to vote, so why waste my time?" Finding a need to justify himself, Critter pressed on, "Jordans don't vote. Only Ike votes, and only for himself."

"I don't understand how he's been able to stay so chummy with the SOD people," Chance said.

"I don't either, but bet on something dirty," Critter said. "You come to see Ike?"

"Soapy. How's she doing?" Chance was nervous now.

"Mopes, whittles, talks to herself, tags along with Delphina." Critter's voice turned wistful at his mention of Delphina's name. The baby was almost due but Delphina still hadn't agreed on a wedding date.

"We're all waiting on somebody," Chance said.

Ike emerged from the auction barn, by habit grinning insincerely. He looked Chance up and down, but withdrew his attention when he saw neither note pad nor camera. He had the knack of making people feel invisible; Chance felt a sudden gust of wind seeming to blow right through him.

"Let's hip-hup down the road," Ike said, and left in the van with son and dog.

Chance stood alone, aware now of a creeping cold in the air. He tried to imagine buds on trees, flowers pushing up from the ground, animals in the earth coming awake. Looking up, he saw Soapy standing on the landing of the auction barn apartment. She was so still that it wasn't until the wind moved the tip of her braid that he was sure she was there, not a trick of his mind. They stared at one another for the longest time. Finally, without a word or a nod of acknowledgment, Soapy went back into the apartment.

Chance made no move to follow. He had nothing to say to her, nothing to give to her, nothing to receive from her. He preferred the images he had of her in the woods to actually seeing her, touching her, working through a self with her. He preferred the thought of the forest, which would always be the thought of Soapy, to the real thing, dark, looming, confused, scary. He got into the Brat and drove back to Tuckerman.

Duty

Ike Jordan was preoccupied as he walked from the auction barn to his van. He was thinking about the speech he would deliver at the special town meeting tonight. And it wasn't until he was in the van that he realized something was wrong. The air didn't move right, there was a smell not his own, not Crowbar's. He turned, and in the back of the van beside Crowbar emerged a figure.

"He's not much of a guard dog," the figure said.

The voice was friendly, but Ike knew something was terribly wrong. He who could sneak up on anyone had been sneaked up upon. The important papers he had left in the folder on the dashboard were gone. Ike moved his hand nonchalantly to the glove compartment. Everything depended upon his cunning. He talked to divert the attention of the figure behind him. He started giving his speech: "This mall will destroy this town as we know it." He raised his voice as his thumb clicked the button on the glove compartment door.

"It's not there, Ike."

Ike turned and saw his own gun pointing at him. Ike, grasping for meaning, made sense of what he was seeing by creating an apparition.

"You don't fool me," Ike said. "I know who you really are. You're Ollie, and you come for your dog."

Professor Hadly Blue had spoken out against the mall. He felt so strongly on the matter that he had, uncharacteristically, signed a petition condemning the mall. He truly believed it would destroy the Darby he'd learned to love in recent years. So he had every intention of attending the town meeting, had even pondered a brief speech: *I'm one of the new people, and I realize that I am part of the problem and not the solution as Darby strives to retain its identity in the 21st century. However* . . . What was he going to say beyond the "however"? Hmm, "Beyond the However" would make good title for an epic poem by Balthazar, the main character in the novel he'd been working on the last twelve years, and with that he rolled out any thoughts about the speech and wheeled in some images for the poem.

He might not have succumbed so swiftly to the whim of his free-wheeling mind had it not been for the fact that he had grown suspicious of some of his fellow mall adversaries. The Magnus company had asked the selectmen to call a special town meeting to decide the rezoning issue, instead of putting it on the agenda of the regular town meeting. Hadly had waited for the reflexive cry of outrage from SOD, but it never occurred. Quite the opposite. SOD, in a prepared statement that was printed in the *Crier* as well as posted about town, endorsed the proposal. The selectmen quickly capitulated, and the meeting was scheduled for the middle of February. Hadly sensed a conspiracy afoot, a betrayal, a sellout. Then, too, he didn't like the idea of going to two town meetings. He composed a terse response to the selectmen for their action: "One cannot live duty-free in a free society, but double duty inhibits the free in the society." Not that he would think of actually sending such a note.

Despite his misgivings, despite the fact that he had worked late that day (actually, he had lingered at the library, lingered at the coffee shop, lingered over a drink with Stillwaters at Murry's), despite the fact that he didn't really enjoy the town-meeting production number and found the atmosphere in the town hall suffocating and shabby, and despite his desire to read tonight, he had made up his mind to go to the special meeting and vote down the mall. Duty was duty.

But when he got home, his day took a turn toward the swamps when he found that the Star Route mailman had left a letter from his estranged lover, Kay Bradford. She had moved in with the director of a Marathon House in Rhode Island. She and the son of a bitchin' beau would arrive this weekend, and pick up the rest of her things. Depressed, Hadly wrote:

> PAINTINGS
> By Hadly Blue (for Kay)
>
> Places I have never seen
> That perhaps no longer exist
> Or have never existed
>
> —muddied oils of New England villages
> By unknown artists which can be had
> Cheap at country auctions—
>
> Might be places to go
> If they drop the bomb
> Or if the world were to go suddenly, permanently
> Bonkers
> Or if you leave me.

Quarter to nine. Oh, dear. He'd lost track of time. The meeting was already more than an hour old. Hmm. He didn't want to walk in late—heck, it might even be over. So instead of going to the meeting, he drank some wine and reread favorite sections of *Pnin*.

Billy and Dot McCurtin had a minor argument before the special town meeting. Dot had shut off the scanner, signaling she meant business about attending the meeting.

"Dot," said Billy McCurtin, "I know how you're going to vote, and you know how I'm going to vote, so the votes cancel each other out. Right? So, let's cancel out the babysitter, stay home and have popcorn."

"You've been out in the world," said Dot McCurtin. "I have been cooped up in this house all day. I am not going to pass up an opportunity to see some people."

"It's because I've been out in the world that I don't have any urge to see any more of humanity tonight, a weekday night, I might add," Billy said.

"I can call the sitter, tell her to stay home, and I'll go to the meeting by myself," Dot said.

"Come on, Dot," Billy said. "I don't want to babysit. And how are our votes going to cancel out if only one of us stays home?"

"That's not my problem. I'm going to the meeting."

"That's not my problem," Billy said, mocking his wife's voice.

"You just don't want to take care of your own children," Dot said.

"I do my duty."

"Yah, just barely. Anybody who refers to caring for his own children as 'babysitting' ought to examine his values, I daresay."

"Examine his values," he said, mocking her again. "You've been watching too much Donahue."

"I may not be out in the world like Mr. Sophistication here, but I do know, for one thing, the votes don't cancel each other out. Since a two-thirds majority is needed to pass the mall, my vote is more precious than yours."

"I still don't understand why you want that mall to begin with," Billy said. "It's going to ruin the town."

"Billy, it isn't the town we think it is," Dot said. "It never was. The town you have in your mind is your father's town, and the one I have in my mind is my mother's town. It doesn't exist today, except in our minds. The town we live in is already ruined. One more chunk of progress isn't going to make it any worse, and it isn't going to kill our idea of the town in our minds. More people, more things to do—I think it's going to be fun."

"Darby as it is today is still a pretty good place to come home to at night, a pretty good place to raise children, and I don't see that a bunch of stores and pizza joints is going to make it a better place."

"Then go to the meeting, say your piece, and vote against it," Dot said.

Smarting a bit for getting beat, for the umpteenth time, in an argument by his wife, Billy McCurtin fetched the babysitter. But by the time the McCurtins arrived at the town hall, Billy had gotten into the town meeting spirit, and he was grateful to Dot for making him see his way toward doing his duty.

Dot McCurtin looked over the crowd, evaluated it, and said to herself, "Mrs. McCurtin, you're the one that should have stayed home tonight."

"Goddamn, aren't you ready yet?" Avalon Hillary said to his wife, who was struggling to get into a dress.

"Don't swear at me, you old fart. I'll be ready when I'm ready," said Melba Hillary.

He watched her remove the dress and throw it in the closet. It dawned on him that she'd gained some weight.

"You're getting fat," he said.

"I was always fat—now I'm fatter. Will you please leave me alone while I find something to wear."

"Melba, I know you're burdened by this—you don't have to go," he said.

"I don't want to go, but yes indeed I do have to go. How would it look if Melba Hillary didn't show up for the special town meeting? Besides, if you ask me, these Magnus people are going to need every vote they can get."

Melba might have signed papers, but she couldn't admit to herself that she was a party to the proposal for rezoning. Although she and Avalon had discussed the matter over and over again, it didn't seem real to her, didn't seem as if anything they said, they decided, they did made any real difference. It was as if Magnus was from another planet; as if she and Avalon were part of some great celestial scheme, beyond their understanding, of which the Magnus people were higher ranking members whom she should feel privileged to follow. The Magnus people were little bitty gods, like apostles or maybe even angels, herself and Avalon two among a chosen few selected to serve them. Unpleasant as she found town meetings, she had a duty to attend this one and vote in a manner that had been predestined for her.

"I suppose . . . I suppose." Avalon ambled off.

It was true what she said, he thought. There was nothing to guarantee that the rezoning proposal would pass. He'd been to enough town meetings to realize that each one spawned a life and will of its own.

Until now, he hadn't given much thought to losing. He was a man who believed in his premonitions (perhaps because they were so occasional), and something had told him the mall vote was in the bag. He reckoned that the evidence supported him. For one thing, Magnus was all business. They'd put a lot of money into the site plans, not to mention the all-expense-paid vacation they had treated him and Melba to. Companies like that didn't turn on the oven just to warm the kittens. They knew what they were doing. And, too, all those new people in town—face it! the ones with the votes—who were forever complaining about the roads and the schools and the lack of programs for the underprivileged, now here was a plan that would solve all those so-called problems. How could they turn it down? Still . . . still. As his brother-in-law Arthur Crabb, the politician, was fond of saying, "These polls are horse manure; John Q. Citizen doesn't usually vote the way he thinks he will, and almost never the way he says he will."

He tried to tell himself that if they lost or if, for reasons he couldn't fathom, Magnus failed to exercise its option to buy his farm, why he would continue with his life as before. But deep down he knew that, with the thought of the money, he had changed, Melba had changed, everything had changed. The town itself had changed. Life would be different for all concerned, mall or no. If the voters could somehow see this, why they most certainly also would see that they might as well accept the mall. So flowed Avalon Hillary's logic.

He judged that his own view of the world had been enriched by Magnus. For one thing, the vacation had been an eye-opener. He'd happened to mention to Mr. Case that Melba had wanted to go to Florida. The next day Case had informed him that Magnus would do them one better than Florida, by paying for plane fare and hotel accommodations for two weeks at the Magnus-Bahama Complex on a South Sea island. Avalon had wanted to turn down the offer. He didn't like the idea of owing anybody anything, but Melba wouldn't hear of it. They went. And it had been a revelation to him. He'd always known that people 'round the world were the same, yet different—everybody knew that—but actually to see this was to feel it, rather than merely to know it.

The people on the island were so friendly that at first he didn't trust them, thinking they were trying to get him to lower his guard so they could pick his pocket. After a couple of days, he realized that, true, they did want to pick his pocket, but only because it was their living. The friendliness was sincere and natural, and had nothing to do with the business of parting the tourists from their money. He'd even copied the friendliness routine, smiling at strangers, saying to white people, "Nice island they got here" and to black people "Nice people you got here."

He liked the way the natives talked. They were dark brown and fertile looking as earth. Somehow he'd expected them all to say "Yowza yowza, boss," so it tickled him, by gosh, to hear them talk English like Frenchmen. It made him realize that, goddamn it, it would do him some good to see a little more of the world than New Hampshire and Vermont.

They lived it up on that island. He drank blue-ribbon whiskey and ate rich food, and Melba—who was never one to push away from the table—had outdone herself: "This ocean air gives me an appetite," she had said.

She had bought them bathing suits and proposed that they lay on chaise lounges by the swimming pool. He'd balked at that idea, but she had talked him into trying it. They went out there and basked in the sun like a couple of goddamn hippos. I'm going to hate this, he had thought, but he was wrong. The sun, the water, the drinks—all were quite relaxing, as he had told Arthur Crabb.

He didn't tell him about the women, although he'd wanted to, even now he was dying to talk to another man about the women. These young women today walked around almost bare-ass by that swimming pool. Back and forth they went, and they lay down, and they giggled, and they swam and dived into the water like fish. You had to be blind not to notice. At first he had tried to do the right thing and look away. It took—oh, maybe ninety seconds—to figure out that not only was there no shame in looking, but that it was expected. Later in the room after some connubials, Melba had said, "My, my, but this vacation has perked you up." It had perked her up, too.

The trouble started when they returned home. The farm looked like somebody else's, the product of some old fool with not enough back left to make a go of it. He'd felt sick just thinking about returning to the work and worry of it. He'd even offered to pay Leonard Crabb, who had watched the place in his absence, to stay on. Lenny had hemmed and hawed. He'd do it if Avalon pushed him, but Avalon could see his heart wasn't in it. The boy wanted his own farm. Avalon said never mind. The thought of the work ahead was disheartening enough, but he was made more uneasy by the fact that the farm itself didn't look right, didn't smell right, didn't feel right. He realized that it wasn't his farm, had never been his. It was his father's farm and his grandfather's farm, and it was going to be Magnus's farm even if they never bought it. His farm had always been a sliver of light in his mind, and it had vanished in the glare of the thought of the money.

Not that he was unduly troubled by the idea of giving up the farm. Indeed, it excited him. He wanted to take the $2.3 million and see more of the world, find a new niche perhaps.

The worry came when he wondered: what if the voters turn down the rezoning article?

"Melba, you ready?" he called.

"Oh, pipe down."

Goddamn, but that woman was getting awful independent.

Selectman Arthur Crabb had about ten minutes before it was time to leave for the special town meeting. He hated "ten minutes." If you had fifteen minutes, you could cut a board, or fill a water tank, or check your compressor; if you had half an hour or more, why you could jump into some real work; and if you had only five minutes, you could start the car, wash the windshield, maybe even play the radio while you waited for the wife. But ten minutes meant fidget and wait, ten minutes of precious life wasted, ten minutes missing in the compost pile of history.

"Mrs. Crabb," he shouted up the stairs, talking in the special code of long-married couples, "do you have your buttons buttoned for the special town meeting?"

"No, Mr. Crabb, I do not. My buttons remain unbuttoned, my stockings unrolled. And why should I? We have ten minutes before it's time to go."

"I know, I know," he mumbled, getting the answer he expected, the answer he deserved. Why was it when you got what you deserved you always felt annoyed, cheated?

Crabb scraped his hands, put them behind his back and walked into the kitchen for no good reason other than there might be a few dishes to wash, a pot to put away, six or eight minutes of work to keep him occupied. The farm had eased him into the habit of work, until one day he realized that there was nothing else but work that meant anything to him. When he wasn't working he felt restless, pregnant with the will to do.

He looked around the kitchen. No dishes to wash, nothing to put away. Mrs. Crabb was a fine housekeeper. Ah, he spotted a scat of stove-wood litter on the floor. He'd go out to the wood shed, bring back some fuel, add to the mess and sweep up. He opened the woodbox. It was nearly full, but he could cram in a few more sticks.

On his way back from the woodshed, he tripped slightly on the porch stoop, and that told him he wasn't entirely relaxed. Perhaps he was a little bit nervous because of the special meeting. After all, as chairman of the board of selectmen, he had to deliver a speech; 'course, it was short. He'd always liked public service. He'd served in the legislature and on the county commission, and now he was a selectman. He wanted to serve; it gave him great pleasure to serve, to do for the people. He wouldn't have dreamed of asking for a raise, like some of those politicians in other states. Indeed, he didn't think of himself as a politician. He thought of himself as a public servant.

Wood in the stove, wood in the box, floor swept up, still a few minutes before it was time to go—okay, he'd start the car now. The bathroom in their house was off the kitchen—the proper place for a bathroom, in Arthur Crabb's view, since it could be kept warm by the kitchen range—and he noticed now that the light was on. He went in to shut it off, wondering whether Avalon, now that he was going to get rich, still worried about things like putting out the lights. He caught sight of himself in the bathroom mirror, and the unease that he had dimly perceived before now conspired to make him take a long look.

My God, what a face! No wonder some strangers quivered when they had to talk to him. He tried to smile—and failed. He had a man's capacity for mirth, and a potato's for expressing it. How harrowed his skin was. In his own mind, he was still thirty. It was only during moments like this that he realized he was sixty, a grizzled sixty at that. Perhaps to do for the people, you had to look the part of a doer. What could be done to make this face appear more kindly, something that would say, 'Here's a fella wants to serve, got the brains to do it, too'? He looked closely at the face. It struck him, then, that he had too much unsightly hair. Oh, he shaved close all right, but he still had hair sticking out of his ears, his nose, and his eyebrows looked fit for dusting the hall. Impulsively, he grabbed

Mrs. Crabb's scissors and snipped away: eyebrows first, then ears and nose. He inspected the mirror. Well, he didn't look thirty, but he looked better.

When he met Mrs. Crabb coming down the stairs, all buttoned and ready to travel, he scraped his hands twice, his unconscious signal to her unconscious mind that something was afoot.

"What?" she said.

"Trimmed up," he said.

"So you did, so you did," she said. "This must be a big meeting indeed for Arthur Crabb to trim up."

They arrived in time to help Bob Crawford straighten the chairs in the town hall. Poor Bob had such weakness for the bottle that his idea of a straight line had some bends in it. Crabb had never acquired vices. He liked Postum from the start, so he saw no need to turn to coffee. He was given tea once, but found it too watery for palatability. As a young buck, he once got drunk at the county fair—come to think of it, he had been with Avalon—and had vomited afterward. Never had an urge to take another drink; never did, except for the punch they gave you at weddings.

He led Mrs. Crabb to a seat. She removed her knitting and set to work. He envied her. She was doing something productive. He sat at the selectmen's table on the stage, glancing at the warrant:

Article 1: To consider whether the town ought to rezone the so-called Hillary farm on River Road from agricultural to commercial. (By ballot)

Article 2: To consider whether the activity commonly known as jogging should be regulated on town roads.

Crabb smiled inwardly when he read the jogging article. Others might know him as a dour, serious-minded man, but Arthur Crabb liked a certain kind of prank. Seeing to it that the jogging article, petitioned for by citizens led by Ronald Thorpe, found its way on the agenda for the special town meeting was an example of such a prank. The jogger issue was about the stupidest thing to come down the pike since whitewall tires on pickup trucks. So Crabb had thought, Why not put the multimillion-dollar proposal in the same pew with the two-cent one? No one would know he had himself a tickle at the mall people's expense.

At root here was the fact that Arthur Crabb had mixed feelings about the mall proposal. On the one hand, because of family obligations he was duty-bound to back it. This he did not find difficult to do, because it was clear as spring rain that the mall would be to the enormous betterment of the town—better schools, better roads, more help for the under-privileged. The town would be able to do for its people. Simple as that.

And, too, he was happy to see Melba and Avalon prosper. There had been a time when he had been mildly jealous of Avalon, because he had better cows. Avalon was a go-getter, an experimenter. He tried out every new idea and gadget; he spent a lot of money on new equipment. He was never sat-isfied. His father had been the best farmer in the valley. Per-haps Avalon had been driven to stay even. As for himself, Crabb had stuck with the old ways, and his herd was not a great producing herd, though it produced, but it was healthy, and he had his markets nicely sewed up because they knew he was reliable. He had no debts; he had money in the bank. He considered himself a lucky man; he considered Avalon an unlucky man because he worried so. Thus Crabb had long gotten over his petty jealousy, and he was happy that Avalon and Melba were going to get their two million, or whatever the hell the figure was. Melba had wanted to tell Mrs. Crabb, but she didn't want to know. At any rate, he hoped the money made the Hillarys happy.

Despite all this, there was something that bothered Crabb about the mall—the location. It rankled him that they wanted to build it on good farmland. Why the bejesus couldn't they put it out in the woods? Covering good land with a department store—the thought galled him.

Bob Crawford, the part-time janitor of the town hall, stood in the rear. He didn't like to sit down. He had an idea that if you sat down too long without a beer at hand you risked injury to yourself—dizziness, folding of the bladder, tightness of haunch muscles. So he stood, near the exit. He cleaned this building, and he knew it intimately. It was old and dry and it harbored grudges: he didn't trust it. If there was going to be a fire, he wanted to be in a position to make a getaway. Or so he told himself. The truth was he planned to sneak out now and then to his car for a nip of Seagram's 7. He'd had a drink before coming in, and currently he was skating on its bright surface. Normally Bob drank beer, but he didn't think it proper to be running off to the toilet every few minutes during a public event. Or so he told himself. Bob Crawford had many excuses for taking hard liquor. Not that he would ever sneak a bottle into the town hall. He didn't believe in drinking in public buildings. It was sacrimonious, a word that he thought he had heard somewhere and which he had trans-lated as a verbal confluence of the words unmannerly, undig-nified and uncivil.

From the way the town hall was filling he judged that the crowd would be nearly as large as expected at a regular town meeting. It used to be that he'd know everyone who came in. No more. There were so many new people. Some he recog-nized as faces behind the wheels of cars; others were complete strangers. As a rule, the new people were school wise and country ignorant. Still, he had to admit they were probably good for the town because, having come here of their own free will, unlike the natives such as himself, why they were more tender toward the town. Growth, progress—supposed to be good, weren't they?

Victor Copley, the moderator, was already on the stage, chatting with the selectmen, scratching his chin with his gavel. Bob liked Vic. He was born and raised in Center Darby, but he married one of the Butterworth girls, and that gave him celebrity status in town. He worked in insurance in Tucker-man. Once in a while he pretended not to see the upraised hands of people he didn't want to recognize, who often were his in-laws on the hill; he was about as fair a man as you could find who wasn't a total idiot.

Avalon Hillary came in with his missus and the Magnus

men. It troubled Bob that Hillary, whom he already considered to be a rich man, stood to gain even more from the sale of his property. They were going to pay him, Bob had heard, ten million dollars. Not fair, not fair.

Bob Crawford still wasn't sure how he was going to vote on the mall. Nothing unusual about that. It ruined the fun of a town meeting to make up your mind too far in advance. He liked the idea of having stores handy, not having to drive to Tuckerman or Brattleboro to buy a pair of pants or a shovel. There was a rumor going around that the state was going to put a liquor store in the mall. Good, good. Old Man Crabb insisted that the mall was going to bring in a lot of property tax dollars. Good, good. Somehow, though, the promise of lower taxes didn't ring sharp. Property taxes had never gone down before; why should they go down now? The fact that the Upper Darby folk opposed the mall counted for something, too. He didn't much like the people up on the hill, but he trusted their judgment. Rich people had education and their hearts were in the right place when it came to what was good, even if their heads were wedged up their asses when it came to what was practical. If they didn't like the mall, there must be something wrong with it.

These things passed through his mind like scenes at a theater, because something told him that the town meeting itself was not real life. Ultimately, it didn't really matter how you voted, he believed. Certain undefined powers that Bob referred to only as "they" held the power. "They" had their way, no matter what "you" did. The beauty of this theory was that it took away any burden of responsibility. You went to town meetings for the show; you voted, but you didn't fool yourself into thinking you would get anything more than two hours of entertainment.

Mr. Thorpe, the TV actor, came in. My word, he was wearing a suit and tie. His very presence seemed to reinforce Bob's conviction that the town meeting was a sort of play. Thorpe had circulated the petition to ban the joggers on town roads. Bob was attracted to the idea. Joggers had never hounded him personally, but he was unsettled by the sight of people running noplace, running for the sake of running. There was something about joggers that shouted a warning. Joggers were like animals that scurried about frantically before some natural disaster, sensing its oncoming, unable to stop it, but feeling the need to exercise their panic. Maybe the world was coming to an end. If so, let it end. Let's not encourage these people running around heralding it. If you're going to die, you might as well go surprised.

The hall was almost full now, Copley was about ready to bring down his gavel, but something was missing. It took Bob a moment to figure out what it was. Neither Squire Salmon nor Ike Jordan had arrived. Bob was disappointed. He loved to watch Ike perform. Not that the man made any sense, but he could hold you with his voice, make you grateful you'd passed the time just hearing him. The show was going to come down to the Magnus people, their lawyers and experts, against the SOD folk up on the hill, and their lawyers and experts. With no Ike, the bullshit would be spread by professionals only. Too bad. Bob shifted his weight from his right foot to his left foot, and prepared to jury the action.

Zoe Cutter was furious with her brother, Ronald Thorpe. Just when she was beginning to become respected here, just when she had worked her way into a position of authority, Ronald had to spring his preposterous proposal to regulate joggers. If there was one thing that she had learned after living several years in this small New England town, it was that while the townspeople tolerated eccentric behavior, even took a kind of macabre pride in its eccentrics—as one takes pride in a wooden leg or any other disability—the price paid by the subject was a sacrifice of influence in the community. They would never take Ronald seriously again in Darby; by association, she too would be suspect.

Zoe was distracted momentarily from her thoughts by the voice of Victor Copley bringing the meeting to order.

"Before taking up the first article, I've agreed to allow Mr. Ronald Thorpe, petitioner for the second article, a few words," Copley said.

Zoe perked up. Perhaps Ronald had come to his senses and was going to withdraw the article from the warrant. She could have frustrated Ronald's silly vendetta against joggers simply by building new kennels away from the road where the joggers jogged, thus removing Ronald's presumed reason for the vendetta: that the joggers disturbed the peace of mind of their dogs. But she realized the vendetta was due less to anger at joggers than to disappointment with his own life. Ronald had no job, no mate. Someone at the network had arranged for the murder of Dr. Dirk Sampson, the character he played on the soap opera *Intensive Care*. Ronald hadn't been able to find work since. He had done what he had always done when in trouble, run home to big sister.

Despite the fact that she was pleased with her circumstance (had no wish to marry again for the fourth time) and felt no particular need of a companion, she was glad to have Ronald in her house. They gossiped at dawn over muffins and coffee; they read the morning papers until eleven o'clock—the *Journal*, the *Times*, the *Globe*, the *Crier*, they made telephone calls; they walked the dogs; they dined out; they entertained friends and were happy to send them away; they built fires in the fireplaces and sipped brandy in the evening, and went off to their separate bedrooms, he to watch movies courtesy of the VCR, she to read; they traveled from time to time. It was a good life. So when Ronald had fastened onto the jogger issue, she had let him have his head, even if it cost her influence in this town.

At least she had been able to sneak in some guidance in the handling of the issue, by hiring a lawyer from Tuckerman to coach Ronald in the legal matters, steer him in his logic, indeed, to write his speech for him. Ronald was used to scripts and direction, and at the moment it was showing. He was performing admirably.

He never mentioned his own personal stake in the issue and argued on behalf of others, mainly on behalf of the joggers themselves. He cited statistics that said persons running along the road risked knee injuries, heart attacks, and collisions with automobiles. He suggested that joggers might demand the town provide sidewalks and footpaths. He argued that joggers displeased the eye, were outside of the New England tradition, and were a poor fashion example to youth. He spoke just the right length of time.

A few people latched onto the speech to express general resentment at the idea of grown up people running in public. Naturally, many joggers rose to defend themselves. One newcomer said it should be dogs, not people, who were restrained, but he was shouted down. Russell Pegasus questioned the sanity of the petitioners, but Ronald kept his composure. Someone asked whether the town legally could enact a jogger-restraining ordinance. Moderator Copley had let matters go on far too long. Finally, someone called for a motion to cut off debate, and the voters, as if realizing they had been wasting time, quickly responded in the affirmative.

The jogger issue was tabled until the regular town meeting. More than an hour had passed. A few voters glanced at their watches and went home.

"We didn't win and we didn't lose," Ronald Thorpe said to Zoe.

"No, *we* didn't," Zoe said.

"You think they'll hold it against me if I leave now?" he asked.

"I believe they will," Zoe said.

With a sigh, Ronald settled in beside his sister. A few minutes later Zoe watched him slip out. The moon would be up, blue light on the snow. She could almost see his fine figure outlined against the horizon, hear him as he whistled the theme song from *The Bridge on the River Kwai*. What was it— "The Colonel Bogey March"?

Final Arguments

Reporter Roland LaChance scribbled in his slender notebook: "Jogger fray sets timidity tone . . . moderator spacey . . . Where's Ike? Where's Reggie?"

Ike Jordan, who had circulated petitions, made speeches at various hearings held by the Planning Board, written letters to the editor of the newspaper berating the mall— Ike was not at the special town meeting. And Reggie, the leader of SOD, was not at the meeting.

In the pause between the tabling of the jogger article and the reading of the rezoning article, Chance left his chair to ask Persephone where Reggie was.

"I'm not sure," she said. "I came down with Garvin. Reggie took the Bronco. He said he was going to pick up Ike Jordan on the way. He said they were going to make a mutual presentation."

Chance returned to his chair. He felt peculiar. He had approached Persephone as a reporter; she had responded to him as one answering a reporter. It was as if he— Chance—had never spoken to her—Persephone.

A minute or so after the rezoning article was introduced for debate Reggie arrived. Chance watched as he whispered something in Garvin's ear. Later, while Charles Barnum was making Magnus's case before the voters, Reggie was whispering to the moderator. Chance could sense that something was up. Reggie was planning a surprise. Chance imagined Ike in the wings, ready to make a grand entrance.

The discussion on the main issue began with the selectmen making an expected, but unexpectedly forceful, endorsement of the mall. Arthur Crabb, chairman of the board of selectmen, read the statement.

"Whereas there is no question in the minds of the Board of Selectmen that the so-called Magnus Mall will broaden the Darby tax base and therefore help relieve property taxes and

"Whereas the selectmen find any detriments associated with the mall such as for example a possible increase in vehicular traffic to be far outweighed by the benefits and

"Whereas Magnus Mall is a nonpolluting industry and

"Whereas Magnus Mall likely will boost the economy of the town and employ local persons

"The Darby Board of Selectmen strongly and unanimously recommends that the so-called Hillary Farm on River Road be rezoned from Agricultural to Commercial to allow construction of the Magnus Mall."

Barnum and Case presented the company's position. Barnum did most of the talking, lapsing into the local dialect, cracking jokes on occasion. Chance saw a mistake in this. From their clothes and carriage, most of the voters appeared to be newcomers or natives who, through education and employment, had lost much of their provinciality, people who had cleaned up their accents, people to whom wry humor was hick humor. As for Case, he lapsed into business jargon now and then, but nonetheless gave the impression of a man who preferred to be honest if he could.

The Magnus strategy included three themes: tax revenue for the town, jobs, and sensitivity to the townspeople's desire to preserve the identity of Darby. Barnum and Case displayed charts and blueprints; they spoke with pride of the company's expertise and solid reputation. Case narrated a brief slide show of Magnus Malls all over the United States. He pointed at the Old World architecture in the Mall in Charleston, the adobe look of the Mall of Southern California, the loglike walls of the Mall of Seattle. The Mall of Central New England would be "strictly Colonial," he said, and showed artists' renditions that included perimeter shrubbery for the building and rounded concrete islands of trees in the parking lot. Someone asked how you could make a broad, flat-topped structure of steel and concrete "Colonial," and Case answered simply that Magnus liked a challenge.

Case ended the company's presentation by promising that Darby residents who qualified would have first dibs for jobs at the mall. "We want to go where we are welcome. If we are not welcome, we will egress elsewhere," he said.

A few people argued vehemently against the mall. But they seemed to be outside of the mainstream, leftover hippies, left-wingers with a dislike of big business—at any rate, left. There was a lull, then. People were waiting for SOD to present its case. When Garvin Prell rose to speak, Chance expected he would make the presentation, but all Prell said was, "Mr. Moderator, SOD would like to speak."

"All right, Mr. Prell," Copley said, and then he turned his attention to the voters. "SOD representatives earlier asked for time to deliver a formal presentation before the meeting. As moderator, I approved this request, provided there were no objections from the meeting. Are there any objections?"

"What is the nature of the presentation, Mr. Moderator?" asked Barnum.

"I don't know," Copley said. "Does anyone from SOD wish to answer the question?"

"Mr. Moderator, we at SOD didn't object while Magnus made its pitch. I think we should be granted the same courtesy," Prell said.

"I wasn't objecting. I was making an inquiry," Barnum said.

At that point, Case touched Barnum's sleeve, and Barnum said, "I withdraw the inquiry."

By that time Reggie Salmon already was moving toward the stage. He made his way slowly; he was wearing a cape over his parka. He looked, Chance thought, like Dr. Jekyll about to be Mr. Hyde.

The people in the hall were arrested by his appearance. Those who knew him were seeing a different version of the man who was known as the Squire of Upper Darby. Those who didn't know him (he hadn't been introduced by name yet) looked closely at this obviously very important person. Whatever the value of Reggie's position on the issue, he would have the attention of the gathered.

Copley stepped aside, and Reggie took control of the rostrum and the microphone. With this act, he had scored a coup. Previous speakers spoke from their chairs in the hall. Case had set up his own equipment for the slide show on the stage, but he had narrated it from below.

"I have something very important, extremely important— and tragic—to report," said Reggie Salmon. His voice was low, but he kept his lips close to the microphone, and he spoke each word distinctly. The effect was the verbal equivalent of someone banging a pipe with a tire iron; each word clanged throughout the hall.

"Before arriving at the meeting, I drove to Ike Jordan's place in Darby Depot. We were to have presented evidence together at this meeting concerning the inadvisability of a mall for Darby. When I arrived, I found not Ike, but our constable and the state police. Constable Perkins informed me that Ike Jordan was dead. Murdered. That's correct. Murdered. Shot twice."

People shuffled in their seats, looked at their neighbors for verification that what they had heard was what they had heard.

Reggie went on, "I have a few things to say about Ike, but first I'd like to ask you all to observe a moment of silence on behalf of his family and his memory. Please stand, my friends and neighbors."

After the moment of silence—which Reggie drew out to perhaps a full minute—Reggie asked the crowd to be seated, and went on with his speech.

"I'd come here tonight to deliver the common arguments against the Magnus Mall, the ones I've been harping on for months and which most of you are familiar with.

"You all know, for example, that the mall is not going to lower your taxes. Oh, it might for a few years, but once the town has to improve the roads, build a new fire station, expand the school and quadruple the police budget, I think you'll see those extra tax dollars from the mall siphoned off into services. You'll be right back where you started from, with one difference. Your taxes will still be high, but you won't be living in the country anymore. You'll be living in a city, with all the city frustrations and problems and, yes, corruption. Being a novice city, we might even get some new kinds of city troubles, unheard of troubles, troubles to make us famous. Who knows?

"Ike was going to talk tonight about the quality of life in Darby. We are a town with so many different kinds of people, and while we have had disagreements, we have not gone to war with one another. We are not a classless society. Just the opposite. We are a society of many classes, without a class that tyrannizes. I don't say we all love each other. I don't say we don't gossip about our neighbors. We do. Gossip makes the world go round. Isn't that so, Mrs. McCurtin?"

That elicited a burst of surprised laughter from the crowd and a deep blush from Mrs. McCurtin.

"We are independent souls in Darby who realize that we depend on one another—for snow plowing, tomato sharing, apple picking, and companionship at sugar-on-snow parties. It's a delicate equilibrium. Who knows which way this world would be tipped if a mall were built? This is what Ike Jordan would have said were he here tonight.

"I'd like to say a few words about Ike himself. It's no secret that I and other SOD members oppose the mall to promote our own interests. We don't deny this. We are proud of our interests. We feel the Jepson Salmon Trust, besides being one of the few places on this planet where nature will be allowed to have its way, will also be a haven to walkers and campers and cross-country skiers and snowshoers, perhaps even to snowmobilers and off-the-road vehicles. Open to all who wish to visit, but not to disturb: this is the promise of the Trust.

We believe the mall will invite too much trespassing by too many people on the Trust. We would then have to close the Trust, police it. This we do not want to do.

"Ike Jordan had no such interest. In fact, in his own eyes, he stood to gain from the mall. He believed that the mall would bring greater tax revenue to the town and that therefore his property taxes would go down. At the same time, he believed that the value of those properties would increase. These are rather large considerations for someone who owned as much property as Ike Jordan. Mind you, we at SOD don't agree. As I've already said, we at SOD believe strongly that the mall will cost the town dearly in tax dollars over the long haul. But, as I say, Ike Jordan believed the Magnus lie of lower taxes.

"Yet, he continued to oppose it. Why? Because to Ike Jordan there was a principle involved. Ike believed in the land, in the tradition of Darby. He openly opposed the mall. It wasn't going to be Reggie Salmon that was going to stop the mall, it wasn't going to be SOD, it was going to be Ike Jordan because the people he reached were going to be the swing votes, the common men and women of Darby, the people who are most hounded by taxes, who might have gone along with the Magnus lie, had not one of their own pointed out that the folly of a mall goes beyond tax benefit or debit."

Reggie waited a while for the echoes of his words to reverberate around the room. He waited until there was a general restlessness among the gathered. He waited until Copley glanced at his watch, then he went on:

"I will now level a very serious charge. I believe that an investigation will reveal a suspect in the murder of Ike Jordan. Who stood to profit from Ike's death? The answer is one entity— Magnus Mall."

There was a great stir in the Darby Town Hall. Barnum jumped to his feet. "I object to this, Mr. Moderator. This is sheer speculation, out and out slander—disgraceful. It will prejudice the outcome of this serious issue for Darby . . ."

"I hope it prejudices the outcome," clanged Reggie's voice.

"Mr. Salmon, your innu . . . innu . . ."

"It's not an innuendo. It's a charge—first-degree murder," Salmon clanged.

"It's slander, in the legal sense. It's actionable, I warn you," Barnum said.

"Sue me, go ahead and sue me," Reggie clanged.

At that point, Copley stepped in and took the microphone from Reggie Salmon.

"My apologies to the voters," he said. "I let this go on too long . . ."

But Reggie Salmon was not finished. The streaks on his face purpled with rage, he grasped the microphone and shouted into it one more time, "Sue me," and then he collapsed on the stage, bringing down the microphone, which magnified the sound of his falling, like pipes thrown down a flight of stairs.

BY ROLAND LaCHANCE
Crier Staff Writer

DARBY, Feb. 16—Magnus Mall officials say the company is no longer interested in constructing a shopping mall in Darby.

The company's decision was only incidentally influenced by dramatic events Tuesday at a special town meeting on the mall in Darby, according to William W. Case, vice-president in charge of new construction for Magnus Mall Group Inc.

"Darby was marginal for us from the start," Case said. "With the town vote and the accusations, it's clear to us that a pall will hang over any mall built in Darby. Therefore, we are prepared to reroute our proposal. I'm sure there are other towns in the area that will be happy to have more tax dollars from a thriving, clean business."

In fact, Case has already accepted an invitation from the Tuckerman City Council to discuss a mall for the city. Earlier, the council was cool toward a mall, fearing it could hurt commerce in Tuckerman's attractive downtown area. However, city officials now are afraid that if the mall is built in an outlying town, the city could suffer a tax loss as well as deterioration of a downtown.

Darby voters Tuesday turned down a rezoning request that would have allowed a mall in Darby, on the heels of accusations by one of the town's leading citizens.

Raphael G. Salmon of Upper Darby, following an impassioned plea to keep Darby rural, accused Magnus of engineering the murder of Isaac O. Jordan, another outspoken opponent of the mall. Jordan was shot to death with his own .357 Magnum pistol sometime Tuesday. Darby Constable Godfrey T. Perkins said the body was discovered slumped at the wheel of Jordan's van in the parking lot of Ike's Auction Barn on Route 21.

Salmon charged at the meeting that Magnus may have had Jordan killed to silence hs opposition. Salmon then collapsed on the stage at the Darby Town Hall and was rushed to Tuckerman Hospital. Minutes later townspeople voted 237–51 against a request to change from agricultural to commercial the zoning of the mall site, a farm on River Road owned by Avalon W. and Melba C. Hillary.

Salmon was reported in a stable condition this morning. Hospital officials declined to specify Salmon's illness.

Magnus officials were furious over the Salmon charges, as were the Hillarys.

Hillary said he's instructed his attorney to file a lawsuit against Salmon when he recovers from his illness.

Meanwhile, police officials have remained silent on the Jordan murder. Jordan's son, Carlton D. Jordan, was questioned at length Tuesday night, but released. Police refused to say whether Jordan's son is a suspect.

Darby Selectman Arthur H. Crabb said today that the town was prepared to file a suit of its own, asking the Tuckerman County Superior Court to throw out the results of Tuesday's vote because of the charges brought by Salmon.

"But if Magnus is pulling out, I can't see spending town money on a court suit," Crabb said, adding that he would wait to see what Magnus would do.

Case said Magnus officials believe they could win a court fight on the matter, but "it just isn't worth it. We are no longer interested in Darby as a host community for a mall. Right now, we're interested in talking to Tuckerman officials, to see what light the end of that tunnel brings."

Surging

Constable Godfrey Perkins was of several minds about the murder. He was sad that someone had been killed in his town, but if it had to happen, he was glad the victim was Ike Jordan. It was well known among police throughout the county that Ike was a professional burglar, but no one had ever been able to get enough evidence on him for a conviction. Ike's death was a bouquet of roses for the town, in Constable Perkins' view.

The constable was the town's only full-time police officer. There really wasn't much to do in Darby. The town had little violence except "domestics," which didn't really count; there were no robberies; there was no organized crime; drug traffic was strictly local; juvenile crime was of the prank variety. The most common crime in Darby was burglary, and nailing the perpetrators of that trade was so damnably difficult that the constable turned over most of those cases to the Tuckerman County Sheriff's Department.

On "murder Tuesday" (a phrase Perkins had borrowed from a movie he'd seen on television), the constable had been planning on attending the town meeting like everyone else when an unidentified telephone caller said there was a body in the parking lot of Ike's Auction Barn. There he had found Ike slumped over the steering wheel of his van, his dog placidly beside him. The dog seemed to be waiting for its master, as if it realized that this body was not Ike, but uncured meat. Perkins opened the door, and the dog jumped out and wagged its tail. There were bloody paw prints throughout the inside of the van. The gun lay on the mat on the passenger side. Perkins suspected suicide. However, when he looked closely and found two holes, one almost dead between the eyes, the other entering the upper lip and shattering Ike's dentures, Constable Perkins deduced that suicide was unlikely.

Perkins was reasonably sure the murderer was Ike's son, Critter. It was common knowledge around town that the two men hadn't been getting along recently, and Critter didn't have an alibi. Furthermore, Perkins reasoned that only someone who knew Ike very well could have gotten in the car past the dog, laid his hands on Ike's gun, and shot him. The final reason for Perkins' suspicion was the fact that Critter was a Jordan. There were dark stories about feuds in the Jordan clan, and as far as Perkins was concerned, Ike's murder was another chapter.

Critter proved to be tough. He first pretended confusion, then sorrow at the death of his father. When Deputy Sheriff Foster asked him point-blank whether he had killed his father, Critter said, "You think I did it? I did it? Really do, don't you?" After that he acted brazenly cocky, proud of the act, proud of getting away with it, as if he knew they didn't have any evidence on him. They had no choice but to set Critter free. Perkins told himself to be patient. Critter would make a mistake one of these days, and he would be there. Maybe it was all for the best to wait out this case. If they had nailed Critter right off the bat, the sheriff's department probably would have gotten the credit.

Who had made the anonymous call to the police? Would Critter have done such a thing? And if so, why? At one point, he telephoned Critter and talked to him for a while to determine whether his was the same voice that had called earlier.

This exercise led nowhere. He just didn't have a good ear for accents and tones and all that. If Critter hadn't called, then someone else knew of the murder. Perkins hadn't told the attorney general's office or the sheriff's department about the tipster. The tipster was his, his ace in the hole.

Crowbar was in the parking lot of the auction barn, sitting in the snow, waiting for Ike, it seemed. Critter Jordan had been watching the dog for several days. He didn't know what to think about the animal, except that its existence stirred him peculiarly. One minute he wanted to kill it, the next pet it. Certain truths began to come round in Critter's mind when a blue van pulled into the lot, and Crowbar wagged his tail and barked in greeting. A stranger stepped out and Crowbar licked his hand. Critter understood now that Crowbar was not waiting for Ike, as he had thought, but for the van. Mastery did not come to a man from his own self but from his things: this was the lesson for Critter.

Critter then toured the auction barn. He had never noticed before what a wondrous place it was, a receptacle for dreams, a church. With each scene, fresh with the newness of insight, recorded by his eyes, filed by the registry of deeds section of his brain, he felt a sense of ownership, of power, Ike's barn, his. He'd clean it out, fix it up.

He thought about that most important of all words in the Jordan way of things, "ascendancy." The idea of constantly striving for ascendancy over kith and kin had always wearied him, but now he saw the pleasure in it—how to describe it?— a surging.

A little later he was in the parking lot, engaged in a staring-down contest with Crowbar, when Godfrey Perkins pulled into the lot with his cruiser.

Perkins rolled down his window. "Just making my rounds," he said, apparently a little embarrassed at finding himself eyeball to eyeball with a man he'd recently questioned. Critter felt the surging.

"Checking me out more like it," Critter said.

"Part of my job," Perkins said.

"How long is the sheriff's department going to keep Ike's van?" Critter asked.

"Until the perpetrator's convicted and sentenced and appealed out, I imagine," Perkins said. "Don't you have a car of your own?"

"I do, I do. But it ain't running right. I'm going to have to get a car," Critter said, and then spontaneously added, "Hey, Godfrey, how about a ride to Tuckerman?"

Perkins was taken aback for a moment, and then paused to consider the situation. Finally he said, "Why sure, Critter. Hop in. I was planning on taking the cruiser for an oil change anyhow."

So Critter got in the cruiser. It was the first time he'd ever ridden in the front seat of a police car.

"Nice here," he said. "The last time I was in this vehicle, I was in the rear and the wire screen fenced the view a bit more than for comfort."

After a couple of minutes, Perkins asked, "Critter, is there something you want to tell me? Something you want to get off your chest?"

"I don't know," Critter said.

"Just between the two of us and the man upstairs, Critter, did you do in Ike?" Perkins asked.

"Godfrey, are you trying to pin this on me because you honestly believe I would dispose of my own father or just because you don't like me?"

"I like you," Perkins said. "I wouldn't harass a man out of spite. I really think you killed him. I'm going to nail you, too. But only because it's my job."

"If I admitted it to you, I mean just to satisfy your curiosity, would you let me have the van?"

"I might . . . I might. What are you nosing around for, Critter?" Perkins said.

"Nothing . . . nothing."

"Are you admitting you did in Ike?"

"What if I did? What if I came right out now and said, 'I

done it?' No way you could come back on me, right? I mean
I'd just deny the whole thing before the judge, and it would
be your word against mine. That ain't no evidence worth a
shit."

"You're right, Critter. That ain't no evidence. But maybe
you'd feel better if you admitted it. Holding a knowledge—
that can be a hurtful thing. Let it go, Critter. Confess. I won't
tell nobody."

"What if I said I didn't perpetrate nothing?" Critter asked.
He was looking out the window. The sky was pretty today,
pale blue.

"Why, you can say what you want. It's a free country,"
Perkins said, disappointment in his voice.

They drove the rest of the way to Tuckerman talking about
what a mild winter it had been.

Several hours later, Critter Jordan was driving back to Darby
behind the wheel of a five-year-old Dodge van that he had
bought on credit from his uncle Donald.

Once on the road in the van, Critter felt a deep and strong
change in himself. It was as if his brain power had increased.
His course in life seemed clear. He was going to have to learn
business ways, start reading and inspecting and factoring and,
if need be, be a hard-ass with the help. He was taking over.

Crowbar was waiting in the parking lot of the auction barn
when he arrived home. The dog took one look at the van, and
his ears perked up. "Hop in," Critter said. The dog obliged
and took his customary seat in the rear.

"It probably don't smell right, but it will, it will," Critter
said. "Wait here. Be right back."

Critter ran upstairs, shocked Delphina by kissing her on
the nose, opened the face of the clock in the living room,
shoved his hand in, came up with a marijuana cigarette, stuck
it behind his ear, grinned at Delphina, and was gone before
she could get her senses about her.

He slid into the driver's seat of the van, advised Crowbar
they were hitting the road, and peeled out. He took a ride
along the river, almost to Claremont. It was dark by the time

he returned. Before going to the apartment he went into the auction barn, snapping on a few lights to look around. When the stuff here was sold, he'd fix the place up and rent space to flea-market folk.

He shut off the lights now and lit the joint. He stood there by the door, in the dark, thinking. Ike had hated marijuana, feared it, and to smoke it in the auction barn gave Critter an immense sense of satisfaction, of accomplishment, as if he were collecting pay for having completed a difficult job.

"Can you smell it, Pop? Stinks, don't it?" The sound of his words reverberating in the auction barn shivered him with a small fear; it was as if his voice were not part of him. For a moment, he expected Ike to appear before him, grinning and awful. But when there was no response to his question, the fear was transformed into surging. He's really dead, dead and gone, gone forever, thought Critter. The marijuana was beginning to take hold now, and he surrendered to it.

Ike is sitting behind the wheel of his van, taunting his passenger, preaching about this and that. The passenger reaches into the glove compartment of the van.

"What's this, Ike—a .357?" he says.

"Quit fooling around," Ike says.

"I ain't fooling, Ike," the passenger says, smiles, and fires— bang! bang!

Critter played this scene in his mind repeatedly, each time making it more vivid, more realistic. At first it was difficult to give the passenger an identity, even unpleasant to consider the passenger as anyone but a nameless drifter. But the more he played the scene, the more vivid it became, yet the less threatening it seemed, like a horror movie that one sees over and over again, until at last, there is no horror, only the tingle of it. *Of course—the passenger is Critter Jordan, son.* He knew that this idea would grow, not only in himself but among his Jordan kin.

Having come to his Jordan manhood, he was in a good position for fulfilling it. What he could get of Ike's estate would give him a strong base from which to provide succor for his kin; their own belief that he had done in Ike would give him credentials in his campaign for ascendancy in the clan.

He sat there enjoying the dark for a long time, then climbed the outside stairs to the apartment. Delphina saw his eyes, shrank before them. She would have to accept him now, on his terms. The baby would be a Jordan.

Ahead, Butterfly .

Soapy Rayno was trying to think ahead. It was difficult to think ahead. You had to imagine yourself in a place and in a weather that wasn't, and the wasn'ts were like big empty drums and you were inside and somebody was pounding on the outside—hurtful, hurtful. But you had to think ahead. You couldn't go on without thinking about going on. Well, you could go on, but if you didn't think ahead, you didn't know where you were going on to, and there were bad places and bad times out there. So you had to think ahead, unless you wanted to stay where you were and let the swell of time carry you this way and that, in wases and wasn'ts and ises and isn'ts and will bes and will not bes. Who wanted that?

My gosh, how was she going to get ahead without Delphina? Delphina had led the way. Now Delphina was hanging back. The baby was holding her back. Critter was holding her back. She was holding herself back. Nobody was going to hold back Soapy. "Soapy's going to get ahead." "I know, honey, I know," Delphina had said.

Must think ahead. "I got needs." "I know you have needs—everybody has needs, Soapy." A woman had soft and hard needs, soft before hard. Soft was always first with a woman. Maybe a kitten. Little purry fella. Something hard, too. Maybe a gun, or some traps. "I gotta, gotta, gotta get some iron." "What?"

Making up your mind to decide where to get ahead to was confusing. "I'm standing on my own two feet, but I don't know where to make them go." "You're not so dumb, Soapy—she ain't so dumb, Critter." She didn't really want a kitten, because you touched them and you wanted to cry, and if you cried it made you wet. No gun, either. Might shoot it off and hurt somebody, and that wasn't getting ahead. Money—she needed to get money. Money was soft, and it was hard. To get money, you had to get a job. To get a job, she needed Delphina. Delphina could get jobs. "Delphina, can I have a job?" "I'll speak to Critter."

Now that there was no more Ike, there was no more Critter. Critter was becoming Ike. Poor Delphina. Critter gave Soapy a job fixing up. She liked fixing up. Thinking with your hands was not hurtful. Nobody committed suicide by shooting off their hands. "They always shoot themselves in the head, because that's where the hurtfulness is." "Soapy, you say the strangest things sometimes."

She didn't like her present quarters in the balcony of the auction barn. She didn't like the barn. It was full of *woo-woos*, Ike things. Ike was in there, *woo-wooing*. She wanted to move back to her tree house, but she didn't have a car and the hitchhiking was poor on the Upper Darby Road, and so she couldn't, wouldn't, have been able to get back and forth from the auction barn to fix up, so she'd have to quit her job, and then there would be no money—no soft and hard. "I'm thinking ahead." "I know, honey." So she fixed up this and fixed up that, and tried not to be afraid of the wasn'ts.

It would have been nice also to be able to learn, to read books and to speak words, to speak words, to speak words. But she didn't know how to go about learning how to learn. "Delphina, I want to learn." "What?" Delphina didn't get it. She could have used some learning herself.

Never mind learning. One thing at a time. Think ahead. Fix up, get money. Soft bills and hard coin. The more you touched the bills the softer they got. The hard stuff you jingled in your pocket, and it felt good. A woman liked something soft and something hard, so it felt good. She was a woman. No one else knew it yet, but Soapy knew it. She felt it. When you feel something, you understand it.

So confusing to think ahead—she tried to tell this to Delphina and Critter on the ride into Tuckerman one afternoon, but the words, the words did not.

"I'm getting ahead and I'm getting behind because nobody is helping me. If somebody could help me, I could learn to learn to learn myself better." "Soapy, me and Critter is going to the department store to buy some baby clothes. We'll meet you back at the car in half an hour. Don't get in any trouble, honey, and please don't run away."

No place to run away to anymore, since Daddy Newhawk was a horse's ass. She walked the streets of downtown Tuckerman. Snow in the city was so unhappy. She stopped at the Chrysalis Restaurant. She wanted to go inside, but she was too shy. She looked through the window, and she got an idea from the butterflies on the walls. A person got ahead by counting. One, two, three, four, five, six, seven, all the way to a million, and then died. A butterfly counted one, zero, a million, and never mind in between. A caterpillar was a caterpillar and nothing else—one, one, one, one—and then it wasn't anything—zero, zero, zero, zero—and then it was a butterfly—a million, a million, a million, a million.

Back at the auction barn, Soapy went through hundreds of magazines stored in a big box. She cut out pictures of butterflies and pasted them on white paper, and she touched them and shut her eyes, and said, "Butterfly, butterfly, butterfly, butterfly."

The
Trust

"Chance, I need you," Persephone had said over the telephone.

Chance drove the fourteen miles from the *Crier* to the Salmon house in Upper Darby. Several inches of snow had fallen the night before, but the sun was out now, the temperature nudging upward into the high forties. The forecast called for a cold wave on the heels of the brief thaw.

When he arrived, he was taken by the abrupt difference between the simple drone of the Brat's engine and the complex sizzle of water dripping into a New Hampshire winter thaw. Icicles fell—drop by drop—from the eaves of the house; snow on a million trees melted like a conscious rain. It made him uneasy.

Persephone met him at the door. She was lightly perfumed and her skin had a sort of dry sheen to it; she was, he thought, like snow—white to a fault. *If I shut my eyes, I'll fall into her.* She took his coat and put it on a hanger, and he got a look at her fingernails. They had been red. Now they were clear, the pink from beneath coming out like the grain of wood on polished furniture.

"You look a little tired," he said.

"I have to tend the damn fires—everything," she said.

"And, too, Lilith's been home, and she's like a baby when I'm around, and I have to do for her, and naturally I have to do for myself. . . . You look rather robust."

"I've been working out at the 'Y'—racquetball."

"Oh, yes, that sport with the 'Q' in it," Persephone said, ghosting away from him.

Chance was surprised to see that Reggie's sickbed was in the living room, before a blaze in the fireplace. The room was overly warm, but Salmon was lying supine under a down comforter. The streaks in his face had almost merged to form a purple-red second skin. His hands were folded before him on his chest. With his eyes, Chance asked Persephone, is this man dead or alive?

"He sleeps," she whispered.

Persephone fixed some tea, and they sat sipping it in the library. The fire had almost died out, and although the room was still warm Chance could feel a deep chill. He remarked on this to Persephone.

"The room is not usually heated," she said. "The cold you feel is from the books and the shelves, the very body of the room. Only the air and the fireplace bricks are warm, but I wanted to come in here because in the summer it's my favorite room. The light pours in all green from the fields. I don't like the blue-white light of winter."

"You're waiting for summer—in Upper Darby? I thought you might travel, get away, after everything," Chance said.

"I might do that, but only after the summer," she said. "My people started coming to Darby during the summers. Summer is what brought them here, what brought them together. Reggie and I fell in love in the summer, by Grace Pond. Summer and love have kept me in Upper Darby. I want to try one more summer here, alone."

"Alone."

"Yes, alone," Persephone said. "What are you going to do, Roland? Where are you going to go? You look adrift."

"Far out to sea. . . . Where's Lilith? Will I get to meet her?"

"She's with her cousin Beatrice. She'll be home in an hour.

She'll say good-bye to her father and return to school. It's going to be a last good-bye, although she doesn't know it."

"What?"

Persephone explained. Reggie was dying. He didn't want to die in the hospital, he didn't want to die at home, he wanted to die on the Trust. Persephone had prepared a shelter for him overlooking the ledges, but Reggie was too weak to hike up the hill and Persephone was not strong enough to get him up there by herself.

"I'm to be the beast of burden," Chance said.

"If you wish."

"When?"

"Tomorrow morning," Persephone said.

Reggie was awake when they finished their talk and went into the living room. Chance and Reggie exchanged pleasantries. Persephone nodded to Reggie—*he knows*—and left the room.

"You're sooo kind to do this for us. I want you to know how grateful we are," Reggie said, with a slightly condescending, matter-of-fact air of politeness, as if he were thanking a handyman for puttying a window.

Chance cast his eyes about and they fell on the fire.

"I like a fire, don't you?" Reggie said.

"I never had a fire. I don't come from a fire culture. I come from an all-electric culture, but, yes, I like a fire. . . . How are you feeling? Something I can bring you?" Chance said, edgy yet enjoying a feeling of voluntary servitude.

"Not suffering at the moment. Feel weak mainly," Reggie said. "I gave you a pretty good story at the special town meeting, did I not?"

"Not bad," Chance said. "Magnus, Hillary—they want to sue you."

Reggie laughed, a dry, triumphant laugh. "Good, good. A lawsuit—something to perpetuate my memory," he said, then began a new train of thought. "I'm looking forward to the hill, the trees."

"It's a pretty hill," Chance said.

"The university people will study it every year," Reggie said. "In four hundred years or so—why rush?—maybe we'll learn what brings a forest to its climax."

Chance remembered something Persephone had said to him during their lovemaking: "What follows won't be better than this, so why rush?"

Lilith came home. She was big like her father and with his grand features, but what distinguished Reggie slighted Lilith. She was just another somewhat pretty, somewhat horsey young woman mass-produced on the high-protein assembly line of American nutrition. She was introduced to Chance and went through the proper how-nice-to-meet-you ceremony, but she never looked at him. She seemed to be laboring to remember as little of him as possible. There was no doubt in Chance's mind that she knew he'd been her mother's lover. Having arrived, she immediately announced that she had to get back to school, and she was almost out the door before Persephone could stop her.

They spoke in whispers, but the hallway funneled their words to Chance, and the words made a sucking sound, like water draining, against the *drip-drip* background noise of the melting that came in through the door that had been left open.

"Daddy may be going to Hanover for special treatments soon, so you may not see him for a while," Persephone lied. "He's really quite ill, and you never can tell. So, go in the living room and give him a hug and a long good-bye."

"What do you mean— 'never can tell'?" Lilith asked, worry and anger in her whisper.

"Just an expression," Persephone whispered brightly. "You know I'm always using the wrong word. Remember when you bought your car and I honestly believed you said it was advertised as an 'okay abused car' instead of an 'okay used car'? Remember?"

Lilith laughed nervously and drifted into the living room. Persephone closed the front hall door, and for a moment the house was silent. Persephone remained in the hall, trying to muster the strength to continue her deception. Chance could hear father and daughter now, Reggie's voice rumbling and indecipherable, Lilith's at once clear and confused, like stream water.

"Daddy, Daddy, why didn't you tell me how sick you were? No, no, don't say that. I know you're sick. You were in the hospital and everything, and, gee, you look so sick. Daddy, Daddy, I love you. Don't die, Daddy. I'm not ready for that. It was bad enough with Grandmother Trellis. I'm sorry. I'll be good. I know you and Mummy fight all the time about where I should be going to school. I don't care where I'm sent—honest. Except I do think it's indisputable that the music department is better at Oberlin. Don't hate each other. Hate me instead, if it helps. Please don't hate me. Daddy? Daddy? Look at me, Daddy. Doreen Riley has a new Porsche. Well, not new, but like new. Daddy? Daddy? Oh, yes, Daddy, yes. Yes, yes, yes, oh. Oh, oooh, oh, Mummy? Never mind. He's all right. You're all right, aren't you, Daddy? Daddy's going to be all right. No, I don't want a new car. I don't care. To be honest, it would be really neat to have a new car. I mean I wouldn't mind if somebody gave me a new car, but I wouldn't spend my own money on one. College is sooo much more important. And I really wouldn't be so gauche as to buy something that calls attention to itself like a Porsche. I'm fine, Daddy. Yes, Daddy. I love you, Daddy. Can you hear me? I love you. I did something, didn't I? I'm sorry, Daddy, I'm sorry."

After Lilith left for Tuckerman, Chance went for a short walk. It was almost dark, and the temperature had dropped. The melting had stopped, the wind was stirring from the north, and the normal rustling and bird sounds of the woods were a comfort. The snow from last night's storm had almost completely melted, but the crusty, old snow beneath was still visible in patches. He walked perhaps a mile along Upper Darby Road and then returned. It was dark by then.

Reggie was sleeping. Chance and Persephone sipped Scotch old-fashioneds in the library.

"I think I'll close off that cavernous parlor room and make this the social room in the house," Persephone said.

Reggie slept on, and Chance and Persephone dined in the library from paper plates. Persephone boiled some spaghetti, serving it with a white sauce and shrimp. They had a salad in place of dessert, and they drank a bottle of white wine with the meal.

Reggie awakened a short time later—frightened. Persephone brought him water, and he took some Demerol pills. Later, when the fright was shrouded, Reggie and Persephone sat holding hands and talking while Chance waited in the library. Lying on the coffee table was a mystery novel; he tried to get into it but kept losing the story line. He put the book down. He thought it indelicate to ask where the television set was, so he picked up another book. He couldn't contain his restlessness, so he raided the refrigerator for a beer. He was drinking it when Persephone came in. She was flushed as a ravished bride.

"I've set up a cot in the living room," she said, her face aglow, happy. "I'm staying with Reggie tonight. You can take the couch in the library." She tossed Chance a sleeping bag and was gone.

He fell asleep almost at once, and almost at once—it seemed—awakened, although actually it was three a.m. It took a moment for him to realize that the sound that had awakened him was Reggie calling out an unfamiliar name.

"Finally, it's not guilt that bars the way, is it, Reggie?" The question came to Reggie in a dream, in a voice he recognized immediately even though he had never heard it before. Like some Planning Board member poring over papers, Reggie reviewed the facts. Ike Jordan had somehow laid his hands on a will in which Trellis Butterworth had second thoughts about the Salmon Trust and had left all her property to her children. If Ike had asked for money like any common blackmailer, Reggie would have paid. But Ike wanted his political support. He wanted to tie the Jordan name to the Salmon name. On behalf of his father and his grandfather, Reggie could not abide this demand. He had done what he had to do, so it was not guilt that barred him now, as the voice had pointed out. It was the fact that Ike, in his sudden surge of fear in the moment before Reggie pulled the trigger, had seen in his face someone else, had called him by a name not his own—Ollie. "Do you understand now?" the voice spoke again. "A man's name is the compass that leads him from one world to the next. Yours has been taken from you."

"Ollie, Ollie, Ollie . . ."

"Wake up, wake up."

He was looking up into the breath of his wife. Persephone?" he said.

"You were having a bad dream," she said.

"Persephone, who am I?"

"Reggie, it was only a dream."

"Persephone, I heard the voice of the Devil. I'm going to hell," Reggie said.

Chance awakened in the morning to the light of dawn. He smelled coffee brewing. He dressed and sat by the fire in the living room, sipping coffee and eating toast. Reggie sat up in his sick bed, staring at the flames.

"Do you want breakfast?" Persephone said to Reggie.

"I'm not hungry."

"Have a little something. You'll need some strength for the climb to the ledges," Persephone said.

Reggie began to weep silently, to himself. Persephone took his head and held it to her bosom.

They set out for the ledges around eight a.m. The cold wave had come in during the night, and the ground and the snow and the air had a crunch to them. Reggie could walk, but he needed frequent rests to go on, and Chance and Persephone practically had to carry him up the steeper inclines. Chance's muscles were aching when they reached the ledges.

Persephone had cut hemlock boughs, made a rough bed with them, and covered them with clear plastic. The melting

snow had formed a puddle in the plastic that had frozen over-
night. Chance shattered it with a kick of his foot, then pulled
the plastic off. Reggie sat cross-legged on the hemlock boughs.
Following Reggie's instructions, Chance made a stack with
dry branches that he broke off pine trees. Reggie started his
own fire, blowing gently into it to get it going.

Chance listened while the fire caught hold and began to
crackle. Reggie seemed to have read Chance's mind, and said
to him, "It's a merry sound, is it not?" His hands were shaking,
but his voice was steady.

Persephone put the canteen beside Reggie.

"I can't open it. I don't have the strength," Reggie said,
and he returned it to Persephone. Her hands were shaking so
that she could scarcely hold it.

Chance opened the canteen. He took the bottle of pills from
Reggie, spilled some into his palm, and held them out like an
offering. Persephone brought the canteen to Reggie's lips as
he took the pills. Water dribbled down his chin. Chance handed
Reggie pill after pill, as Persephone gave him water.

"I've been so awful to you," Reggie said to Persephone.

"Yes, you've been awful," Persephone said. She was beginning to weep.

Chance withdrew about a hundred feet to the trees above
the ledges, so that Reggie and Persephone could complete
their parting in private. From here, their backs to Chance,
they looked like a couple on a stroll, taking a moment to rest
and look at the view. This side of the hill still basked in shadow,
but the valley below and the western hills in Vermont were
bright with morning sun.

The sun was washing up the slope of the hill now. It high-
lighted the bluish glaze of ice over the snow and the snow
crystals beneath shining through. It was as if a woman with
fair, almost translucent skin had tiny jewels implanted underneath that skin, and as she walked into the light one could
see, for the first time, the faint blue of her veins and the sparkle
of the jewels. This aspect of snow seemed both familiar and
strange to Chance. He had seen this kind of snow before, but

he couldn't remember where or when. Such snow had no name. In order for a thing to be fixed in the mind, it had to have a name.

Below, Reggie and Persephone had joined hands. It seemed to Chance that they were receding from him, as if he were on a boat and the current was pulling him away.

Red Herring

"Always fun to swap lies with you, Charles," William Case said.

Charles Barnum winced. It seemed to him that the word "lies" could be heard throughout the restaurant. Furthermore, Case's friendliness was disturbing. When the mall had been beaten worse than Barnum had expected, he believed he would be fired as Magnum's local attorney. Now here came Case taking him to lunch, telling him he was a fun guy. Something was wrong here. It just wasn't natural for a business exec to accept defeat graciously.

"You look a little nervous," Case said. Barnum didn't like the tone. Too cute.

"Just anxious to learn what and where next for the mall," Barnum said. One of the secretaries in the office had brought in some doughnuts, and he had gone after them like a starving man. He felt as if he had eaten a Mae West. "Besides, I need a bromo and nap," he added, but Case seemed not to hear that.

"We have a long way to go, and I believe we have arrived," Case said.

What the hell is he talking about? Barnum wondered. He'd have to take a stab. "Good-bye Darby, hello Tuckerman," he said.

"Darby was hello–good-bye from the start. And from the start, Tuckerman was the only target," Case said, smiling as one dispensing interesting gossip.

"What? Am I hearing what I'm hearing?"

"Magnus never wanted Darby. Think about it," Case said, still immensely pleased with himself.

"Darby was a red herring for Tuckerman," Barnum said, belched, excused himself, and went on. "Magnus wanted Tuckerman all along, but with resistance from the city government, the going was going to be rough."

"Correct," Case said. "We decided to go whole-hog in Darby, to scare the dickens out of the Tuckerman City Council."

"But, Bill, what would Magnus have done if we had won in Darby?"

"Just between you and I and the great developer in the sky, Charles, when you went home at night and discussed this with your dear wife, did you say, 'Honey buns, we've got it sewed up in the shade in Darby'?"

"Well, frankly . . ."

"Well, frankly, I bet you said Magnus didn't have a prayer at town meeting, not with a two-thirds vote required. Which was why you kept trying to steer us down the variance road. You were doing your job. Do what the client wants, but let him know, too, what you think is the correct flight plan, eh?"

"I should have guessed." Barnum was ashamed.

"Don't feel bad," Case said. "Harriman was afraid you were so good, you might have won us the vote anyway. But, thanks to Squire Salmon, it was easy for us to pull out of Darby."

"Now what?"

"The time is ripe to sell the mall to Tuckerman," Case said. "This is where a mall should be. There was never any real doubt about that."

Barnum was beginning to relax now, although he could still taste the doughnuts. "And what's yours truly's role?" he asked.

"No role. You're fired."

"What?" Barnum shouted, and Case was laughing aloud, the laugh slashing through the entire Chrysalis Restaurant.

"If you could see your face—are you burned up," Case said. "Waitress, oh, waitress. Bring this gentleman a glass of water to cool him down."

"This is not funny, Bill," Barnum said. He was too sick to feel violent. It must be nice to be a felon, he thought. If somebody does you dirt, you beat the hell out of him, and then do the time in peace and quiet. It was better than watching your animosities eat up your insides over the years.

"I'm sorry, Charles, I couldn't help myself," Case said. "Everything is going to be all right. Magnus is going to pursue an option on that piece of land across from McDonald's. Since, as I understand it, you have a direct interest in this parcel, we thought you might want to negotiate on your own behalf instead of ours. Magnum certainly would appreciate you putting in a good word before the primary owner, although something tells me that word is going to be spelled c-a-s-h."

Barnum should have been relieved, indeed cheered, since he stood to make a tidy sum, but he was still upset. His stomach was better, but he had this peculiar, discombobulated feeling, as if something—he didn't know what—had been taken from him. He glanced around the room, as one looking for an exit in case of fire. He spotted Mrs. Reggie Salmon lunching happily with the college professor from Darby, Hadly Blue. Didn't waste much time on trivialities like grief, those old-rich types.

The waitress arrived and turned toward Case, who waved her to Barnum.

"I'll have the steak sandwich, a side order of french fries, and a Dewar's with soda," Barnum said.

"I'll have the shrimp salad, just water to drink," Case said.

Whisper My Name

Reggie Salmon had asked to be buried on the Trust lands, but in this he did not get his way. Persephone had him laid to rest in the family plot beside their infant son. She didn't mourn Reggie, nor did she need to. She had been mourning all those months his body had been alive and his spirit lost to her. As far as she was concerned Reggie had been dead a year. Already the memory of that last year was fading. The Reggie of her memories would be a healthy Reggie, the Reggie she had loved and who had loved her.

As for Chance, something had touched him up there on the ridge. With Reggie's passing, he had felt the touch of the sky, the touch of the land, the touch of the snow, and something else he couldn't say. It was courage. It came to him in a gush of grief, grief for what had died in himself at the passing of old Joe. It came to him as a sense of purpose, to find the truth about himself and accept the consequences. It came to him as love for Old Joe and Genevieve, no matter what they had done to him, and as love for Soapy Rayno, who, he could see in the clarity of the moment, needed him as he needed her.

He drove to Manchester because that was where Old Joe and Genevieve were from, and at the city hall he found his birth certificate. It said he was the natural son of the LaChances. But why was he told he was adopted and why did his parents leave Manchester? The answer that came to him was that someone in Manchester knew the truth. He talked to his grandmother LaChance. She wouldn't tell him the details, only that something bad had happened and it was best he didn't know.

Old Joe had said he'd been conceived in Tuckerman County, and Chance had interpreted that as meaning he'd been born there. Now he realized his mistake, and he searched the *Crier* files, looking closely at the papers nine months before his birthdate. On page five, in a story of about six column inches with a twenty-four-point headline, he found the answer. A woman and her husband had stopped at a wayside park on Route 21. Chance guessed the spot, a place where you pull off in some trees. There was a picnic table, some trash barrels. Two men beat the husband unconscious and raped the woman. Chance went to the police station. The assistant chief, who had been a patrolman then, remembered the crime and the woman's name—LaChance. The two men had never been caught.

Chance put together the rest of the story. Old Joe was sterile. When Genevieve became pregnant, she decided to keep the baby. Old Joe couldn't bear to live with the lie that he had fathered her son, so he had invented a lie he could live with—adoption. The three of them—Old Joe, Genevieve, and The Devil—worked out a deal.

Even if somehow the man who had raped his mother and had fathered him could be caught and identified, Chance could never think of him as father. He would never be able to think of anyone as his father. He had no father, he had never had a father—this was the truth. But he could rejoice in one thing. The mother who was the only mother he had ever known was his mother. He was not ready to see her, embrace her son to mother, but that day would come. He would have to put his own life in order first. With that, his thoughts turned to Soapy Rayno. He had to redeem himself before her.

• • •

Clovis Shard, managing editor of *The Tuckerman Crier*, was trying to explain to his favorite reporter why he was leaving the newspaper.

"It's not the fact that NewSSpot and Magnus are owned by the same conglomerate, or even that Mrs. Chubb knew all along," Shard said. "No pressure was ever put on me or my reporters to slant the news. Isn't that so, LaChance? Nobody told you how to write your news stories, did they? No, it wasn't that, although I personally do regret the unfortunate coincidence and the fact that Mrs. Chubb chose to keep the matter a secret. It did gall me to have to read about the connection in *The Brattleboro Reformer*, and I did gag when Magnus took out an option on the Tuckerman property owned by Mrs. Chubb's canasta partner. But I believed her when she said she had no knowledge of the deal until it was announced. No, LaChance, it wasn't NewSSpot and Mrs. Chubb and her crummy little canasta conspiracy. A little joke—there was no conspiracy; we have no evidence of such. No, it wasn't any of those things. It's the fact that I got this offer to run the *Grand Ford Journal* outside of San 'ntone. It's a great little newspaper. They have this terrific petrochemical issue brewing. Bunch of ranchers and farmers are going to court over some mineral rights their kin sold years ago to the oil companies. If they win, it could turn the country's mineral rights laws upside down. Great little issue—you'd love it, LaChance. Why don't you kiss off the *Crier*, and come to the great state of Texas with Clovis? Grand Ford is a magnificent town. Terrific. Did I tell you there's a possibility I'll move into the publisher's job next year? Yah. Well, whatever. I'm through with the gypsy journalist life. This is it, Graaand Ford! . . . My frozen cursor, look at the time. Don't you have any work to do?"

"I have plenty of work to do," Chance said.

"Okay, kid, buzz off. I've got a deadline to meet."

Minutes later Chance was on his way to Burlington.

He returned that night, but he didn't go home. He went to the auction barn. Delphina met him at the door. She was holding her baby in her arms.

"Who's this?" Chance said.

"This is Ollie Jordan," Delphina said.

"I want to see Soapy," Chance said.

"She don't want nothing to do with you no more," Delphina said.

"I have something that belongs to her," Chance said.

The feel of wood brought Soapy comfort; the shaping of it suggested meaning. So she had been whittling. She had started with a potato masher. Once she had felt the thing come round to itself, it was no longer necessary to touch it or even to think about it in order to know it. It was simply a potato masher. A word stayed-put a thing in the mind. She was whittling a salad bowl spoon when she saw Chance. She knew without his speaking that something in him had changed. He was full of feeling.

She also knew without his speaking that she was going to go with him.

"Everything will be all right," he said.

She put some of her belongings in back of the baby truck, and they were off, headed for . . . she didn't know where. Didn't care.

Under way, she looked at him closely. He had been holding back all these months, and now he was letting out.

"Talk," she said.

"What shall I say?"

"All."

And so he began, and his words were like a favorite music to her—*some things refuse to break, some things refuse to fall*—at first soft, like being touched, then hard, like knowing something, then finally neither soft nor hard, but like water flowing over a mossy rock.

He told her about himself, where he had come from, and how, for reasons he didn't understand, he wanted to stay in Tuckerman County. He told her how he had gone to Burlington and found Newhawk and half-threatened, half-persuaded him into parting with his name. He handed her a note from Newhawk.

"Can you read it?" Chance asked.

Soapy looked at the note. The words were solid as sticks. The note started with a "Dear Sheila" and was followed by the words, "I'm sorry. I've been a bad father, and I promise to do better." It was signed "Newhawk," and underneath, in print, he had written his true name—her name.

She spoke the name aloud. On the drive to Tuckerman in Chance's baby truck, she steeped herself in the thought of the name.

When they arrived at Chance's apartment, she noticed something different about the feel of the night air. It was southern air, moist air. Spring was coming.

The apartment was clean and neat, like Chance himself. She saw that he folded things and put them away, and this realization unaccountably thrilled her in a small way, as when she'd happened upon a bird's nest decorated with some red and green yarn.

They didn't have to speak. He had some kind of plan, and she was part of it, and she succumbed to it, as once—mistakenly—she had succumbed to Daddy's plan. But there would be no mistake here. She sensed that here her trust and wisdom were one.

He undid her braid and let her hair fall about. It used to be she would spend much of her free time combing her hair, looking at it, seeing in it the child she had been. Chance washed her hair three times, and then she sat in a chair and he brushed and combed out the snarls. He brushed for half an hour until the hair was dry and shiny. She could feel her hair around her, soft and clean, falling over her shoulders. This was not the hair of a child. This was the hair of a woman.

When her hair was clean and dry Chance spoke.

"I watched the honey and red colors come out as I brushed it—it reminded me of sunlight coming through the trees," he said, and he kissed her hair.

He filled the bathtub with water and undressed her. She soaked in the tub while he washed her face.

"I always liked the small 'r' of your upper lip," he said, and kissed her gently on the mouth.

She shut her eyes, and he washed her body, first roughly

with a face cloth, then more delicately and carefully with his hands.

He pulled the stopper from the tub, and she listened to the water draining, its sound like her image of the panting retreat of a chased deer. He undressed and they stood under the shower together like stones under a brook. Only after they were both clean and dry and in the bed did he look at her as a woman and touch her as a woman.

She could feel his breathing change, like exciting weather in the offing. She put her arms around him, and they kissed. She could feel love and knowledge come together, and she spoke his name aloud.

Deep in the soft-hard-soft-hard-soft-hard rhythm of love, she said, "Say it, say my name." And he whispered it again and again.

CRIER WEDDING ANNOUNCEMENT

Sheila April Salmon and Roland Joseph LaChance were married June 25 in Upper Darby at an outside ceremony in the woods of the Jepson Salmon Memorial Trust.

Parents of the bride are the late Antoinnette Rayno and Monet Salmon of Burlington, Vt. Parents of the groom are Genevieve LaChance of Santa Fe, N.M., and the late Joseph LaChance.

Delphina Jordan was matron of honor, and Clovis Shard was best man. Other members of the wedding party included Melba Hillary, Avalon Hillary, Persephone Salmon, Estelle Jordan, Carlton Jordan, Terry Dayton, and Hadly Blue.

The reception was held at the Jordan Auction Barn in Darby.

The bride will be enrolled in the fall at the Tuckerman County School for Special Students.

Her husband, a former staff writer for the *Crier*, recently was appointed caretaker of the Salmon Trust lands.

Following a honeymoon in the Southwest, the couple will live in the Druid-Kauffman caretaker's residence on the Trust lands.